THE
N E X T
V I C T I M

Also by William Sanders:

Journey to Fusang
The Wild Blue and the Gray
Pockets of Resistance
The Hellbound Train

WILLIAM SANDERS

THE

NEXT
VICTIM

ST. MARTIN'S PRESS   NEW YORK

Design by Judith A. Stagnitto

Library of Congress Cataloging-in-Publication Data

Sanders, William, 1942-
    The next victim / William Sanders.
        p.   cm.
    "A Thomas Dunne book."
    ISBN 0-312-08861-2 (hardcover)
    I. Title.
PS3569.A5139N48   1993
813'.54—dc20   92-40798
                                                    CIP

First Edition: February 1993

10 9 8 7 6 5 4 3 2 1

TO MATT
FOR HANGING IN THERE

AUTHOR'S NOTE

I have taken certain liberties in this story with geography and other factual matters. For example, there is no such town as Yuchi Park, and Tulsa has no newspaper named the *Courier*.

The character of Reverend Jack Redfield is *not* intended to represent any living, or dead, evangelist.

Everything else in this book is similarly fictitious, except that there really is a state of Oklahoma. Some say there is also an actual city of Tulsa, but around Cherokee County we tend to dismiss that as a mere ugly rumor.

THE
N E X T
V I C T I M

The call came in at 11:25 on the night of June 2. The voice was male but other than that it was so weak and shaky that it was impossible to tell anything about the speaker.

"Listen," the caller said, "there's a dead woman in a house at 6833 Minkolusa Drive."

"Sir," the dispatcher said instantly and automatically, "what is your name and where are you calling from?"

"She's been shot," the caller said. "Shot," he repeated. That was when the dispatcher realized he was crying. "She's just lying there on the floor. My God."

The dispatcher said again, "Sir, please, what is your name? We must have your name."

"No," the voice said, sounding even weaker, as if the man had already begun to lower the receiver from his mouth. "No, I can't. . . ." There was a brief fumbling rattle, and then a click, and then a dial tone.

That was how it was told to me, anyway, much later on, when such details no longer mattered. And so far as I know that was how it went down, but you can never be sure how much to believe. After a murder, the truth is always the next victim.

ONE

It was nearly ten in the morning when I called but the secretary said Mr. Brandon hadn't come in yet. I left a message for him to call me and hung up, thinking how nice it must be to be successful and important. It had been a long time since I'd had a real job—as various people liked to remind me—but I seemed to recall that there had been a certain expectation that I, and my wage-slave colleagues, would show up at something like a specified time.

I wasn't upset about Brandon not being there, though. The only time I'd met him, he'd seemed like a nice enough guy; and the information I had for him was almost certainly going to ruin his whole day. I wasn't sorry to get to put that off a little longer.

While I was waiting for him to call back I got out my harmonica and spent a few minutes trying to play "Smoke Gets in Your Eyes." Might as well ruin my dog's day while I was at it.

The phone rang while the dog was still trying to decide whether to go hide in the bedroom or just lie on the floor and shudder. I let it ring a couple of times while I studied the mouth harp, which had been sticking on the low reeds. The shiny metal cover plates were badly dented. Replacement time, too damn early and my fault this time. I said, "Shit," and picked up the phone, and it was Brandon.

It didn't take me long to make my report. It hit him just about as bad as I'd figured it would. You could hear it happening in his voice. "You're sure?" he said at last, as they always do. "I mean, no chance it could be a mistake—"

"No." I hated to be abrupt with him but I wanted to get this over with. "Your daughter is in Chicago, occupying an apartment with one Bruce Latimer, a.k.a. Bruce Brutal, drummer for a band calling itself Lizard Puke. She never went near that summer camp, and the people who run it never offered her a counseling job and in fact never heard of her."

I paused while he made faint incredulous noises at his end and then I said, "Mr. Brandon, you need to know that the whole thing was clearly planned far in advance, well before the high school year ended. The tickets were bought two months ago, she took the money out of the bank in several increments, and she went to a lot of trouble setting up an elaborate plan for various friends to cover for her. She wasn't dragged off against her will, and she didn't just yield to a moment's youthful impulse."

He started to protest. I said, "All I'm telling you, Mr. Brandon, is that this is clearly something she *wants* to do. Since she's also eighteen, that sort of limits your possible responses. If you follow me."

He thought about it for a minute or so. I hoped he did follow me. I didn't want to have to come right out and say, "Look, if your sweet little daughter wants to open her sweet little thighs for a twenty-seven-year-old social mutant with a tarantula tattooed on his forehead, there's not a God-damned thing you can legally do about it."

I didn't have to say it. He hadn't gotten to be one of the big kahunas of the Tulsa oil scene by being thick. Instead he asked me a few questions about Bruce Brutal, and I told him what I'd learned—not a hell of a lot, and none of it good—and then, as I'd known he would, he tried to hire me for a different kind of job.

I said, "Sorry, Mr. Brandon. That sort of thing isn't my line

2

of work. Anyway, Chicago is a long way outside my territory, and it's not a good town for an outsider to go the strong-arm route."

I waited while he tried to up the ante. Before he could get the bid high enough to overcome my remaining fragments of judgment, I said, "Mr. Brandon, I can give you the name and phone number of a man in Chicago who can help you better than I could. If you're really sure you want to do it that way."

An uneven sigh came through the phone. "I don't know. What do you think I should do?"

"You could try calling her. Or going up there yourself. You know, try to talk with her." Tag Roper, family counselor. "Couldn't hurt."

He sighed again. "Obviously I haven't talked with her enough over the last few years, or she wouldn't do something like this."

I wondered. My impression—as an outsider, to be sure, one who has gotten through four decades without becoming ancestor material—has been that teenage girls sometimes just hit a point where their hormones swamp their brains and then it doesn't matter what happens or doesn't happen at home; all anyone can do is stand by and wait for the craziness to burn itself out. Come to think of it, you could say the same about middle-aged men. Maybe that's why you hear of so many scandals involving middle-aged men and teenage girls.

Brandon said, "Well, I'll get your check off today, of course. I assume you'll want some extra compensation for your trip to Chicago. Travel expenses and so on."

"I didn't go to Chicago," I said. "I did it from this end, with a few phone calls. It wasn't all that difficult."

"Oh? Remarkable. Well—"

When he'd hung up I looked at the dog, who was staring at me with his usual expression of near-terminal depression. Or disgust, maybe. I didn't blame him. I could have bagged Brandon for a few extra yards of bogus travel expenses, easy as breathing. He'd never have asked for receipts, not with so much else on his mind, and he'd never have missed it either. And God knew I could have used it. I wonder about me sometimes.

It was true, though, that locating Dawn Brandon hadn't been all that hard. No teenage girl runs off without maintaining some kind of contact with her friends from school. For a modest bribe, the editor of the school newspaper had given me the names of a dozen of Dawn Brandon's closest friends. Half of them had turned out to be out of town, and the others had lied to me with the fluttery-eyed innocence and practiced consistency of CIA officials facing a Senate committee, but I'd found the weak one fast enough. I'd known there'd be one. Even Jesus Christ couldn't get twelve guys together without one of them turning snitch.

Actually that was unfair to poor little Nguyen Van Drang, who had given it her best shot. Unfortunately her mother, with reactions formed in Saigon under two different police states, had responded instantly and totally to the crudely-veiled threat in my telephone voice. I'd had to listen to several minutes of screeching in Vietnamese and a sound that might have been a slap, and then Nguyen had come on the line again, her voice muffled and tearful and the quality of her English badly deteriorated. She'd had to give me the phone number and address in Chicago twice before I got it right.

Not, on the whole, one of my prouder moments; which might have been part of why I hadn't been able to get it up for a low-grade ripoff of an apparently decent man whose world had just turned to shit. I gave the dog the finger and said, "Get a job, Harry," and he let off a long slobbery sigh and went to sleep.

I looked at the harmonica again. I knew what I'd done to it, though my memory of the exact details was a little vague. Two nights ago, it had been, out on the parking lot of the Putty Tat Club, where I'd been looking for somebody for somebody else. The old classic Hohner Marine Band non-chromatic harmonica is a simple and sturdy instrument, but it was never made to load fists with. And hadn't been all that good for the purpose, either; my right hand was still a little sore.

On the other hand, sore fingers made a good excuse not to do any work this morning. Maybe all day. I looked across the little room at my desk, with the stack of paper covered in double-spaced typescript and the much bigger stack covered in nothing, the yellow legal pads with illegibly-scrawled notes, the reference books boosted from the Tulsa library, the scattered defunct Bic pens, and, squatting malevolently in the middle of the world, the fancy typewriter I'd bought in the rush of euphoria when they'd accepted my first book and everything was finally going to be all right because now I was a Published Author and would soon be a famous one besides. And obviously I'd need first-class equipment to write all those best-sellers. . . . I don't remember, now, whether I'd figured on winning the Pulitzer and the Nobel in the same year or maybe spacing things out a little, but I know I had it all figured out.

There was a rattling sound at the door. I got up and walked over and opened the door and reached out to get the mail from the cheap little metal box on the front of my trailer, getting a whiff of rotten air that told me the wind was from the northwest again. Yuchi Park, where I live, is far enough out from metropolitan Tulsa that you can usually take a deep breath without needing to make out your will first, but when the wind is right you can still get strongly reminded that Tulsa is one of the most polluted cities in the United States. I slammed the door quickly, not pausing to look around outside, and looked through the mail.

It didn't amount to much. One of my unofficial clients had finally gotten around to sending me a long-overdue check; even now, he'd stiffed me for half of the agreed-on price. That was okay; I'd known he'd do it, so I'd doubled my rates. The Goldentone Tanning Salon informed me that I had just won a free introductory session.

Everybody else seemed to want something from me. Southwestern Bell wanted money, as if I hadn't spent enough over the years bribing their employees to let me see long-distance records and billing files. My congressman wanted me to remember all he'd done for me. Western Writers of America wanted me to pay my dues.

The last envelope bore the printed logo of the Buckner Publishing Group. I knew what it had to be about. They'd let my first book go out of print a year ago and, by contract, the rights were supposed to have reverted to me by now, but they were being a pain in the ass about it for no apparent reason beyond simple inherent fuckheadedness. I tossed the envelope onto the desk, unopened. I'd read it some time when I was more in the mood to lose the will to live.

Just as the envelope hit the desk and skidded to rest next to *History of the Colt Revolver,* somebody knocked on the trailer's front door.

Immediately Harry started barking, in a loud and threatening voice but without bothering to get up off the floor. I stepped over him and opened the door.

A genuinely beautiful young woman stood on the flimsy metal steps, hand raised to knock some more. She said, "Mr. Roper? Taggart Roper?"

I said I was. She said, "Your name was given to me by a friend. I hope you can help me. I don't know where else to turn."

I looked at her for a minute. She was maybe twenty years old, medium height, with pale skin and small, neat features. She had large light-blue eyes and thick honey-blond hair that came down past her shoulders in back. She had on a light-blue summer dress that showed her shape to good effect. It was quite a shape. I closed my eyes and opened them again. She was still there.

I said, "If I go into the city and rent myself a dingy office in a run-down building and get myself a desk and a swivel chair and a shoulder holster, will you come there and say that again?"

She said, "What?"

I said, "Never mind. You'd better come inside and tell me about it."

Two

Harry had quit barking now in order to concentrate on lurching to his feet and thrashing the air with his tail. I grabbed him by the collar as our visitor came in the door. There was no chance at all of his biting her or anyone else, but I could tell he was about to kick into his manic phase; another minute and he'd start jumping on her and licking her and, quite possibly, humping her leg. Not that I couldn't sympathize with the impulse.

She said, "What kind of dog is that?"

"His mother was mostly chow, I think," I said, dragging him toward the bedroom. "His father was in the armed forces. Come on, Harry."

She sat down on the buttsprung couch and watched as I shoved him into the bedroom. "Harry? Is that his name? Why Harry?"

I pushed the bedroom door shut and, with a little effort, got the balky latch to click. Ignoring Harry's scratching and whining, or trying to, I said, "Sorry to tell you, but when you get a look at the back of that skirt you'll know why Harry. I should have warned you about sitting on the couch."

I paused, considering the social options. Tradition said offer her a drink, but this one didn't look quite legal drinking age and anyway it was a bit early. I said, "I've got coffee but it's last night's. Want me to make a fresh pot?"

She shook her head. "No, thanks." Her voice had the clarity of youth, without a trace of that combination Southern-Midwestern accent you get in Oklahoma. She started to open her purse. "Okay if I smoke in here?"

I shrugged. "Go ahead." With the wind from Tulsa, she couldn't make the carcinogen level much worse anyway.

She dug out a pack of menthol cigarettes and stuck one in her face and ignited it. At least the antismoking movement has had one effect: people nowadays either smoke or they don't, but they've just about quit trying to look sophisticated or sexy when they do it. She held her cigarette and smoked it with none of the fancy movie tricks with which the girls of my generation had dislocated their wrists.

She was looking at my desk now. "Hey, wow," she said, "do you write?"

I admitted I did. She said, "Had anything published?"

Years of practice allowed me to mask the wince; all sorts of otherwise nice people think nothing of asking that, though I can't understand why. I mean, if you told them you were a doctor, would they immediately ask you if you'd ever actually treated any sick people? I said, "Yes. Two books, a few magazine pieces."

"Wow," she said again, sounding genuinely impressed. "Shelby didn't say anything about you being a writer."

Shelby? I barely remembered him: a small-time entertainment entrepreneur, owner of a couple of night clubs and a kind of disco, promoter of the occasional rock concert. No heavy connections that I knew of. I'd done a small job for him a year or so back. "Shelby sent you here?"

"He suggested I come see you, yes."

Evidently I hadn't impressed on him the importance of not giving out my name and address without checking with me first. On second thought, he could send these over by the busload. I dumped a stack of books onto the floor and sat down in the decrepit armchair facing her. "How do you happen to know Shelby?"

"My boyfriend works for him," she said. "Bouncer at one of his night clubs."

Oh well. "And what did he tell you about me?"

"That you do . . . unusual jobs, sometimes. That you're dependable and trustworthy." Her eyes were giving me the slow up-and-down, as if she still hadn't decided whether the package came up to the advertising.

"And a man of true grit? Never mind," I said hastily as she looked confused. "Well, Miss, Mizz, uh—"

"Amy Matson," she said. "Call me Amy."

"Okay, Amy. Whatever Shelby told you, I better lay it out for you before you tell me anything. I'm not a private detective, or a public one either. As you see, I'm a freelance writer." More free than lance lately, but no need to bring that up. "Now and then, I supplement my income by doing certain odd jobs, just as Shelby told you. But the point is, I don't have any legal status at all. Anything that requires standing up in court to testify, or submitting a formal written report— such as divorce or child-custody cases—I can't touch."

She was nodding. "Okay, no problem. What I need done," she said, "it's nothing like that. Only I think it may be kind of, like, illegal."

Kind of, like, unsurprised, I sat back and folded my hands and tried to look dependable and trustworthy. "Tell me about it."

"My mother," she said, "died three weeks ago."

I jerked upright. "God, I'm sorry—"

"Oh, it's all right." She made a dismissive gesture with her cigarette and then her mouth kinked down a little at the corners. "I mean, it's not all *right*, but I'm pretty much over the bad part. I never knew her very well. I'd be a phony to act all broken up now."

She stopped and began looking around. After a second I got it. "Here," I said, picking up an empty beer bottle from the floor and passing it over. Nothing like quality furnishings to make a solid impression on a prospective client.

—

9

She dropped the rest of her cigarette into the bottle, where it sizzled, filled the bottle with thick bluish-white smoke, and died. She said, "My mother was murdered."

Oh, shit. I said carefully, "If you really believe your mother was murdered, you ought to talk to the police. Say what you like, they—"

"No, no," she said impatiently. "She *was* murdered. Shot. It's official and everything. Person or persons unknown. It was even in the paper, they tell me. And don't worry, I'm not trying to hire you to find out who did it or any corny shit like that."

She made that little grimace again. "My mother was a whore, Mr. Roper. I mean for real. She laid guys for money, all right? Made damn good money doing it, too. She must have been what they call a call girl, at least when she was younger. She kept me in a high-priced boarding school from the time I was seven, and after that she came up with the bread to get me into Sarah Lawrence for the last three years. Not to mention money for good clothes so little Amy could hold her head up among all the little rich bitches. Most of whose mothers," she added, "were basically doing the same thing she was doing—sleeping with assholes for their money—only they had the papers to make it legal. Never mind."

She got out her pack of smokes again, looked at it, and then put it away without lighting one. "Which I guess is why the Tulsa cops aren't exactly busting their asses trying to find the killer," she said. "It figures there'd be any number of possibilities, and not much chance of ever getting the right one. Even I know that hookers are always getting murdered by, what do they call it, their johns."

I couldn't think of a damn thing to say. I kept quiet and let her roll.

"Like I said," she continued, "I never really knew her, not the way most kids know their moms. Now and then, maybe three or four times a year, she'd come see me—after I got into Sarah Lawrence, we'd meet in New York somewhere, have dinner, shop, stuff like that. She didn't want me coming down here where she . . . worked, and all. This last three weeks, after I came down here for the funeral, that's the longest I've spent in this part of the country since I was a little kid. Boy, it's going to be longer than that before I come back, too. What a dump."

If she meant Tulsa, I didn't feel inclined to argue with her. Something struck me and I said, "If you've only been here three weeks, how come you've got a boyfriend working for Shelby?"

"Oh, Larry drove me down from New York. School had just let out anyway, and we'd been planning to drive out to California for the summer, when they called me about Lorene."

"Lorene?"

"My mother. That's what I always called her," she said. "So anyway, when it looked like I might have to stay here awhile, Larry went looking for work. Tried out as a bartender at Shelby's place, got hired to bounce instead. He's only been there about a week."

Somehow that part about calling her mother Lorene got to me. This was turning into the most depressing story I'd heard in years.

"Lorene used to call me on the phone," Amy said, "usually pretty late, usually when she'd had too much to drink. I never paid much attention to what she was saying. It was generally the same stuff over and over. I'd just hold the phone and let her blubber."

My face must have shown something. Amy looked a little self-conscious. "Well," she said defensively, "that's what she did, she blubbered. You couldn't call it anything else."

She got out the smokes again and this time she did light one. When she had it going she said, "One thing she almost always brought up, though—this routine about how no matter what happened, I'd never want for anything, because she had this special . . . something, better than an oil well or a gold mine or blue-chip stock. Her secret weapon, she'd call it, or sometimes she'd call it our insurance policy."

Amy snorted softly. "For a long time I just figured she was talking about her trade—you know, that guys would always pay top dollar to do it with her—but I finally realized that couldn't be it, not any more. I mean, she was still pretty and all, but Jesus, she was getting sort of *old*. She would have been forty this month."

11

I shifted my forty-year-old bones, which suddenly felt very stiff and creaky, into an easier position. "She never gave you any indication as to what it was? This secret of hers?"

"No. And she'd only mention it when she was drunk, so you couldn't make much sense of anything. I tried to ask her a few times when she was sober and she clammed up on me, really stonewalled. Said it was better I didn't know. Then," Amy said, "back this spring—I remember it was just before spring break—she began talking about a major new angle she was working on. 'Our insurance policy just got a lot better,' she said. And she said that if anything happened to her, she'd make sure I'd have something to take care of me."

Her face took on a distant look. "You know," she said, "that was the last time I ever talked to her. The last thing she ever said to me was, 'I've fixed it so you'll have some chips to cash in if I cash in my chips.' "

I said, "She talked about something happening to her?"

She shook her head. "Hey, I know what you're thinking, but you're on the wrong track. She wasn't afraid she was going to be killed. I knew at the time what she was talking about, because she'd talked about it a lot before. Lorene was worried she was going to catch AIDS," Amy said. "In her line of work, you can't exactly blame her."

She picked up the empty beer bottle and tapped the ash off her cigarette into its throat. "Now," she said, "she's dead, and I know this is going to sound like hell, but she died at a damn bad time for me. Sarah Lawrence isn't a cheap school. I'd gone through my bank balance and maxed out my credit cards by the end of the school term. Lorene always sent me a big check at the start of summer, but this year she waited a little too late. Now I'm living in a shitty weekly-rates motel room that you wouldn't keep that dog in, and if Larry hadn't gotten that job with Shelby I don't know what we'd do. *He* doesn't have any money, that's for sure. His parents don't even speak to him."

She looked at me through a curtain of smoke. "I can't even get at her bank account or anything, until some legal bullshit gets taken care of. Apparently she never left a will. Also they tell me the county or somebody may try to grab all her stuff because it's the proceeds of an illegal business. And it doesn't help that I've never had a clue who my father was."

"I'm starting to see where you're going with all this."

"You probably are. Whatever Lorene had going for her, I haven't been able to find out what the hell it is, let alone cash in on it. What I want," she said, "is for you to try and find out what the big secret was, where she was getting all that extra money. And, maybe, how I go about tapping into it."

I thought it over for a minute or so while she burned more of her cigarette. The only sound was the clatter of the geriatric air conditioner and Harry's whining from behind the bedroom door.

I said finally, "Has it occurred to you that—no matter what your mother was or wasn't worried about—this mysterious 'insurance' of hers could still have had something to do with her death? And that if you start trying to take up where she left off—"

"I could be asking to get dead too. Yeah, I've thought about that. But," she said, "if it looks too hot, like if she was screwing around with the Mafia or the CIA or something, I'll just drop the whole thing and get the hell out of this Godawful town. In fact that's one more reason I need to know what she was into—in case it was something that's going to make trouble for me."

"But," I said, "you figure I shouldn't mind poking around in something that may have already gotten one person killed. For—I don't know how much you expected to pay, but it doesn't sound as if you're in a position to make any offers I'd have much trouble refusing."

She reached out and slowly and deliberately dropped her cigarette in with the corpse of her first one. "What I thought," she said, "was that you could maybe ask around—Shelby says you've got all kinds of contacts—and see if you could pick up anything we could at least go on. And maybe you could get into her place and see what you can see. For all I know the big secret is something that's lying around the house in plain sight. I doubt if the cops made much of a search. They're just writing it off as another dead hooker."

She reached into her purse and brought out a little red wallet. "I've got two hundred and fifty dollars left," she said. "I'll pay you that much just to take a shot at it. If you do find whatever it is, and I manage to cash in on it, I'll give you a fair cut."

I watched as she took out a small tight roll of bills. "When you've done as much as this buys," she said, "and I'll accept your call on that, you seem like a straight guy—when you hit that point, if you still haven't found anything, I'll just say I took a gamble that didn't pay off."

I looked at the money. Damn little pay for a lot of trouble, to say nothing of possible risk. I said, "I hate to say this, but—"

There was a knock on the door. Amy Matson jumped slightly. In the bedroom Harry began barking again. I stood up and said "Excuse me," and went and opened the door.

A small, dark, white-haired man in bib overalls stood at the foot of the trailer steps: old Mr. Berryhill, from the house up at the corner. He was holding out a big yellow manila envelope. "Mailman delivered this at my place," he said. "Think it's yours."

He'd walked a quarter of a mile in the heat of a June day to bring me a misdelivered parcel that most people would have just put back out for the mailman to pick up next day. Even for an old-school Creek, that was pretty good. I said, "Thanks," and took the package, and he bobbed his head and grinned and headed back toward home.

The manila envelope was stuffed nearly to the bursting point; the staples that held it shut were starting to give way. It was pretty damn heavy, too. I shut the door and turned around, looking at the glued-on mailing label. I was pretty sure I knew where it was from and what was in it, but I looked anyway. After all, people throw their hands over their heads when a building falls on them.

I ripped the stapled end open, gouging my fingers on the staples, and reached inside and pulled out a thick bundle of typescript, held together with rubber bands. The rubber bands had chewed ragged little notches in the margins of the outer pages. The top sheet bore a tasteful letterhead identical with the logo on the mailing label.

I read:

Dear Taggart:

Thanks for giving us a look at CEREMONIES OF THE HORSEMEN. The writing is good, the characters interesting, and the research genuinely impressive. I had never before heard of the colonies of ex-Confederates in Mexico, or their involvement in the Mexican civil wars.

Unfortunately I'm afraid it's not for Climax House. There's just no way for us to market something like this right now. The background is too obscure, and the style too "literary," for the category-Western field. And historical fiction, except for women's romances, is dead these days.

Sorry I can't be more encouraging. Good luck in placing this one elsewhere.

Best,
Roger Froman
Associate Editor

P.S. If you're going to keep submitting this, I strongly suggest you rewrite it in third person— first-person narration went out twenty years ago.

I went over and tossed the bundle onto my desk. Amy Matson said, "Bad news?"

I grunted at her and sat back down in the chair. She said, "I thought writers all had agents that handled their stuff for them."

I closed my eyes and rubbed the bridge of my nose with two fingers. "I'm . . . between agents right now," I told her. "The one I had—let's say we developed some compatibility problems."

That wasn't even close to the facts, but there was no way in hell I was going to tell this kid about my troubles with my ex-agent. Her own story had been depressing enough for one morning.

"Listen," I said, opening my eyes, "if I come across anything that looks like evidence concerning your mother's murder, I'll have to turn it over to the police. I may be able to do that without involving you, but I can't give guarantees. Know anything about Oklahoma prisons? There's no way I'm going to play around with accessory to homicide or concealing evidence, not for two and a half yards."

"Does that mean you're taking the job?"

I stared at the bundle of typescript on the desk. "I guess it does." What the hell. "Give me the address where your mother lived. Better give me the name of the motel where you're staying, too, so I can reach you if I do find anything."

"I'll write it all down," she said.

THREE

For once Wiley Harmon was at his desk when I called, which was so remarkable as to be slightly unnerving. In a town like Tulsa, with the summer heat starting to make the residents even crazier than usual, finding any cop sitting down at headquarters is a major event. Even a cop like Wiley Harmon.

He said, "Hey ho, Taggart my man. You hear about the new charity Richard Pryor and Michael Jackson are forming? Gonna call it the *Ig*nited Negro College Fund."

The wheezy laugh that followed was so coarse, so dripping with overall grossness—so Wiley Harmon, in short—that it almost seemed as if I could smell the blast of rancid breath that undoubtedly went with it. I said, "You told me that one already. Repeatedly."

"Shit. I ought to know better than to tell you a joke like that over the phone anyway. No fun when I can't see that liberal flinch. Or the guilty expression when you realize you laughed at it."

"My flinch reflexes burned out years ago, being around you. Listen," I said, "I need to talk with you."

"Ah hah." His voice dropped to a more discreet volume level. God knows why; the times I'd been in his squadroom, you could have had Arnold Schwarzenegger playing the drum part to "Inna-Gadda-Da-Vida" on a Cadillac fender, and the people at the next desk wouldn't have heard it over the racket. "I take it," Wiley Harmon said, "this ain't something we need to kick around over the phone."

"Probably not. You want to get together this afternoon?"

He let off a long damp sigh. I realized suddenly that he sighed almost exactly like Harry. "Man," he said, "it's not a good time. All kind of shit going on around this town right now, and half of it seems to go across my desk. Plus Birdshit is watching me again. Unless this is something really hot—"

"No. At least I don't think so." Harmon's troubles with his boss, Lieutenant Bradshear, a.k.a. Birdshit, were the stuff of legend and folk tale; no use making things even worse over some oddball story about a dead whore. "Later?"

"Be a lot better for me, yeah. Say tonight, eight or so? At the Copper Bottom?"

I said that would be fine and hung up. Actually it wasn't fine; it meant I wouldn't be able to do anything about Amy Matson's problems for the rest of the day. And here it was just getting on toward noon.

I looked at the desk. Obviously I wasn't going to get out of trying to write this afternoon.

Well, I still hadn't had any lunch. Or breakfast either, come to think of it. That would soak up a good deal of time, especially if I also made a fresh pot of coffee; and with any luck, there wouldn't be anything in the refrigerator and I'd have to make a trip to the store. Another hour there, easily. . . .

I got up and headed for the little half-walled alcove that the trailer designers figured was all you really needed for a kitchen. Halfway there I remembered something else, and went to let Harry out of the bedroom.

I got into what you might call the odd-jobs business pretty much by accident; I sort of slid backwards into it over a period of time, and there was never any point at which an actual decision was made.

It wasn't like the writing. I always knew I wanted to write, even back in high school. The only career goal I'd ever had before that had been to be the Lone Ranger, and I'd dropped that as soon as I was old enough to understand why this wasn't a realistic ambition.

It's funny, you know. There were three of us little bastards who hung out together all through high school, and all three of us knew exactly what we wanted to do with our lives. I wanted to be a writer, Elton Fester wanted to be a rockabilly singer, and Rodney Callahan wanted to be a social delinquent.

(We did occasionally dabble in one another's milieus: I played mouth-harp accompaniment to Elton Fester's parking-lot renditions of Roy Orbison hits, Rodney Callahan taught Elton and me how to pick locks and hot-wire cars and fight dirty, and one night Elton and Rodney got to fooling with my typewriter and produced a kind of collaborative novella, unfortunately never completed, which began: "He pushed it in another inch and it was then that Sue Ellen realized that she hated every bone in his body.")

It was generally agreed by the teachers and other authority figures that the three of us would come to No Good End. Which just goes to show how wrong such judgments can be. I haven't exactly stayed in touch with the people I went to school with back in Coffeyville, Kansas; but now and then I run into somebody, or a relative sends me a newspaper clipping. And the last I heard, Elton Fester was leading a moderately successful country-rock band in Memphis and had a record out, and Rodney Callahan was doing time in Texas for armed robbery.

As for Tag Roper, I got into writing through the usual tradesman's entrance of journalism. After college, and a brief government-sponsored excursion to Southeast Asia, I went to work for the Tulsa *Courier* and wound up spending seven years as a police reporter—during which time I got to know a lot of people on both sides of the legal fence, and picked up various useful bits of knowledge about how things really work.

I quit the paper when my first book came out; and even when the book promptly vanished without a trace in the lightless depths of the American book market, I didn't let myself get discouraged. All I needed was a slightly better break, a publisher that would understand what I was trying to do and promote my work properly.

When the second book did even worse than the first, though, and the bank statements started looking like Saddam Hussein's popularity ratings, I finally realized it was time to wake up and smell the mold spores. Somehow I was going to have to develop an alternative source of revenue until the publishing industry and the book-buying public got around to recognizing my unique talents.

I don't even remember the details of the first job. Somebody I knew happened to need to find out something that nobody was supposed to be able to find out; I happened to know another somebody—it wasn't Wiley Harmon, though it probably should have been—who could get at the desired information. Not long afterward, yet another body looked me up and said he'd heard about that little job I did and would I be interested in making a few more bucks doing something similar?

As I recall, the first few gigs were only slightly illegal. The preachers are right; the small stuff is how it starts.

A hooker told me once, "From the time I found out I could get paid for it, I never looked back."

Yuchi Park, where I live, is a little less than thirty miles from downtown Tulsa as the crow flies. If the crow has to get there in a decrepit Camaro, it's a bit farther. To get to the Tulsa side of the Arkansas River, you've got a choice of two bridges, both about equally out of the way. Since the roads and streets around the Tulsa area also tend to be under some form of construction at any given time, getting into town can be a dramatization of the old joke, "You can't get there from here." When the river floods, as it does at least once every spring, Tulsa becomes a galaxy far away.

It was, then, quite a bit after eight-or-so by the time I finally showed up at the Copper Bottom. Wiley Harmon seemed to have made himself comfortable while waiting. The table in front of him was littered with Busch empties and the ashtray was overflowing.

"Hey ho, Roper," he greeted me. "Set your ass down and we'll order a round of whatever you're buying."

Somehow, Wiley Harmon's appearance always came as a slight shock to me, even though I'd known him for nearly ten years; I always thought of him as fat, and I couldn't seem to get my mind to believe that he wasn't. He was a little on the stocky side, all right, and he could have used some regular exercise, but he was built more like a bear—a smallish bear; he only stood five-five—than a hippo.

Maybe it was just that there's a common stereotype of a certain kind of fat cop, slovenly, cheerfully corrupt, foul-mouthed and given to bigoted language and offensive jokes; and Wiley Harmon fit the pattern so perfectly in every other possible respect, you expected him to be fat too.

I sat down as he waved to the waitress. "Don't expect too much in the buying department," I said. "The current job is pretty low-budget stuff so far."

"Oh, well, don't sweat it. Couple more beers," he said to the waitress, and to me, "We'll chalk it up to old times. Shit, I still figure I owe you."

Years ago, while I was still new on the police beat, I'd written up an incident—a minor but violent bust of a pair of stickup artists—in such a way that Harmon had come out looking considerably better than the facts warranted. I'd just been milking my story, trying for the front page; but the Department had been in the middle of some political heat at the time, so Harmon's superiors had been grateful for the favorable publicity. In the end he had received a commendation, which had been of great value to him in his later brushes with Internal Affairs. For me, the investment in goodwill had paid off many times over.

"Before you lay the story on me," he said, "I got to go take a leak. Back in a minute."

While he was gone I glanced around the place. It had been a while since I'd been here.

The Copper Bottom, as you might guess from the almost unbearably clever name, is a cop bar. I mean, nobody makes you show a badge to get in; but the occasional civilian who does drop in, either unknowingly or in search of social variety, tends to leave quite soon and not come back.

There's something about a cop bar, if you're not a cop, that isn't like anywhere else in the world. You walk in and maybe a few people look at you, maybe some others don't, nobody says anything or gives any sign of hostility or even real interest—but from the minute you walk in, you're enclosed in an invisible, hermetically sealed capsule, and very soon you find it hard to breathe in there. You're a foreign particle; you don't belong.

No, there *is* one other experience that is almost exactly like it: when a straight man walks into a certain type of gay bar. Not one of those leather bars, or a gilded cage full of ferns and twittering queens, but the sort of gay bar that looks exactly like any other bar, where all the customers look exactly like anybody else—there, and only there, do you get that same impenetrable force-field cutting off the outsider.

I wasn't quite an outsider at the Copper Bottom; a good many of the regulars knew me from my reporter days, and some of them still appreciated things I'd written about them. And then, too, I'd been there a lot of times with Wiley Harmon, although being an associate of his wasn't necessarily the best endorsement you could have. Still, I felt alone enough to be glad when he got back from the can.

"Boy," he said, sliding into his seat and leaning his elbows on the table, "am I beat. Hell of a day. Hell of a *year,* so far. Christ, this always has been a tough town, but it used to be just ordinary shit—normal holdups, burglaries, couple of guys get drunk and shoot each other, you know. Stuff you could *understand.*"

He rubbed the area above his forehead where his hairline was starting to pull back to a new line of defense. "Now," he said, "we got all this weird shit. Fucking worthless nigger punks got these damn gangs, blowing the shit out of each other every night—which wouldn't be so bad, only they also blow the shit out of everybody else in sight. Fucking worthless *white*-ass punks got these Nazi skinhead groups going, painting swastikas on walls, not to mention the Klan coming back strong and backing them up. Fucking Indians used to at least have sense enough to stay out of that shit, but now they're getting pissed off at these fucking wetbacks that we're starting to get from Mexico, going to be some shit there pretty soon. Plus they got that big powwow in Mohawk Park coming up in another week, you watch, there'll be fights all night and we'll be up to our noses in drunk blanket-asses, probably have a stabbing or two, too."

You had to admire Harmon in a way; his racism was so seamless that it took in the entire *human* race. And yet this was the same guy who'd taken it on himself, at considerable risk to his career and maybe his life, to get the goods on a little ring of secret Klan members among his fellow-cops. This was also the guy who'd taken out his off-duty revolver, while watching the televised videotape of the Rodney King beating for the third or fourth time, and blown the picture tube out of his television set. True, he'd gotten the set as part of a payoff from the biggest fence in Tulsa, but still. . . .

The waitress brought our beers and I paid her. She was Indian and pretty, and as she walked away Harmon watched her hips and said, "Nice ass," but only in a perfunctory sort of way. He liked them fat. I mean, *fat.* Once he'd shown me some nude Polaroid shots he'd taken of his current squeeze. She'd looked as if there ought to be a one-legged sailor sitting on her back, stabbing her with a harpoon.

He said, "You hear about the two California faggots driving through Oklahoma, stopped at one of those Indian trading posts? They got all excited and blew twenty bucks."

I didn't even bother groaning. He said, "So tell Uncle Wiley."

"You used to work Vice, right?"

"Oh, yeah." He sipped his beer, looking reflective. "I spent a long hitch with the Pussy Posse. You know, you'd think that would be a pretty good deal for a guy like me, but it was a disappointment. There's just no serious money in it, in this town. You know the way the whores move around?"

I nodded. Tulsa's prostitution scene is a little unusual. There is no clearly delimited, tacitly recognized area of established vice, like Boston's Combat Zone or The Block in Baltimore.

Instead the hookers move around like nomads, working a neighborhood until the police start leaning on them—usually because the cops in turn are getting leaned on by some citizens' group—and then moving on to fresh pastures. Even the strip joints and porn shops are scattered over a wide area, often turning up in residential neighborhoods.

"You can't get a decent pad going," Harmon said, "before they drift on to some other asshole's turf. And there's all this constant pressure to shut down the whores and the skin bars and like that, because this town is ass-deep in these big-time television preachers like Oral Roberts and Jack Redfield, and they get the citizens to raising hell and then you have to make a lot of busts to get the heat off. Nobody's gonna pay shit for protection, they know they're gonna get knocked down anyway next time some Bible jockey gets a wild hair up his ass. So," he said, getting out a cigarette, "what's your angle? Gonna write a book about whores? I think it's been done."

I told him about Amy Matson's visit and what she wanted. He listened with that total attention really expert cops develop—and, whatever else you could say about him, when he wanted to be a good cop Harmon was as good as they come—and at the end he said, "Hm. Lemme think a minute."

I sat there and kept quiet while he drank his beer and looked off into the smoky dark air. His face was blank as a plaster wall, but inside his head, I knew, he was sorting and filing what I'd told him, digging in his memory for whatever might be relevant. As he'd told me many times, a crooked cop has to be more organized than an honest one, just to survive.

"Okay," he said at last, "I remember Lorene. Of course I remember when she got whacked—wasn't my division caught the case, thank Christ, but I know the guys who wound up with it. This call came in just before midnight, dispatcher said it was a guy, sounded shit-scared. Assumption is that the caller was the one who did the shooting, but it might have just been some poor asshole, maybe a regular john, came to see her for some reason, found her dead, got up enough balls to call it in and then ran like hell. She was shot twice in the chest. Thirty-two automatic, as I recall. You want the details, I can get you a look at the files, but it's gonna cost you."

"No," I said. "Not at this point, anyway."

"What I meant, though," he continued, "I remember her from when I was on the Pussy Posse. She was damn good-looking for her age, I'll tell you. Had a hell of a shape on her. I never got any off her myself, you know the kind I go for, but my partner nailed her now and then and he said she was really hot stuff."

He shook his head. "But I guaran-fucking-tee you she never put that kid through those fancy schools on what she made hustling. She did okay, because she didn't have a drug habit to support or a pimp to take her earnings, but she was never a first-string call girl, even when she was younger. And like the kid said, there's a limit to how much a whore can make once she gets past thirty or so, unless she's got some kind of specialty act. Anyway, this isn't Vegas or Frisco, the really big money just isn't in Tulsa any more, not since the oil business went to shit. The kind of money those schools get? No way in hell."

"Which," I said, "means she *did* have something extra going for her."

"Right. Something that paid regular solid dividends over a lot of years." Harmon looked briefly wistful. "Sounds like a hell of a setup . . . and," he said, his eyes serious now, "I don't have to tell you the odds-on explanation. Considering the business she was in, and all."

"Blackmail?"

"Fucking A. Can't think of anything else it *could* have been, really. If she'd been dealing dope on the side, something like that, I'd have known about it. Well," Harmon said, "she wouldn't have been the first whore to get the idea of soaking some well-heeled john by threatening to send his wife a photo or two of him getting his tool cooled. Unusual for it to go on that long, but not impossible."

His expression grew thoughtful. "Of course, she could have been working more than one guy, but I think I'd have heard about it if she'd been running a regular racket. After all, I been a cop in this town just about as long as she was working her side of the street. Damn," he said, "it's kind of a surprise. Lorene always had a good rep for being square with johns—no lifting their wallets, no badger games." He laughed shortly. "Hell, I sent a fair amount of business her way over the years, never had any complaints."

The waitress drifted by. Harmon said, "Get us a couple more of these, will you, babe?" When she had gone he said to me, "And now let's consider the implications, Taggart my man. We got a whore blackmailing some person or persons unknown. We got a whore found dead with a couple fresh holes supplied by person or persons unknown. Doesn't take Sherlock fucking Holmes to see a possible connection, does it?"

"It's occurred to me."

"Yeah, I bet it has. That kid must be paying you damn good money. Either that or she better give fantastic head, because you're about to start dicking around with some really bad shit here."

He tilted his head. "How much *is* she paying?"

"You don't want to know," I said. "It would depress you. It already depresses me."

The waitress brought our beers. Harmon looked at me until I paid her. "Tell you something," he said when she had left. "You go nosing around in this thing, you find anything, anything at all, looks like evidence—"

"You'll get it," I said. "I already explained that to the kid."

"Yeah," he said, "you explain things to these people, but they don't really listen. We both been down that particular road a few times before, right? But *you* listen to *me,* Roper. Any time you got a dead body in the picture, you can't fuck around."

He studied me with dark hooded eyes. "If I was the right kind of a cop," he said, "what I ought to do would be take this story of yours to the guys working the case. Let them talk to little daughter and then tear that house apart down to the fucking nails, see if they could find anything to lead to the son of a bitch that did it."

I didn't say anything. After a second he sighed. "Of course, if I was that kind of a cop you wouldn't have talked to me to

---

26

start with, would you? All the same, I can't sit on this forever. You don't find anything in a reasonable time—say this time next week—I'll have to pass along an anonymous tip. You got me?"

I nodded. "Fair enough." I wasn't going to stay on it longer than that for the kind of money Amy Matson was paying anyway. "Thanks," I said.

"Shit. You just watch your ass. Don't leave any tracks, in case my heroic fucking brothers in blue do come back for a closer look."

"I'll watch it."

"I don't know," he said. "Somehow I got the feeling you're about to step off into deeper trouble than you ever knew there was. Somehow I think before this is over you're gonna be so far in over your head, you're gonna look like Prince Namor the fucking Sub-Mariner."

FOUR

Lorene Matson's place was a small white frame house on a quiet street in the eastern part of Tulsa. In the dim light of early morning the neighborhood had a respectable but slightly shabby air; it hadn't gotten really seedy yet but it was working on it. It was the sort of neighborhood where you'd expect to find people who worked at the oil refineries or the McDonnell-Douglas plant, not a full-time prostitute. But then Wiley Harmon had said that she seldom took clients to her home, preferring to work in hotels and motels.

It was a good neighborhood from my point of view, anyway. On that street my beat-up old white Camaro would look right at home.

It was just shy of five in the morning when I got there. For clandestine purposes in a residential area, you can't beat the gray-light time. At night, people are edgy and alert, and liable to notice a light in a house that ought to be dark. In the daytime, you can get spotted going in or coming out, and cops may make note of a strange car parked on the street.

But around five in the morning, the human engine tends to run at its lowest idling speed. Most of the people on the street—especially in a working-class neighborhood—are going to have to get up in another couple of hours to go to work, while the few night-owl types will have been in bed for an hour or so. Either way, nobody wants to get out of bed to investigate anything. Even if you make some sounds getting in, or the dogs start barking, the neighbors will just roll over and curse into their pillows and go back to sleep. And the cops tend to be tired and less alert, getting close to the end of their shift; chances are they're sitting somewhere in an all-night place drinking coffee and not paying for it.

The one real drawback is if you've stayed out till midnight drinking beer and talking with Wiley Harmon. Do you set the alarm clock—allowing for the hour or so it's going to take you to get to the target area from your place—and try to catch at least a few hours of sleep, knowing you're going to wake up groggy and stupid and dick-tromping clumsy? Or just stay up the rest of the night, gulping coffee, so you get there wired up like an electric chair with your bladder aching and your teeth itching?

Decisions, as they say, decisions. As with most other decisions in life, whichever you choose, you'll wind up wishing you'd done the other. This time, for no particular reason, I'd stayed up.

The block was bisected by a rough, narrow, unpaved alley, lined with hedges and fences and a couple of garages. I nosed the Camaro down that and stopped in back of Lorene Matson's house and sat there a few minutes, studying the layout, making sure nobody was moving about in the area and satisfying myself that the car wasn't visible from the street. A little extra caution never hurts. After all, carelessness on a simple B&E put Gordon Liddy into the joint and Richard Nixon into the routines of a whole generation of stand-up comedians.

Maybe, I thought, I should have found a pay phone and called the cops and told them there was a crime taking place. That way I'd be certain of at least an hour to work uninterrupted.

Everything stayed quiet. There weren't even any dogs barking. A big gray cat did come sauntering down the alley, but it didn't so much as look at me. I pulled on a pair of cheap plastic gloves, got out of the car, and walked across the alley to the chain-link fence that ran behind Lorene Matson's house. There was a gate, not locked. It opened easily and silently. A couple of minutes later, after a bit of persuasion with simple tools, so did the back door of the house. Rodney Callahan would have been proud of me.

I stepped quickly inside, closing the door behind me, and stood for a moment orienting myself. The interior of the house was nearly dark, lit only by a faint gray dimness coming in the windows. While I was standing there, somebody came up and knocked me on my ass.

In the movies and the books—including the ones I write—the guy gets hit over the head from behind and knocked unconscious. It didn't go that way at all. There was just a dark, vague figure that came out of the gloom in front of me, and a fist that slammed into the pit of my stomach, very hard. That was plenty. The air went out of my lungs all of a whoosh, my vision went red and then black, and I crashed back against the wall and slid down along it and curled up on the floor, not unconscious but close to it.

A moment later I heard the front door open and close. Then everything was quiet again except for the blood booming in my ears.

After a couple of subjective weeks, I managed to get some air into my chest, and my vision seemed to be getting back to normal, though it was hard to tell in there. I didn't jump up and charge off after my assailant, though. I didn't do a damn thing but lie there and hurt for quite some time.

I got to my feet at last, holding my stomach and clenching my teeth against the pain, and when the room quit dipping and swaying I pulled the flashlight out of my pocket and had a look around. I was in the kitchen. I went over and threw up into the sink and then washed my mouth out and splashed a little water on my face, and after that I felt better. Not good, but better.

I didn't look out the windows for a glimpse of whoever had punched me out; he had to be long gone by now. I wondered who the hell I'd just run into in the dark. Traditionally the murderer is supposed to return to the scene of the crime, but I'd always figured that was bullshit—I'd never heard of one actually doing it, and neither had any cop I'd ever asked. Still, it was possible that somebody else had been here looking for Lorene Matson's mysterious ace in the hole, and the killer would seem a logical candidate.

More likely, I decided, it had been some petty-ass burglar who'd learned that the house was empty. Word would be out that Lorene was dead, and hookers know junkies, who know thieves.

Whoever the son of a bitch was, he knew how to throw a punch. It had been a shrewd blow, too, far more intelligent than clubbing me over the head. A blow to the top of the head can have unpredictable results; one victim may fall down dead and another, hit in exactly the same way, may turn around and beat the shit out of you. But a solid punch to the solar plexus will disable any man alive, and as a bonus the victim can't cry out. Or do much of anything else.

The kitchen wasn't very big, and a table and chairs against one wall showed that it was also the dining room. The windows were fitted with Venetian blinds and I made sure they were tightly shut before I switched on the light. Luckily the electricity hadn't been turned off yet. The refrigerator held only the usual sad odds and ends of leftover food, most of it pretty grim by now, and I closed the door fast against the smell.

I made a quick superficial search of the kitchen, not really expecting to find anything in there, just touching bases. Then I moved on to the living room.

It was pretty creepy in there, with that damn body outline still in place on the carpet. There was a dark spot that had to be a bloodstain, not all that big considering; with a small, underpowered weapon like a .32 auto, most of the bleeding tends to be internal. She'd been standing in the middle of the living room when she got it, but I couldn't guess which way she'd been facing, or where the killer had stood.

Taken all in all, the house was nothing like what I'd expected. The furniture was adequate but inexpensive; the walls had been done in cheap off-white latex paint, and the pictures on the walls were the sort of printed reproductions you see in motel rooms. I'd had a mental picture of decadence and glitz, kind of a one-whore whorehouse. This could have been the home of an underpaid kindergarten teacher or an unmarried librarian.

I worked my way on through the house, room by room, getting the feel of the place before attempting any sort of real search. All the rooms had Venetian blinds and heavy curtains, so I didn't have to worry about lights being seen from the street. No doubt, working as she did at night, Lorene Matson had felt the need to be able to darken the interior during the daylight hours while she slept.

The bathroom medicine cabinet contained nothing more interesting than a bottle of PMS-formula Midol and a tube of K-Y Jelly. Of course any serious drugs would have been seized as evidence, or simply stolen, by the cops on the scene.

Even the bedroom was nothing all that exotic; there was a big water bed, but the sheets were regular white ones and not new. The only signs of the late occupant's business were the flashy outfits hanging in the closet, and several drawers full of fetishy lingerie and various toys, props, and gadgets. Even there, the effect was relatively conservative; there were no handcuffs or whips or the like.

Clearly, whatever Lorene Matson had been up to, she hadn't been using the proceeds to live in high style. In fact, it looked to me as if she'd been channeling all the take into Amy's support and schooling, while she herself lived off what she made whoring. I might have gotten a little sentimental over the thought, if my gut hadn't hurt so bad.

From what I could see, the house hadn't been tossed with any real enthusiasm or purpose. The cops appeared to have poked around a little, but in an unsystematic, half-assed way. Most of the signs of search activity—drawers open, stuff on the floor—were in the bedroom, which, since the murder had happened in the living room, suggested prurient rather than professional interest.

And if my mysterious attacker had been a-burgling, he'd missed a lot of fenceable merchandise: a TV, VCR, stereo, even a few loose bills on the bedside table. I must have interrupted him before he could get to work.

On the dresser were several framed photographs: a portrait of Amy, a baby picture that was probably Amy too, and one of a pretty, dark-haired woman that I figured was Lorene Matson. She didn't look much like Amy. There was also a small photo, a little faded, of a man, a woman, and a child standing in front of a house. From the clothes and the hair styles, the picture had been taken some time in the early fifties. I guessed that this was Lorene Matson with her parents. On a stray impulse I pocketed the picture, thinking vaguely that Amy might like to have it.

There was nothing in any of the dresser or bureau drawers, nor were there any packets or envelopes taped to their undersides. Nothing was up under the water bed, behind the pictures on the walls, or inside the toilet tank. After a moment's thought I went to the closet, remembering something I'd seen once while covering a drug raid.

Sure enough, part of the closet ceiling formed a crude hatchway for emergency access to the attic space. It wasn't a trapdoor, just a loose panel that could be lifted and pushed aside, barely big enough for a man to squeeze his head and shoulders through. I had to stand on a chair and then climb up onto the closet shelf, hunched over like Quasimodo, to get at it at all.

The air that drifted down through the opening was musty and full of dust. I didn't try to climb through; I just stuck my arm up into the darkness and groped. My fingers touched rough wood and protruding nails and cobwebs. I tried not to think about exposed wires and black widow spiders. And then, by God, I had something.

When I pulled it down through the hole and had a look, I found that I was holding a flat metal box, maybe a foot square and a couple of inches deep, with a hinged, tight-fitting lid. The lid was locked. The whole thing was surprisingly heavy.

I started to work on the lock, but then I stopped and put the pick back in my pocket. The hell with it; if this wasn't what I'd come for, I was still going to take it home and find out what it was. And the light would be getting stronger outside. Time to go.

I closed the crawl-trap carefully and did what I could to restore the closet to its original appearance. I put the chair I'd stood on back in front of the dresser, had a quick look around to make sure I hadn't missed anything, and got the hell out of the dead woman's house.

Back home, I poured a cup of last night's coffee, warmed it in the microwave—faster than heating up the whole pot—and sat down at the table and went to work on that metal box.

The box was full of papers, and a mixed bag they were. I dumped them out onto the table, wondering where I ought to start. There were photocopies, varying in condition and clarity, of various legal and medical records, several bearing seals of official certification. There were bills and receipts and canceled checks and an Oklahoma birth certificate. There were a number of letters, with and without envelopes, all in the same strong clear hand, all signed with the same name. There was a one-page typed statement, stiffly formal in wording, signed in the same hand as the letters.

There were also two regular business ledgers of good quality, their pages covered with columns of tiny, severely neat figures. One was completely filled and the other had only a few blank pages remaining. Each entry—and there were a *lot* of them—consisted of a date and a number from three to five digits.

I drank some more coffee and sorted the stuff into a number of piles on the table top, trying to make it all tell me something. It was harder than it should have been because I'd been up all night and my midsection was a solid bowling-ball-sized ache. Even with my brain running rough, though, the basic implications of all this paperwork just about stood up and shouted in my face.

Amy Matson had mentioned that she'd never known her father's name. Well, I knew it now. The papers in the metal box proved it twenty times over. I'd studied a lot of records in the last few years, doing background genealogical research for historic fiction, and I'd never seen a package this complete. Hell, I wasn't sure I could have come up with this much proof of who my own father was.

The funny thing was, the name was somehow familiar. It wasn't anybody I knew, but I'd heard it somewhere before. But my memory wouldn't quite retrieve the information this morning, and I pushed the feeling of near-recognition to the back of my mind, where it settled down to gnaw at the insulation on my nerves.

Just now, I was far more interested in the unexpected picture that had begun to emerge from the letters and the ledgers, and the wording of the statement in which the father acknowledged that Amy Matson was indeed his child.

Like Harmon—and Amy, too, I suspected—I had assumed that Lorene Matson's game had been blackmail. And maybe it had been, but I couldn't be at all sure of that from the evidence in front of me.

It seemed to me that what I was looking at could just as easily represent the willing efforts of a man to do the right thing by his out-of-wedlock daughter and her mother. True, there was no indication of any schedule of court-ordered child-support payments, but that didn't necessarily mean anything; more than one anonymous father has made and kept unofficial arrangements because it wouldn't do for the story to come out in court.

Certainly there was nothing in the letters to suggest that he had felt any resentment toward Lorene Matson, or was being leaned on in any way. Of course, there were fewer than a dozen letters, and the last was dated eleven years ago, but the tone made me wonder. One read:

Dear Lorene,

Here is the tuition money, along with something for clothes, as you wanted. I am sorry for the delay but I had to find a way to cover the withdrawal.

Painful as all this has been, it does please me to hear that our daughter is doing well in her studies. Whatever has happened between us—and nothing, I know, will ever make it right—I do not want her to suffer. She is merely the innocent victim of our sin.

I will try to get the next payment off to you more promptly.

As always,

There followed that big looping signature I was getting to know so well. And, God damn it, where *had* I heard that name?

It didn't sound to me like the words of a man being squeezed, except by his own conscience. But then maybe he was just trying to keep a good face on the situation, rationalize it to himself; maybe he didn't want to admit he was getting bled. Or maybe he'd started out voluntarily trying to meet his obligations and later on it got too heavy for him and Lorene rolled out the blackmail artillery.

It was certainly easy to see how the ongoing nut could have gotten burdensome. Even at a casual glance, the ledger entries added up to extremely serious money.

Finally, along about eleven in the morning, I gave it up for the day. I was just too damn groggy to go on; my brains had turned into a cheap grade of expanded polystyrene. Whatever stories were hidden in all this ink, I wasn't going to find them until I'd had some sleep.

I put everything back in the box, along with the picture I'd taken—I couldn't think, now, why the hell I'd boosted it—and stowed it in my desk drawer. I got myself a beer out of the refrigerator and went into the living room and switched on the radio and dumped my ass onto the couch to try and wind down.

My aching stomach wasn't all that happy about the first swallow of cold beer, but the second settled nicely in and the pain began to recede a little. Harry came over and climbed up on the couch beside me and laid his head in my lap and I scratched behind his ears and drank more beer, while the radio filled the room with twang and boom and pleasantly corny lyrics about heartbreak and infidelity and highways in the rain. Charlie McCoy came on with a wailing mouth-harp arrangement of a Hank Williams song about a lonesome train whistle and I remembered I still hadn't gotten a replacement for my own defunct Hohner. Not that I'd ever be able to sound like Charlie McCoy, not if I had a thousand years to practice and a brand-new harp every morning.

The music ended and I listened, half asleep and a bit annoyed, as a string of commercials started. A man with a high, fast, hysterical voice told me now was the time to get the deal of a lifetime on a new pickup truck. A woman with the plastic-sex sincerity of a 900 number told me I should get on down to some damn place for the best price on Western wear in the Tulsa area. Harry and I looked at each other and I drank more beer.

Then a strong, ringing, manly voice, hypnotically rhythmic in cadence, blared from the speaker, while in the background an organ began playing "Sweet Hour of Prayer":

"Friends, have the cares of daily life begun to crush your spirit? Are you confused, bewildered, unable to see the way? Do you feel alone and helpless in this harsh modern world?"

"Harry," I said, "have you been telling this guy about me?"

"Jesus said, 'Let not your heart be troubled,' " the voice went on. "Hear the good news of the full gospel! Learn how Jesus can make your life over! Listen every weekday at three o'clock on this station, and hear the truths of God's word, expounded by Reverend Jack Redfield of the World Faith Tabernacle! And don't forget to watch "The Jack Redfield Hour," every Sunday morning—"

Well, now I knew where I'd heard that name before.

FIVE

The *Courier* had moved into a new building since my reporter days, a shiny modern affair of glass and metal with the general shape of an upended brick and half the esthetic appeal. The building wasn't the only thing that had changed; half the faces I saw on my way in were strangers. There was even a uniformed security guard at the entrance who gave me the bad eye and seemed to be considering stopping me on general principles. In my day, at the old place, all we'd had was an elevator operator, and he was usually asleep.

It was pretty depressing, all in all; it made me feel ancient, almost prehistoric. I wasn't sure I'd even evolved speech yet, let alone writing. I almost looked down to see if my knuckles were dragging the floor.

I found the office I was looking for, after a bit of searching. The door was open so I walked in. A woman in a red dress was standing behind a big desk, her back to the door, bending way over and doing something in a file drawer. I stood and admired the way the red fabric stretched smoothly over the curves of her bottom. Bullshit; what I was admiring had nothing whatever to do with fabric.

She straightened up at last and turned around. She was tall

and slender and dark-skinned, with large brown eyes. Long thick black hair came down past her shoulders. She looked at me and said, "Can I help you?"

I said, "I'm looking for Ed Leavitt," and then I said, "For God's sake. Rita. Rita Ninekiller."

She frowned for a second. "Do I," she said, "no, wait . . . Tag?"

Then we both just stood there for a few seconds grinning at each other like a couple of damn fools. It had been a while.

Rita had come to work for the *Courier* during my last year there. We'd been in different departments so we'd never worked together, but eventually we'd gotten acquainted; and, in time, we'd started going out together. It had been a pretty irregular relationship, even though we'd gotten on well and, the few times we'd slept together, things had gone better than all right.

We had been what Ernest Hemingway called "victims of unsynchronized passion." When I started seeing her I was still walking-wounded from a broken engagement that had gotten very ugly at the end; and by the time I'd started to recover, she had fallen for a junior editor who was charming, handsome, and married. At the time I'd left she'd still been seeing him.

Finally I said, "So now you're what, Ed Leavitt's assistant?"

"No," she said, "I'm Ed Leavitt." She quirked a long black Cherokee eyebrow at me. "I mean, this is my office now. Ed's down in Oklahoma City covering the legislature and the other crooks."

"They gave you Ed's job?" Christ, the *Courier* had sure as hell changed; in the old days women never got above flunky level except in the society section. And a fullblood Indian woman at that. . . . "Well," I said, "congratulations."

"You too. On your writing. I read your first book," she said. "Really good, and I don't usually like Westerns."

"It wasn't supposed to be a Western," I said. "It was supposed to be a historical novel about the Civil War in Oklahoma. The publisher—" I shrugged. "There were Indians in it, and people riding around on horses, so these New York types decided it must be a Western, and that was how they packaged it."

"I wanted to read your second one," she said, "but I never could find a copy for sale."

You and the rest of the population of North America. This was getting to be a painful conversation. I said, "Come by the trailer some time and I'll give you a copy."

"Maybe I will. I'd like to see Harry again."

We did some more standing around looking silly. At last she said, "If you need to talk with Ed, I could give you his number—"

"Actually," I said, "you can probably help me just as much as he could have. Maybe better." Something had just come to me. "They had you on church news for a while, didn't they?"

"Yes." She looked puzzled. "Don't tell me you've gotten born again or something."

"What I need," I said, "is some information on Reverend Jack Redfield."

She folded her arms and gave me a long level stare. "I've been hearing some things," she said. "About how you're not just writing these days. They say you've been doing some strange jobs on the side."

"It's gotten to the point," I said, "I don't know which side the side is on. If you know what I mean."

"You're on one of those jobs now?" she said. "That's why you want to know about Jack Redfield? It's not for something you're writing?"

"Does that make problems?"

"No. I just wondered if the stories were true. What did you need on Redfield?"

"General stuff, that's all. Nothing deep, not at this point anyway. What I'm after," I said, "is some kind of handle on the guy. Whatever will give me a clear picture of him—not so much his operation, or his religious ideas, as what kind of man he really is."

"Hm." She shook her head. "That's just about the last subject I'd have expected Tag Roper to be asking about. But sure, I can give you a hand. Let me dig a little. When do you need the word on the Blessed Rev?"

"Pretty soon," I said. "What about tonight? Dinner?"

40

She looked me up and down slowly, smiling. "Tag," she said, "tell me the truth. You can't really afford to take me to dinner right now, can you? Not on the strength of whatever weird little job you're on."

"Hell, no," I said. "But I'd have had to buy Ed dinner if he'd done the digging for me. And, all right, I wanted to take you out."

"I've got a better idea," she said. "Come by my place this evening about seven and I'll make dinner for both of us. And we'll talk about the Reverend, and—whatever."

"Sounds good to me," I said.

By the time I walked out of the *Courier* building, it had been more than twenty-four hours since I'd opened that damn metal box, and I still didn't know what the hell I ought to do. Do? Christ, I wasn't even sure what to *think*.

It didn't help that the thinking machinery was running on a slightly lean mixture today. I was in a weird, out-of-it state, the result of having my sleep patterns hopelessly disrupted. I'd fallen asleep on the couch—spilling the rest of the beer on the floor; I still hadn't done anything about the mess, although Harry had lapped most of it up—and awakened just at sunset, when Harry had started licking my face and whining to be fed.

I'd gotten up, fed Harry his kibbles and myself a cheese-and-stale-white sandwich and another beer, and lurched back to the bedroom for more hours of sleep. It wasn't very good sleep; my gut was sore where I'd been hit, so that I couldn't seem to find a comfortable position, and there were some dreams I was still trying not to remember.

In the dead hours before dawn I'd gotten up, sweating and fuzzy-tongued and all my joints stiff but one. And sat at the table until daybreak, drinking coffee and staring at the papers from the metal box; and finally, just as the sun was coming up, I'd gone out to the Camaro and driven for a couple of hours on various back roads, going nowhere in particular, just trying to clear my head. That usually works for me. This time it hadn't.

From one angle, the answer was simple: tell Amy Matson the story, give her the box and its contents, and let her decide what she wanted to do about it. After all, she'd paid me to find something, and I'd found it; and God knew she had a right to know the truth. I wasn't exactly looking forward to telling her—how the hell was I going to say it? "Amy dear, I've found your long-lost daddy. He's a big-time television preacher and he may have blown your mama away." Still, I was going to have to find a way to do it, sooner or later.

The problem there was that I didn't know Amy Matson that well. I didn't know her at all; and therefore I didn't know how she might react to my news. It seemed entirely possible that she'd do something impulsive and uncool, like going to the cops or the press—and if she did, some of Wiley Harmon's colleagues were going to come looking for me, and they wouldn't be after autographed copies of my latest novel.

The obvious alternative was to turn the whole package over to the law. Harmon would find a way to get the evidence into the system without leaving any tracks to my door—he'd done it before—and I'd be off the hook. If Amy Matson didn't like it, well, I'd warned her this might happen.

And yet, God damn it, the whole thing felt—I don't know, not exactly wrong, just vague and uncertain, like driving on a slick road. As many times as I'd examined the papers in that box, I still couldn't make them add up to a clear and unarguable pattern. There was no doubt at all that any police investigator would see evidence of a powerful motive to commit murder, and maybe he'd be right. But I couldn't shake the feeling that this wasn't as simple as it looked.

It was a hell of a dilemma. By turning the box's contents over to the cops, I might be bringing a king-hell nightmare down on a poor bastard whose only crime had been to try and do the right thing. Even if he wasn't convicted—even if the case never went to trial—the publicity would probably destroy his evangelical career.

On the other hand, by sitting on what I'd found, I might well be helping a murderer—an evil, hypocritical son of a bitch who knocked up whores and murdered them while hiding behind the Bible—get away clean.

All of which was what had brought me at last to the *Courier,* looking for an old associate who'd been a minor expert on the local prime-time-religion scene. I didn't really know if it would help me make a decision, but somehow I felt that I ought to find out more about Reverend Jack Redfield before I went any farther.

And now, as if my mental processes weren't already chaotic enough, about half of my brain cells had gone on strike on this whole Redfield-Matson business. They said they didn't want to think about television preachers and dead hookers any more; they wanted to think about seeing Rita Ninekiller again. . . .

When I turned down the long gravel drive that goes to my trailer, I saw that a small light-blue car was parked in my lot. I drove up beside it and stopped and a husky young guy in jeans and a Guns and Roses T-shirt got out and came toward me as I opened the Camaro's door.

He said, "You're Taggart Roper, right?"

I finished getting out of the car while he finished coming up to me. He was, I guessed, somewhere in his early twenties— maybe not even that; it's getting so I have trouble telling with the young ones, which has got to be a bad sign. He had curly reddish-blond hair and a tan and lots of muscles. He had the sleeves of the T-shirt rolled up over his shoulders so everybody could see more of his muscles. His hands were shoved in his back pockets and he walked with a rolling, dig-me-man-I'm-bad motion. I sighed to myself. For some reason I didn't think I was going to be glad to meet him.

When I didn't answer right away he said, "So what'd you find out?"

I closed the Camaro's door and looked him over a moment longer. "So far," I said, "I haven't got the faintest idea what the fuck you're talking about. Or who the fuck you are. If anybody."

He moved his head impatiently. "My name's Larry," he said. "Amy's like, my old lady. What'd you find out? About the stuff she paid you to check out?"

His accent was almost but not quite New York. Jersey, maybe. I wondered where Amy Matson had met him. If he was a college student I was Zoltan, the King of the Gypsies.

I said, "My arrangement with Amy was that I'd get in touch with her when I had something to tell her. I don't believe your name came up."

"Yeah, well," he said, "I didn't know she went to see you till after it was too late, or I wouldn't of let her. Tell you something, fella, I was just about ready to come over here and get that two hundred and fifty back, that she gave you. Here I am working all night at that fucking night club of Shelby's, supporting both of us, and she gives a month's rent to some hillbilly hustler, doesn't even ask me first."

He spat on the ground. "But she bitched and moaned and I said okay, give this guy a chance. Now I'm here and I'm asking you, what'd you find out?"

"And I'm telling you," I said, "my deal was with Amy. She's the one who paid me, she's the one I talk to."

"Huh," he grunted scornfully. "You talk with her, you do it through me from now on. You got that?"

This was getting a little hard to believe. I said, "Son, you need to do something about these old-fashioned male-chauvinist attitudes of yours, you know that? This is the nineties, for God's sake."

His eyes changed. You couldn't pin it down more precisely than that; they just changed. He took a step toward me and his hands came out of his pockets and the muscles along his arms rippled briefly. "Listen," he said, "I don't want you to talk to me like that." His voice had suddenly gotten much higher, like Mister Rogers on speed. "You don't *ever* talk to me like that, right?"

I had his number now. I'd met the breed before, more times than I could count. A flipout, Wiley Harmon would have said.

Nobody seems to know what makes a flipout tick. You run into them at all social levels, in all sorts of places, from pool halls to corporate boardrooms. They've got one thing in common: given the necessary trigger—and it often takes very little—they can go from calm, reasonable behavior to flat-out rabid-wolverine craziness in absolutely no time at all. The surest way to trip the flipout's switch is to oppose him, to fail to give him his way, on any matter at all.

I didn't know whether this one was a natural flipout or had gotten that way with chemical assistance—cocaine in particular turns normal people into instant flipouts, and speed is nearly as bad—and at the moment I didn't particularly care. He was fifteen years or so younger than me, he had the size and the reach on me, and he was obviously in fantastic shape; and right now he was on the cusp of flipping out.

I started to speak and he said, "Now are you gonna tell me what I want know? Or are you gonna give me some more shit about it's none of my business?" He shifted his weight forward onto the balls of his feet. His nostrils were flared so wide it was like looking into the muzzles of a double-barreled shotgun. "Because, motherfucker, what if I *make* it my business?"

I stood still for a moment. "All right," I said. "Calm down, Larry. I'll show you what I've got."

His face went through a couple of shifts. "Yeah?" He seemed uncertain whether or not to be happy that I'd caved in. He'd been ready to start kicking ass and now he wasn't going to get to. "You got something?"

"In the trailer," I said. "Come on."

"All right." The warning light was still on in his eyes but a different expression, one of intense interest, was taking over the rest of his face. "This better be good," he added.

I climbed the trailer steps and unlocked the door. Harry was barking now, his already big voice amplified impressively by the trailer's thin metal walls. I said, "Better let me go in and put my dog up, or he'll go for you."

"I ain't afraid of your fucking dog," Larry said, but he didn't sound entirely sure about that. "Don't get funny, man, I'll be right behind you."

"Fine with me," I said, opening the door, hearing Larry starting up the steps as I stepped inside the trailer.

When I turned around he was just reaching the top step and his face and upper body were coming through the doorway. That was as nearly perfect as anything was likely to get in this life. I slammed the door, getting all my weight behind the slam. There was a loud tinny crash, and also a sort of soggy thump, all at once.

I opened the door again. Larry was still standing there on the top step. His facial expression had gone very blank. There was blood beginning to spread over his upper lip and his nose seemed to have changed shape.

While he was still in position I did my best to kick a field goal with his crotch. At the last instant he moved a little—I think his knees started to buckle—and the kick missed his groin and caught him in the lower abdomen instead. That was okay too. His eyes got really wide and his hands went toward his belly and he said, *"Gah,"* in a hoarse voice and fell off the steps.

As his ass hit the grass I said, "That's what if you try to make it your business, asshole."

Harry crowded out the door past me, barking frantically, and jumped onto Larry's chest and began trying to lick his face. I said, "Larry, Harry. Harry, Larry. Excuse me a minute."

I went back to the bedroom and got the shotgun out of the closet and came back. Larry was trying to get to his feet but Harry kept knocking him down. He drew back a foot and I racked the shotgun's action with a loud *clack-clack* and said, "You kick my dog, there's going to be a whole crowd of you."

The shotgun wasn't loaded, but Larry didn't know that. I didn't think he'd be interested in finding out experimentally, either. Very few men are. He looked at me—his eyes seemed to be slightly crossed—and I said, "Get in your fucking car and get out of my yard. Harry, come here."

I had to call Harry a couple of times—we didn't get company all that often, and he was excited about having a new friend—before I could get the stupid bastard to let Larry get to his car. A few minutes later, though, there was a long plume of reddish-yellow Oklahoma dust moving up the drive toward the main road. From the sound of it, Larry's car didn't seem to be a very good one. But his technique might have been a bit off just then.

I put the shotgun on the couch and had a look at my door. As I'd feared, the flimsy aluminum had been bent out of shape. I had to wrench and grunt a bit to re-shape it before it would close properly. There was a distinct dent in the middle. The dent contained a small smear of what looked like blood.

Going back to the kitchen to get a rag and the 409, I wondered if I'd been a little hard on Larry. But the hell with him. He'd picked a really bad time to crowd me; I had too damn much on my mind today to bother with macho-man punks.

And—though I hated to admit it to myself—it had made me feel infinitely better to get to hit somebody. Maybe I should write one of those self-help books about it. *Punch Your Way to Peace of Mind.* Best-seller material for sure.

Six

Rita Ninekiller's apartment was on the south side of Tulsa, part of a whole block of two-story, eight-unit condo buildings that hadn't existed back when Rita and I had first known each other. The total area of her place was probably no bigger than that of my trailer, but I figured you could have bought a whole lot full of secondhand trailers like mine for what this place cost. Nice to see that one of us had moved up in the world.

"Tag," she said, meeting me at the door. "Come on in. Oh, great, this is your other book?" She took it from me and looked at the title. *"Steps of the Sun.* Another Western?"

"It's about an old mountain man and a party of settlers in Oregon," I said. "But the publisher—"

"Don't tell me. It takes place west of the Mississippi and it's got horses and Indians in it, so they knew it had to be a Western."

"Something like that. Also I already had one Western on the market—it said so right on the cover—so obviously I was a Western author. Believe me," I said, "you think newspaper people can be thick, wait till you try doing a book."

She nodded. "It's the same with Tommy." She gestured around the room, at the paintings on the wall. "He's an Indian artist, so they expect teepees and buffalos and war dancers in feathers."

Rita's brother Tommy Ninekiller was a painter, pretty well regarded within the Indian art scene. I recognized several of his paintings that I'd seen at Rita's old place, years ago, scenes of Cherokee life in early times—stickball players, men building log cabins, women pounding grain in wooden mortars. There were also some I hadn't seen before. Next to the door was a big flat-wash watercolor of a bunch of Indians struggling on foot and horseback through drifts of snow: the classic Trail-of-Tears picture, long a standby theme of the cornier tourist-trap artists. Except that Tommy had placed a cartoonist's balloon over the head of one of the Indians in the foreground, and the words, "Are we having fun yet?"

She saw what I was looking at and laughed. "Tommy's moved in some new directions," she said. "Getting more satirical, maybe more political. Look at this."

"This" was an oil painting, done in a heavy, somehow disturbing style, showing a human skull wearing a Plains war bonnet. The eagle feathers had been replaced by dollar bills. The title on the frame read *Come to the Powwow*. I said, "Christ."

Rita said, "Well, come on in. Dinner's nearly ready."

Dinner was built around chicken breasts done in some kind of orange sauce. I mean it was orange in color, not that it had orange in it, although for all I knew it might have. I said, "What do you call this?"

"Chicken Climax." She grinned. "You know the secret to making a chicken climax?"

"Tell me."

"Plenty of foreplay." We both broke up briefly and I spilled a little of my wine and said, "Sorry."

"It's all right," she said. "God, Tag, it feels good to have to clean up after a man. After a certain anal-repressive son of a

---

49

bitch who never dropped a crumb in his life and wouldn't say shit if he had a mouthful. . . . Oh, hell," she said. "I'm doing it, after I always said I wouldn't."

"Doing what?"

"Talking to a man about another man. You know. Forget I said anything," she said. "Finish your chicken."

She'd lost me about three sharp turns back, but I nodded and kept eating. After a minute she said, "At least you didn't ask me if this was an old Indian recipe. Every *yoneg* I've cooked for always wound up asking me that, no matter what I fixed. I could serve lox and bagels and cream cheese, or linguine marinara, and they'd say it: 'Is this an old Indian recipe?' "

Yo-ne-ga in Cherokee means merely "white" but *yoneg,* the way a modern Cherokee uses it, is closer to "honky." I said, "You forget I'm a *yoneg* myself."

"Oh, hell, no, Tag, that's one of the things I always liked about you. You're almost the only white man I ever met who didn't claim to be part Indian. That always comes next," she said, "right after the question about the recipe: 'Did you know my grandmother was a Cherokee princess?' I get so tired of that bullshit."

She snorted. "Of course nowadays you get these New Age types. They've got a whole new angle on being a pain in the ass. They tell you they were Indians in a previous incarnation. That, or they've been channeling the spirit of a dead medicine man— who for some reason speaks fluent English. Last New Year's," she said, "at the staff party, I got in some trouble when our new city editor's fiancée told me she'd been an Indian in a past life and I'd had a few and I said, 'Yeah, I bet you were a butthole then, too.' "

I laughed. She said, "Sure, it's funny to you, you don't have to put up with it all the time. Remember last year, that movie? White people all went crazy. Every *yoneg* I met wanted to talk about *Dances with* fucking *Wolves.* I'd tell them, look, I'm a Cherokee, I don't know a damn thing about Plains Indians, we lived in log cabins and hunted deer and grew corn and raided the Creeks before those Plains guys ever saw a horse. For God's sake, I'd say, would you ask a Sicilian nun what she thought of

Fiddler on the Roof because Italians and Jews are both white? And they'd look at me and smile and nod and ask me some damn thing about Custer or Geronimo or something. I'm telling you, Tag, I still don't understand how we lost."

She picked up the wine bottle. "More wine? Don't mind me, Tag, I'm just wound up and you were nice enough to be here to unwind on. It's been kind of a long day," she said. "Come on, have another glass and then we'll go talk about your preacher."

There was a cardboard box on the coffee table. It was full of books and paperback pamphlets and a lot of photocopies of newspaper stories. I sat down on the couch and stared. "Christ," I said, "you didn't screw around, did you?"

She deposited herself in a chair with a smooth graceful motion. She had on a shortish blue-green dress and I had a fine view of her legs, which were as splendid as I'd remembered, but I still felt a slight twinge of disappointment. I'd been sort of hoping she'd sit down beside me on the couch. Deep down inside, I suppose all men are still sixteen.

"I didn't know what you were after," she said, "so I collected everything we had that looked potentially useful. Probably most of this is irrelevant for your purposes, but you can sort through it at your leisure." She grinned. "What's the old Carson show gag? Everything you could possibly want to know about Jack Redfield is in that box."

I wanted to bet it wasn't; there was at least one pretty important fact about Jack Redfield that I was damn certain wasn't in that box. But I kept quiet. I might eventually tell Rita the story, but it wasn't time yet.

She rummaged around in the box and pulled out a few books, trade-size paperbacks and a couple of hardcovers. One of the hardbacks bore a dust-jacket photo of a middle-aged man in a suit. I said, "Is that Redfield? I don't even know what he looks like."

She passed the book over and I studied the picture for a moment. I'd been expecting some red-faced, wild-eyed shit-kicker in a bad doubleknit suit, but this guy had a thin, rather sensitive face and a sort of academic appearance; he might have been a professor at some small college. Rimless glasses and graying, thinning hair added to the effect. Good suit, though. The book was titled *Doing His Will: The Story of Reverend Jack Redfield*. The imprint was one I didn't recognize, probably a private press.

"That one's the authorized biography," Rita said. "Then here we've got a couple of collections of his sermons, and this is the book he wrote a few years ago on the deterioration of moral values in the United States."

"He say anything about the publishing industry?"

"This stuff comes in all the time," Rita went on. "That guy's got a publicity-and-promotion operation that a lot of rock stars would envy. And, of course, he's not the only one. I don't have to tell you that Tulsa has gotten to be one of the big centers for these characters, and they all make sure the newspapers get copies of everything they crank out. Naturally it all goes into the wastebasket, except that we hang on to a fair sampling just in case we need it for background. Like if there's a scandal."

"A scandal? Involving a TV preacher? What an outlandish thought." I lobbed the book back into the box. "Okay, I'll take all this junk home and look it over. Meanwhile, tell me what you know about this guy. Better yet," I said, "tell me what you think."

"Hm. Well, anything I tell you will be pretty superficial, of course—" She looked at the box and then at me. "How about something to drink? My analytical processes need a little lubricating."

"My listening processes have the same problem."

"Bourbon?" she said, getting up and moving toward the kitchen door. "I remember you drank bourbon in the old days."

"You remember anything I *didn't* drink in the old days? Well, except for those candy-ass liqueurs that make you want to brush your teeth after each shot. . . . Bourbon's fine," I said. "Couple of rocks in with it, if you would."

While she was in the kitchen I looked through the contents of the box. Besides the books, there were lots of little booklets— tracts, I guess you'd call them—with titles like "God's Plan for

Man" and "How Can You Be Born Again?" Surprisingly, there didn't seem to be a lot of political material, unless you counted an interesting-looking item titled "Caring for God's Creation: Christians and the Environment." Even more surprisingly, I didn't see any overt pitches for contributions. Rita came back with the drinks just as I was leafing through "Alcohol: The Devil's Brew."

She handed me a glass that contained a couple of ice cubes and a very worthwhile level of good-smelling whisky. She'd brought herself one, too. "Reading the good word?" she said, sitting down in the chair again.

I tossed the tract back into the box. "Not quite what I'd expected," I said. "In some ways, at least."

She nodded. "Yes, Redfield's different, that's for sure. Most of these blow-dried TV Bible thumpers are just redneck hustlers out for a buck, with a scattering of genuine loonies and more than one outright fascist. They grow up hungry out in the boondocks, they don't make money fast enough selling vinyl siding or used cars, so they get themselves ordained in some obscure denomination—maybe buy a mail-order diploma—and start making the rounds. If they get hot enough, eventually they go on radio and TV, preaching a lot of simplistic mumbo-jumbo backed up with misquotes from the Bible. Most of them promise all sorts of miraculous cures and material rewards in return for cash contributions—"

"I suppose they don't put it quite that way."

"The hell they don't. Obviously you've never watched some of these shows, Tag. Oh, the majority aren't quite that crass—they talk about 'prayer requests' and 'giving to the Lord's work' but even the more sophisticated ones generally manage to suggest that God is going to hear your prayers a lot clearer if you send some bread to His spokesmen."

She leaned back and sipped her bourbon. "Jack Redfield, though, is something else. He started out typically enough," she said. "Grew up on one of those lonesome, windswept farms out in Kingfisher County in the early fifties. Raised mostly by his mother, a fanatically devoted pillar of some minority Pentecostal sect. His father had given up farming for the oil business and was gone a lot. And made it pay off, too. By the time young Jack Redfield was nine or ten, Eugene Redfield had made himself a serious pile off some oil deals that, I understand, are still paying royalties every year."

She looked thoughtful. "I suppose that's the key to what makes Jack Redfield different. He's never been driven by money hunger, like so many of these people. He's always been comfortable, never had to worry about where the money would come from. So," she said, "I've always assumed that he's sincere in what he's doing, because he doesn't have any need to run a hustle. In fact he's never needed to do any work at all, except what he wanted to do."

I said, "My impression is that the sincere ones can be the worst. The craziest, I mean."

"Oh, sure, tell me about it. Don't forget, I grew up in a super-conservative Cherokee Baptist family. My grandfather got mad when my parents let Tommy and me go to stomp dances, said they were 'devil worship.' But," she said, "all that oil money also paid for a good education. Eugene Redfield died just before his son finished high school, but the legacy he left put Jack through college and then a top eastern seminary. As a result, the Reverend is considerably more literate, less narrow, than most hard-core Bible Belters."

"Big time, is he?"

"Oh, my God, yes. He doesn't have as huge an empire as some of the megastars, but then he hasn't gotten in trouble by overreaching, either. He's big enough," she said. "Jack Redfield Ministries has a whole complex of buildings down in southeastern Tulsa, big staff of full-time workers—in fact they're a major employer in the area. There's that World Faith Tabernacle, where they do the shows—in theory it's Reverend Jack's church, but actually it's as much a television studio as a real church, though they do have a live congregation. They also print and distribute those tracts, run a recording studio for gospel music and inspirational tapes, counsel unwed mothers on alternatives to abortion, operate a shelter for the homeless—I couldn't name all the things they do. And then there's the mail operation. I'd guess more mail passes through the Ministries offices than through some Third World countries."

"They go for mail-in donations?"

"Yes, but not as voraciously as most, and the money seems to be handled honestly. Three different bunches of TV news types have tried to catch them dirty, and even '60 Minutes' drew a blank."

She gestured toward the box. "Plenty of details in here, if you're really interested. There's a brochure that goes into all the Jack Redfield Ministries operations."

I said, "What about his personal life? Now, I mean?"

She gave me a quick keen look. "Still looking for angles? As far as anybody seems to know, he's even cleaner on the private front. Married for twenty-some years to 'a Missouri girl' as *Mrs.* Martha Redfield—they don't go for these modern designations, these people—describes herself in her extremely rare interviews. No children that I've ever heard of."

"He lives here in Tulsa?"

"Actually I think his place is across the line in Broken Arrow. Down there along the river, anyway, where they're building those expensive estates. Why the hell," she said, "would people spend that kind of money to live next to a river so polluted an atheist could walk on it, one that floods every spring? *And* almost permanently downwind of a city with one of the worst air-pollution indexes in the country?"

"If they're so rich," I said, "why ain't they smart?"

"Right." She looked down into her glass. "Refill time. You?"

I held up my own glass. "Just a bit."

She went out to the kitchen and came back holding a bottle. Jim Beam. I let her refill my glass. The ice cubes had melted but that was okay.

When she had seated herself again she said, "Actually, that's quite an interesting little family scene at the Redfield place, or so I've heard. The old lady is still alive and living with them."

"Redfield's mother?"

"Right. I met her once, just to shake hands, while I was on the church page. Terrifying person," Rita said. "Looks at you with these hard little eyes like she's evaluating your whole life and character and doesn't like a damn thing she sees. Here, I'll show you."

She bent over the coffee table and dug into the box's contents. "Here we are." She handed me an eight-by-ten black-and-white glossy, a professional-looking group portrait. "They also keep us supplied with publicity photos, whether we ask for them or not."

I recognized Jack Redfield, though he looked a little older than he had on the book cover. Next to him stood a small, pale woman, pretty in a bloodless sort of way. She looked slightly nervous; she looked as if she looked that way a lot. On the other side of the Reverend was a tall, absolutely erect woman in a plain dark dress with no jewelry or ornaments whatever. She had white hair and her face was lined about the mouth and eyes. I said, "This is the mother?"

"Amanda Redfield," Rita said, rattling the remains of her ice cubes. "In the mortified flesh."

I saw what Rita had been talking about. The older woman's face was scary even in a photograph. Not that she was ugly; you could tell she'd been a hell of a fine-looking young woman and even now she might have been considered handsome for her age. But it was a hard, cold face, the face of a person who never cut an inch of slack for anyone, including herself.

There was another figure in the photograph, standing off to one side, almost in the background; a big, powerful-looking man with the shoulders of an adolescent mastodon. He had a broad, heavy-boned face that appeared to have experienced several collisions with solid objects. I said, "Who's the fullback? Family?"

Rita laughed. "No, although I think he wishes he could be. That's Melvin Rains, a.k.a. Mad Mel. Former heavyweight pro wrestler, martial artist, and stunt man, until he heard the Reverend speak—he says—and got born again. Now he's head of security at the Jack Redfield Ministries complex and on the Redfield revival tours, and personal bodyguard to the Reverend and his family. Also," she said, "member and leading light of the Christian Martial Arts Association."

"You're putting me on."

"I swear. He's in this national organization of chop-socky types who go around putting on demonstrations and delivering sermons to anyone who'll watch, usually church youth groups. Break bricks with their fists, put their heads through boards, then explain how Jesus gives them the strength of ten. Or something like that," she said. "Mad Mel has a special elite group of his own, called Black Belts for Christ—if you're ready for that—right here in the Tulsa area. Most of them work on the Redfield Ministries security staff."

I put the photo back into the box. Rita said, "You're not going to tell me what you're working on, are you?"

"It's better I don't, right now. I'd have to make you swear not to use it yet, and you'd go crazy sitting on it."

She crooked an eyebrow. "That hot?"

"It could be." I finished my bourbon. "So," I said, "what's been happening with you? I don't think we've covered that yet."

"Hell, you don't want to know. Or if you do, I don't feel like telling you tonight." She raised the bottle. "More?"

I hesitated. "I better not," I said reluctantly. "Not if I've got to drive home. Friday night traffic out my way, you know what it's like."

I set my glass down on the coffee table. I said, "And I do have to drive home tonight. Don't I?"

We looked at each other for a long time. Something had just come into the room with us. I don't think either of us was surprised. I think we'd both been waiting for it all evening.

But at last she said, "Yes. I guess you'd better go on. This time, anyway." She sighed. "I can't tell you how good it's been to see you again, Tag. An awfully big part of me wants to tell you to stay. And after all, it wouldn't be the first time for us, would it?"

"But?"

"But," she said, "I don't think I'm quite ready to take it any farther tonight. It's been a long time, Tag. A lot of things have happened to me, I'd guess a lot of things have happened to you. I don't know about you, but I need to think it over."

I nodded. "Okay," I said, getting to my feet. "Your call. See you again?"

"Count on it," she said. "I'll be out of town for the weekend, but call me any time after that."

I picked up the box from the coffee table. "I'll do that," I said.

Back at the trailer, I dumped the cardboard box on the floor beside the couch and went into the alleged kitchen and got out my own current bourbon supply. Jim Beam again; my bottle wasn't as old as Rita's, but what the hell, youth deserves a chance too. I went back and stretched out on the couch and unscrewed the lid and dosed myself a little, not bothering with ice or glasses.

Harry came up and stuck his nose up close to my face and said something in dog. I said, "Hey, Harry. Are you glad I came home?"

He whined faintly and I said, "I'll tell you straight out, good buddy, *I'm* not glad I came home. You can thank Rita that you didn't have the place to yourself tonight." I tilted the bottle again and let another increment of Jim trickle down my throat. "You remember Rita, don't you?" I asked Harry after a minute. "You were just a puppy the last time she was here."

Harry walked away and began sniffing the cardboard box. Probably smelled Rita's perfume on it. I said, "Nothing in there for you, Harry. Just a bunch of paper. What we really needed around here, huh, more paper."

He stuck his muzzle down into the box and made sure I was telling the truth. Then he looked at me with an expression of bemused incomprehension: what the hell *did* I want with this junk?

I said, "I'll tell you, Harry. There's this man I've never met, and right now I'm in a position to ruin his life, maybe destroy him completely. So I went looking to find out more about him. I guess," I said, realizing it at last, "I was hoping to find out he was some kind of a sleazy son of a bitch, so it would make it easier for me to drop the hammer on him."

Harry climbed up onto the couch and made a snuffling sound

and stretched out beside me. I said, "Yeah, I know, Harry. Life just isn't that accommodating, is it?"

There was a sudden percussive rattling on the trailer's aluminum roof and sides. A brief gust of wind shook the windows.

I hoisted the Jim Beam again. They say getting drunk alone is bad, but hell, there are times when staying sober alone is worse.

SEVEN

The rain went on all weekend. A couple of times it slackened up to light-drizzle level and I went out to the supermarket and the liquor store, but even then the streets were slick and the spray thrown up by the other cars' tires was as bad as the rain itself. It never got heavy enough to threaten flooding, but my yard did get a little boggy. When I let Harry out to take one he sank in up to his ankles. Or whatever dogs have.

I spent most of the time going over the material Rita had collected on Reverend Jack Redfield. By now I wasn't really expecting to learn anything that would make any difference; I was just curious, and it was an excuse to stay away from the damn typewriter.

I'd blown my own act Friday night, with what I'd said to Harry. One of the best reasons to have a pet around is so you can tell it things you can't tell anyone else; but it must not be a very good sign when you find yourself telling the dog things you don't want to tell yourself.

Damn it, I *had* been hoping—maybe subconsciously, but hoping—to learn that Jack Redfield was a rotten son of a bitch so I could dump on him with a clear conscience. So maybe he's innocent of killing Lorene Matson, so fuck him, he's guilty of *something,* right?

Which is very bad thinking, and I was ashamed of having caught myself at it. It's that sort of twisted logic that causes a jury to convict a man for killing his wife because the prosecutor proved he was screwing around with his secretary, or to let a rapist walk because the victim once posed for stroke pictures. Even if Jack Redfield had turned out to be a two-hundred-proof asshole, a phony who couldn't wipe his own butt without stealing some of the take, it wouldn't have proved that he had anything to do with Lorene Matson's death.

And, of course, the reverse was also true: just because he seemed to be a reasonably sincere and decent man, it didn't necessarily follow that he hadn't killed her.

Or had it done; there was that possibility too. I found myself looking, more than once, at the flat brutal face of Melvin Rains, and wondering how deep his loyalty to the Reverend ran. Remembering, too, that powerful, professional-grade body blow I'd walked into in that darkened house on Minkolusa Drive. . . .

The call was still mine, and nothing in the box of literature was going to help me make it. Still, I flipped through the tracts, studied the newspaper and magazine stories, and even read a few chapters of the biography, just for the illusion of doing something. What the hell, there was nothing I could do until Monday anyway.

The first chapters of the book were fairly interesting, in the sharp clarity with which they described what it had been like growing up on that lonesome Southern Plains farm. I'd always thought it must be a hell of a life out there on that endless flat country, where the sky is so huge and deep you feel as if you might suddenly fall upwards into it. Maybe that was why young Jack Redfield had gotten interested in religion; in country like that a man can feel so insignificant that he needs to feel that someone or something bigger is watching over him. After all, a lot of the world's religions came out of desert and plains country.

The book contained a number of black-and-white photos, and I studied them for a while, particularly the ones from his

---

childhood. The father, Eugene Redfield, appeared in only one picture, a group shot; a big, smiling man in a hat that shaded his eyes. He was out of focus in the picture and, I suspected, in the lives of the others as well.

The mother, however, was another matter. Amanda Redfield somehow dominated every picture she was in, even when she was standing in the background. As I'd guessed, she'd been a splendid-looking young woman. There was a well-composed photograph of her standing in the yard of a big farmhouse, with a baby in her arms that I assumed must be the infant Reverend. She looked happier then, her expression softer than in the later pictures.

By Saturday evening I had a fairly clear picture of Jack Redfield's life story—both the authorized version and what I could read between the lines—and a working understanding of the organization he was running, which was indeed impressive. I also had a basic grasp of his religious beliefs. Basically, God truly loved me, but didn't want me to do *any* of the things I enjoyed doing, and if I didn't shape up He would sooner or later with great regret do some things I wouldn't like at all.

There were no gimmicks, no promises of wealth or health— one of the tracts all but said faith healing was a scam—or bizarre practices, and, for a change, no right-wing political rhetoric. In actual content, there wasn't much in Jack Redfield's message that would have been out of place in any fairly conservative Fundamentalist church. What put him outside the mainstream was the exuberant, tacky-flashy style, and the sheer mind-boggling size of the operation. One news writer had said that the Jack Redfield Ministries complex in Tulsa might be the Protestant world's closest equivalent to the Vatican; apparently it was damn near an independent city-state up there across the river.

But nothing in any of this told me what I wanted to know: was Jack Redfield the kind of man who was capable of murder?

And, of course, the answer wasn't there because the question was bullshit. No one knows what kind of man is capable of murder. There are plenty of people—including many homicide cops—who will tell you that any man, or woman, is capable of murder under the right circumstances.

In the years I'd worked the police beat, I'd seen a lot of murderers brought in, and I'd never been able to detect a pattern. I'd seen killers with white hair and others too young to shave. I'd seen those who'd done it for love and those who'd done it for hate and those who couldn't tell the difference. I'd seen a couple of pre-teen bubblegummers who'd tied a woman up and poured gasoline on her and set her on fire just to watch her burn; I'd seen a quiet, soft-spoken middle-aged man, with one of the most angelic faces I'd ever encountered, who'd poisoned his elderly mother for the insurance. I'd seen a young couple brought in for killing their newborn baby, and a poor, shaking old man who'd shot his wife because she had cancer and he couldn't stand to see her suffer. And I'd seen more than one cop walk away with no worse than a reprimand after a shooting that would have been called murder if anyone without a badge had done it.

All I could ever tell they had in common was that none of them seemed to feel they'd done anything really wrong; they all seemed to believe they had done the logical thing under the circumstances. Some of them felt bad about the way things had turned out, but none I'd talked with had felt they'd had a choice. You did what you had to do.

Sunday morning I watched television. That was something I hadn't done in a long time.

"The Jack Redfield Hour" followed pretty much the standard format, beginning with a choir in white robes singing old hymns in slick, rather irritating modernized arrangements. A youthful fivesome—two smiling lads, two smiling lasses, and a smiling androgyne at the piano—did a song about going to heaven, in harmonies that suggested they were going there by elevator. A middle-aged black man with a truly astonishing basso voice did a spirited solo of "Deep River." Mad Mel Rains came on in a white karate suit and spoke briefly "to the young people watching," telling them to treat their bodies as temples of the Lord and not abuse them with drugs, alcohol, or smoking. He was even uglier on the screen than in the photos.

The show was very professionally produced. The camera work and the lighting gave the effect of a big church sanctuary, practically a cathedral. You had to watch closely to see that the World Faith Tabernacle was just a somewhat bigger and fancier version of an ordinary TV network studio. Or that Reverend Jack's live congregation wasn't that much bigger than, say, David Letterman's; there were lots of close-up shots of happy, exalted-looking faces in the pews, but very few of the whole crowd.

Everything obviously had been rehearsed to precision level. The announcer, a handsome young man with a natty suit and the relentless enthusiasm of a strip-joint emcee, kept the pace brisk and the energy high, until at last it was time for Reverend Jack himself to appear.

By now I'd begun to wonder what the big deal was. But then Redfield started to speak, and I didn't wonder any longer.

His voice was powerful, but that wasn't it; he spoke in neat phrases, using simple vivid images to make his points, but that wasn't it either. It certainly wasn't the content of his sermon, which was ordinary to the point of banality. Jack Redfield had something that went beyond the details. He could have stood there reciting decimal places of *pi* and nailed you to your seat.

They've tossed that word "charisma" around until it's become almost meaningless, but the real thing still exists, and Redfield had it. I hadn't seen enough of the TV preachers to know if any others had the gift, but I'd seen it elsewhere; John Kennedy had it, and Martin Luther King, and they say Franklin Roosevelt had enough of it for ten men. And, of course, Hitler and Castro and Mao; the talent seems to be fairly evenly distributed on both sides of the good-guy-bad-guy line. Even Charlie Manson, in his way. . . .

Hell, I don't mind admitting it: Jack Redfield had *me* going, just a little bit, toward the end. Me, who had over the years broken all the Commandments except the one about erecting graven images. Me, who hadn't been inside a church since 1979, and then only to view the spot where the choir director had shot the senior deacon for fooling around with the organist.

And me, more to the point, who knew about Lorene Matson. For a couple of minutes there, it just didn't seem to matter.

When the program ended—the white-robed choir lined up belting out "God Be With You Till We Meet Again," the Reverend standing in front of the big mahogany altar with arms spread wide in a gesture of benediction, and the 800 number flashing at the bottom of the screen—it was a little while before I could move, and not entirely because Harry was lying across my lap. Finally I got it together enough to get up and locate the Jim Beam and pour myself a healthy dose. My hands, I discovered, were not absolutely steady.

You go around thinking of yourself as a very tough, cynical, hip sort of person, and it's always a bad shock when you find out they can get to you too.

And I still didn't have any answers to the questions that mattered.

Sunday evening, after the rain finally stopped, I was out in the yard with Harry when the phone rang. I went inside and picked it up and it was Rita Ninekiller.

"I've been thinking about you all weekend," she said. "Can you come over? Or would you like me to come there?"

"I'll come there," I said. "My place is a mess. Give me a little time to clean myself up."

"Hey," she said, "I'm not pushing, am I? If you'd rather not—"

"You're not pushing," I said. "I'll be there."

It was dark by the time I climbed the steps to Rita's place and knocked. She opened the door and reached out and took my hand and pulled me gently inside. She had on a white wraparound terry-cloth robe that stopped halfway down her thighs. The only light came from a lamp in the far corner, filling the room with a soft orange glow.

Her hands went to the buttons of my shirt and then to my belt buckle. I kicked off my cheap running shoes without pausing to untie them. Neither of us spoke as we got rid of our clothes. Underneath the white robe she was naked. Her skin was the color of apricots in the dim light.

We moved to the couch, still not speaking. Only when I had mounted and penetrated her did she begin to make a low, hoarse, wordless sound in the back of her throat, growing louder as our rhythms matched and began to accelerate. Bucking at last in climax, she cried out something in what I thought must be Cherokee. I lay on top of her, spent, and felt a series of rippling shudders pass through her body. "Oh," she said finally, "that was good. I'd forgotten how good we were together."

After a while we went into the bedroom and made ourselves comfortable. "Boy," she said, "I've been kicking myself in the ass all weekend for letting you leave here the other night. First thing I did when I woke up Saturday morning, I went into the bathroom and looked at myself in the mirror and said, 'Rita Ninekiller, have you lost your damn *mind?*'"

She propped herself up on one elbow beside me and put her hand on my chest. The long thick black hair flowed down over her small hard-pointed breasts. "All this time," she said, "all the bad moves I made with my life, I always told myself I should have hung on to Tag Roper. The only man who ever slept with me and never tried to control me, never tried to use me to make himself look good or feel big, never played any kind of bullshit games. Then you show up one day and for God's sake, I nearly let you get away from me again."

"I wasn't going anywhere."

"Yeah, well, I didn't know that. Cherokees are supposed to be smart Indians, but you sure couldn't prove it by the way I act." She lay back and put her head against the side of my chest. "You knew why I finally quit seeing you, just before you left the *Courier?* About me and Chandler?"

"I heard."

"Yeah, I bet you did. I bet everybody on the staff heard. Young woman running around with a married guy, everybody always knows. Too bad somebody didn't kick my ass," she said. "I don't know what the hell got into me. No, I know what got into me, all right. I just don't know why I kept letting him put it there."

"Bad?" I said, watching her face.

"Not quite as bad as being buried alive with the shingles. That's about the best I can say. . . . It wasn't just the usual pain and strain that goes with that kind of affair, Tag, although God knows that was bad enough. He *owned* me," she said, "or he thought he did, and I let him get away with it for nearly two years, so I guess he was right. He told me how to dress, how to wear my hair, even gave me books to read and records to listen to—and then asked me questions about them to make sure I'd had the right reactions. It was like he saw me as a package of raw materials that he was going to turn into this perfect woman he had in mind."

I said, "It's hard for me to imagine you accepting that sort of thing."

"Christ, Tag, it's hard for *me* to imagine it, even now. It's not like I was some impressionable eighteen-year-old trainee, after all. I was twenty-five with an M.A. in journalism, I'd been around the block a few times. I knew what he was doing to me, God damn it," she said, "and I kept letting him do it. I'd swear I wasn't going to see him again, and then the phone would ring and next thing I knew I was waking up next to the son of a bitch and trying to get out of bed to go to the bathroom without waking him because it was odds-on he'd have some remark to make."

She shook her head. "I don't know what his secret was. He was good-looking, sure, but no more so than plenty of other guys. He was good in bed, but so busy admiring his own technique that he hardly seemed to notice my responses. And he didn't string me on with any bullshit about leaving his wife and marrying me, either. I'll give the bastard that, he was honest in his way."

She raised her head and looked at me. "Is this bothering you?" she asked. "Me talking about another guy when I'm with you?"

"Not if it's what you want to do."

"See? That's a Tag Roper answer. Chandler, man, he wouldn't stand for me talking about you or any other man, ever." She sighed. "But he could be so incredibly damn charming. When I did or said something that pleased him, that met his expectations, he could turn on that smile and my insides would just melt. I think it was some kind of natural talent, you know? Tommy's good at painting, you're good at writing, Chandler happened to be good at controlling people. And the worst of it," she said, "I don't think he ever realized what he was doing. I think his ego was so enormous he just assumed that that was the natural order of things, for any woman to want him to take charge of her life. I think he thought he was doing this poor backward little Indian girl a favor."

"What finally happened?"

"He got a chance at a better-paying job in California," she said. "That's how it ended. I never even managed to break it off on my own. I think that's what hurts worst."

She reached up and stroked my cheek. "And so, the other night when you were here, I went a little bit gun-shy. Part of me wanted you to stay, just as I said. But another part said watch out, remember last time."

I said, "You do realize I don't have a damn thing to offer anybody right now."

"Oh, that's okay. I'm not after any kind of commitment," she said. "I'd just like it if we could be there for each other now and then. You know?"

She sat half up and turned, crouching over me, her hair hanging down and brushing my chest. "And now," she said, "that's all the talking I want to do for a while. Unless you've got something you want to talk about."

"No."

"Good. Right now this is what I want to do," she said, doing it.

Early in the morning I got up without waking Rita and put my clothes on and let myself out. Monday morning, the start of a workday and a workweek for her, while I had nowhere to be and nothing to do at any particular time; the rhythms of our lives this morning were going to be too far out of synch to try to mesh them even briefly. We seemed, in the phrase of my college years, to have something going, but I couldn't see any sense in pushing our luck just yet.

I drove home the long way, taking the back roads south of the river, watching the sun come up over the flats. Birds flew up in front of the Camaro in flapping, croaking flocks. At the intersection with the main road I pulled into a little cafe for a piece of good pie and a cup of bad coffee. There was a wire rack beside the cash register with a hand-lettered sign: TAKE ONE— FREE!!! The rack contained religious tracts from the Jack Redfield Ministries Press. I recognized a couple from the stuff Rita had brought over.

Back home, I let Harry out and went inside while he did his routine in the yard. The cardboard box still sat by the couch. The metal box lay on the table. Should have stashed that somewhere, I thought. Larry was probably capable of coming back and breaking in while I was away.

Next to the metal box lay the little framed picture I'd taken from Lorene Matson's bedroom. I must have forgotten to put it back with the other material, last time I'd had the box open. Shaking my head at my own carelessness, I popped the metal lid open and glanced down at the picture. The child's face stared solemnly up at me from between the two adults. It was Lorene Matson, all right; the features were recognizably those of the woman whose portrait I'd seen on the dresser. The shape of the nose and eyebrows, and the line of the chin, were the same.

Hard to imagine, I reflected, that this rather ordinary-looking little girl had wound up leading such a lurid life, and come to such a squalid end. She must have had some plans and dreams for the future; surely they hadn't included becoming a full-time prostitute and then the victim of a murder. To say nothing of bearing a child whose father was so rich he even owned his own religion.

I said to the picture, "You deserved better, kid."

I looked at the photo a few minutes longer, and then I said, "Ah, fuck it," to nobody in particular, and went over to the phone and called Wiley Harmon.

EIGHT

Wiley Harmon said, "Jesus *Christ,* Roper, you got any idea what you're screwing around with here? I thought you had better sense."

We were sitting in his car on a McDonald's parking lot in south Tulsa. I hadn't wanted to be seen at the station and he hadn't wanted to come to my place because he hated dogs. This had seemed as good a rendezvous as any.

He said, "I don't have to tell you, Roper, you been around. Certain places, there's certain groups of people you just don't fuck with. Don't piss them off, don't even do anything to make them notice you're alive. In Boston it's the micks, in New York it's the hebes, in Jersey it's the guineas, in Frisco it's the queers. And in Oklahoma, especially *this* fucking town," he jerked his head in a motion that somehow took in all of Tulsa, "it's the Christers. You know they call this town the buckle on the Bible Belt. Hell, yes, it's the buckle on the belt, and the cup in the fucking jockstrap too."

He tapped the side of the open metal box in his lap. "And what you got here," he said, "is dynamite. Dynamite my ass, make that a tactical fucking nuclear device. Saddam Hussein would given his left nut for a bomb like this. When it goes off they're gonna hear it clear across the country. I can hardly wait."

I said, "Wider implications aside—and I hear what you're saying—what do you think?"

"You mean speaking strictly as a cop looking at possible evidence? Forgetting for the moment who we're talking about and the shit that's gonna fly when this comes out? That ain't easy, Roper. But"—he rubbed the balding area at the front of his scalp—"just looking this shit over for the first time, I think the son of a bitch waxed her. Or had it done, maybe, he's sure as hell got the money to buy a pro hit. A thirty-two auto isn't really pro equipment, but it's possible. . . ."

He stared out through the dirty windshield. "You know, Roper, when you talked to me the other night about this, I got kind of curious, and the next day I went and had a look at the file. And I got to say I couldn't make myself entirely happy about it being a regular whore killing. Most of those happen in the bedroom—a john gets pissed off about the price or because she won't do something he wants, take it up the ass or something. Or, lots of times, you get a guy's simply crazy. Wigs out when he sees her with her clothes off, or he's an S and M freak and goes over the edge, whatever. Got your share of religious full-mooners, too, hear voices telling them to kill the sinners for Jesus. Anyway," he said, "you generally find the stiff in the bedroom. And oftener than not she's all slashed up, because for some reason you get more knives than guns in these cases."

He turned to look at me. "But Lorene was found in the living room with all her clothes on—and not her working clothes, either, you know what I mean. Just jeans and a sweatshirt and sandals, like she wasn't figuring to be working that night. Also," he said, "like I told you, she didn't work much out of her house."

"That was the impression I got."

"Yeah. And whoever did it was standing a little way inside the front door. No signs of forced entry—either she let the fucker in or he had a key, so either way it was likely somebody she knew or at least was expecting. No signs of a struggle, nothing to indicate the shooter was there any length of time—

stray hairs, strange butts in the ashtray, anything like that. Way it looks to me," Harmon said, "this son of a bitch just came in and stood there and shot her, bang bang, and left, didn't leave anything but a couple of thirty-two empties and a dead body on the carpet. Well, it wasn't my case, I didn't say anything to anybody. Chalk it up as a whore killing, who gives a shit? Nobody around this fucking town. But now we got somebody who had a solid motive to waste her—"

"Do we?" I asked. "He paid up faithfully for years, why kill her now?"

Harmon shrugged. "She got greedy. Tried to raise the ante."

"Except this is Jack Redfield we're talking about. He could have paid three or four times his regular nut with no pain."

"So," Harmon said, "it was something else. Maybe she was gonna go public. You know, kid's nearly through school, she's tired of hooking and living in a cheapshit little house while he's got it made, she decides to sell the story to one of those magazines or something. Been a lot of broads made good money, even got careers started in show business, telling the world how some sleazebag preacher or politician or singer done them wrong."

I thought that over. It was a possibility that hadn't occurred to me. And should have; one of the reasons it's so hard to make a living in my line of work is that the publishers keep handing out all the money to people with scandalous confessions to make.

"Understand," Harmon added, "there's plenty of questions ain't been answered yet, ain't even been *asked*. It'll be interesting to find out if the Reverend can tell where he was the time of the crime. And it'll be extremely fucking interesting to see if his voiceprint matches up with the dispatcher's recording of our anonymous call-in that started this whole thing off."

I said, "What's going to happen next? Will they pull him in?"

"Nearly anybody else, you bet your ass they'd pull him in. Some bad-looking nigger or Indian off the street looked this good for a homicide, only question would be will he get AC or DC. Seeing who it is, though," Harmon said, "I dunno. They'll handle it with the old kid gloves, you can be sure of that. Whatever they ask him, they'll ask real polite. At first, anyway."

He closed the metal box with a sharp snap. "What I'll do," he said, "I can get this into the hands of the guys working the case, your name won't have to come up. I'll tell them I got this package came in the mail, I figure the broad left it for safekeeping with some other whore—you know, get it to the cops if anything happened to her—and the whore remembered me from when I was with Vice. They'll buy it. I know these guys pretty well, they ain't Dick Tracy material."

"And then?"

"Fuck do I know? Something this hot, no regular cop is gonna move on it without going upstairs for instructions. It could get bucked all the way to the top. Could wind up, the Chief and the D.A. sitting down together on this one, each one figuring how to grab the publicity for himself and lay all the heat on the other asshole. Interesting to see how all this comes out. I got some leave time coming, I just may decide to go visit my brother in St. Louis, this shit gets hairy-assed enough."

"Any chance of a coverup?"

"Hell of a good chance, if there wasn't all this money involved—the IRS is gonna get real interested in where that money came from and was it ever declared, and they don't give a shit whether they piss off the Rev's followers—and if the daughter wasn't running around town, liable to talk. You see her, tell her watch her ass, don't talk to *anybody*. She's kind of a loose cannon just now. But," Harmon said, "even if they do try to bury this, it'll come out. You know the department. Leaky as an old man's dick."

"If they do take Redfield down," I said, "what are his chances?"

"Assuming they don't find anything else to go with this, and assuming the Rev doesn't break down and confess the minute they lean on him—hey, it happens—I don't see a conviction. This stuff you found looks like hell, but it ain't evidence he snuffed her. It just establishes a possible motive. Tell the truth,"

Harmon said, "I wouldn't give you a nickel on this even going to trial. Unless the prosecutor decides to cut himself some publicity, could be Redfield won't even be indicted."

He got out a pack of cigarettes and extracted one. "I got to quit smoking these things," he said, "price has gotten out of the fucking world. Wasn't for those Indian smoke shops, I don't know how I'd get by. Anyway," he went on, sticking the cigarette in his mouth and fumbling for his lighter, "even if he never spends a night in the slammer or stands in front of a judge, the Rev's in deep shit. Even if he walks, he's history in the preaching racket."

He paused to set fire to the cigarette. "History, hell, he's fucking *archeology,*" he said. "Been too many scandals in his business lately, people getting fed up with it. Lots of people out across the country thought this guy was different, and they gave him their loyalty and their bucks. That's something else," he added, "the loyal contributors're gonna wanta know just where the money came from to make those payments to the late Lorene. They ain't gonna be real thrilled, they get the idea their donations went to pay off a whore."

He stopped and stared at me. "Hey," he said, "what I said a minute ago, about the daughter. You figuring to tell her all this?"

"As soon as I can get hold of her," I said, "after I'm through talking with you."

I'd stopped at a copy shop, on the way to the meet with Harmon, and made photocopies of everything in the metal box: one set for Amy Matson, one for me. Well, everything but the ledgers, which would have taken forever; I'd settled for a few sample pages there. I didn't see any reason to tell him that, though.

"Better you than me," he said. "Well, like I said, tell her to be careful who she talks to, what she says. This thing's a long way from over. Could get pretty weird, you know?"

He dragged at his cigarette. "Christ, Roper," he said disgustedly, "don't bring me into any more jobs like this, okay? Nothing but trouble and I can't see a buck in it anywhere for either of us."

"Sorry."

"Yeah," he said. "You used to have better sense."

Amy Matson said, "My *God,*" for the twentieth or thirtieth time in the last hour or so. Then she said, "And now the cops have all this too, and they're going to bust this Redfield guy?"

"I don't know what they're going to do," I said, "but they've got the information, and presumably they'll do something."

"Wow," she said. "This is all pretty heavy for me to deal with, you know? First I find out my father is still alive and I'm right in the same town with him, *and* he's some kind of television holy-roller preacher. And now maybe he's going to go to jail or the electric chair or something. Jesus," she murmured as if to herself, "nobody back at Sarah Lawrence is going to believe this. Talk about what did you do over your summer break? My *God.*"

We were sitting in the motel room she shared with Larry. I was using the room's one chair, while she sat on the bed, the photocopies of her mother's secret papers spread out all around her. The room was pretty seedy-looking and the whole motel had long passed its even adequate days.

Larry was nowhere around. She'd said he was down at the club, doing some work for Shelby. I hoped it was a full afternoon's job. There was an empty beer bottle on the chipped nightstand and I thought I might be able to take him with it if I got in some early moves, but I didn't want to find out.

Amy said, "I guess you had to give all that stuff to the cops, huh? I mean," she rushed on, "I don't guess there's any way you could have kept quiet and let me kind of, like, take up where Lorene left off."

I probably stared. She looked embarrassed. "Oh, shit, I didn't mean that. Not really," she said with a nervous little laugh. "I wouldn't even know how to go about putting the squeeze on somebody like that if I wanted to." She ground her cigarette out in the ashtray on the nightstand. "It's just that I'm having a lot of trouble right now. I've been trying to find a job, but there don't seem to be many available. And I don't really have any job skills."

She gestured around the room. "And I can't take it here much longer. Larry's getting really impossible to live with. It didn't help that you beat him up," she said, and grinned slightly. "Hey, I know how he gets sometimes. . . ."

She sighed. "One more year to go at school, and it might as well be ten. God knows when, or if, I'll be able to come up with the bread to finish and get my degree. I guess you think I'm pretty spoiled and selfish," she said, "and maybe I am, but right now I'm having to adjust to some major lifestyle changes, you know?"

I said, "Aren't there any scholarships, anything like that, you could apply for?"

"Maybe. I don't know. You apply for something like that, they require you to document your parents' finances for the last year or so. Can you imagine me doing that?" She looked off through the wall for a moment. "Listen," she said, "does this state have, like, the death penalty?"

"Yes," I said, puzzled. "Why?"

"Because if he did it, I hope they do it to him. I hope they strap him down and shoot electricity through him till he's dead." Her face was suddenly very bleak, the skin tight over the cheekbones. "I'll make them let me watch."

She looked embarrassed again. "Boy, listen to me. Two months ago I was circulating a petition for a group that wanted a constitutional amendment outlawing the death penalty. Just shows how your thinking can change."

"You understand, it's not at all certain that he killed her. I've got some doubts about that myself."

"I don't care." The bad look was back again. "After what the son of a bitch did—here's me growing up without any family at all, here's Lorene doing it with God knows how many creeps just to stay alive, and all the time here's this asshole getting rich running some cheesy bogus-religion scam on TV, conning these yokels out of their money and living it up big and not giving a shit about us. You know what? I hope he *didn't* do it, and they fry him *anyway*. It would serve him right."

I didn't bother to correct her on any of what she'd said. She wasn't trying to be reasonable or fair now, she was trying to get a handle on an almost unbearable load of pain and shock.

I stood up. "You've got my phone number?" She nodded. "And you know where I live," I said. "If there's anything I can do to help—"

"Sure," she said. She was crying openly now. "And thanks, Roper."

I didn't know what she had to thank me for. In her place, I don't think I'd have thanked me. I took out my wallet. "Here," I said. "Considering how everything turned out, I'm going to give you back your money."

She started to protest. I laid the folded bills on the night-stand. "Take it," I said. "Don't let Larry know you've got it. Maybe it'll help get you through until . . . something breaks."

She nodded. "Thanks," she said again. Her voice was blurry with tears. "I'll pay you, though. Just as soon as I, like, get it together."

Going across the parking lot toward the Camaro, I wondered what was going to become of her. I wondered, too, when the hell I'd gotten so noble. But my conscience, such as it was, had enough to handle already.

I drove home and let Harry out to take one and stood for a minute looking at the mess in the living room. Finally I went over to the desk and sat down and dug out my address book and rummaged around under the desk for a big manila envelope. A short time later I was heading back out to the car, carrying the addressed parcel. I should have time to get to the post office before they closed. *Ceremonies of the Horsemen* wasn't going to get published lying on my desk.

What was it Elvis Presley used to say? Whatever else happens, you've got to take care of business.

Rita Ninekiller said, "Son of a bitch. So that's what you've been working on. No wonder you didn't want to tell me about it."

I said, "Actually, I knew I could trust you—"

"Huh," she said. "Don't be too sure. A story like this? Don't be too damn sure."

77

We were on the couch in my living room. Harry was lying between us with his head in Rita's lap and a look of ecstasy on his face. Rita shuffled through the stack of photocopies one more time and laid them carefully on the end table.

"But now," she said, "you're through with your part of this business, right? I can go ahead and use the story, it won't make problems for you?"

"None I can't handle." Wiley Harmon wasn't going to be too pleased to find out I'd given the information to a journalist, but screw him. "If you can do yourself any good with the story, go for it."

"Oh, it'll do me some good, all right. The truth is, I've been sort of under the gun ever since I took over Ed Leavitt's desk. Some of the Old Guard still don't think a woman can hack it. This," she said, "will knock certain people on their reactionary asses."

I nodded. "Glad to help."

Something must have come through in my voice. She gave me a sudden intent look and reached over and laid a hand on my shoulder. "Hey, Tag," she said. "You're having some problems with this, huh?"

"I don't know—" I shrugged. "It's bothering me some, yeah. I can't quite convince myself that I handled this thing right."

"I know what you're going through," she said. "I've never been involved with the police, but a couple of times I've had to make a decision like that—whether to use information, or run a story, that I knew was going to cause a lot of pain and trouble for someone who might not deserve it. You remember that bribery case?"

She began stroking the side of my neck. "Quit trying to second-guess yourself, Tag. You did the right thing."

"Say that again a few times," I said. "About me doing the right thing. You say it enough times, maybe I'll even start to believe it."

She laughed very softly, deep in her throat. "You're a good man, Tag Roper," she said. "But I promise not to tell."

* * *

That was Monday.

Tuesday afternoon, around five or so, I was sitting at my desk, trying to stare some words onto the blank sheet of paper in my typewriter, when the phone rang. I picked it up and it was Wiley Harmon.

He said, "Thought you'd be curious about the results of the voiceprint comparison. Seeing as you've turned into such a concerned fucking citizen, and all."

It took me a few seconds to register what he was talking about—my mind was still back in the nineteenth century, out on the Staked Plain with a Comanche war party—but then the stuck relays closed and I said, "Oh, right, the dispatcher's tape. You mean they've already pulled Redfield in?"

"Shit, no. Why would they need to do that? They had all the sample of his voice they could want," Harmon said. "They just tuned in to the three o'clock radio program."

"They can use that?"

"It's his *voice,* for Christ sake. Oh, it's not absolutely guaran-fuckingteed certain, and I don't guess it would stand up in court if the judge got picky, but it'll do till they can do the job by the book."

"And?" I realized suddenly that my hand was sweating where it gripped the receiver.

Harmon chuckled. "Go change your pants, Roper. They got a match," he said. "It was him."

Nine

During the days that followed, all hell, to coin an original phrase, broke loose.

The *Courier* broke the story—Rita told me later that management came close to losing their collective erection at the last minute, but not quite enough to kill something this hot—but the other Tulsa papers, and then the Oklahoma press and then the national media, were right behind. In an astonishingly short time the press and TV people were disembarking at Tulsa International by platoons and companies and battalions, all intent on covering what promised to be the juiciest scandal of the season.

If the authorities had had any inclination to brush this one under the rug, there was no chance of that now. It was officially admitted that the Reverend Jack Redfield had been questioned by the police in connection with the slaying of a Tulsa prostitute named Lorene Matson, though everyone was at great pains to deny that he was actually a suspect at this point. It would have been nice if this had been England, where they could simply have said that the Reverend was "assisting the police in their enquiries."

It had been a dull month for news. This story had everything—murder, sex, a charismatic television evangelist, sex, a mysterious illegitimate daughter, sex, money, sex. . . .

The reaction from the rest of the TV megapreacher crowd was loud and predictable. Quite a few of the competition had been trying to cope with scandals of their own; having an "erring brother" (in the phrase of more than one sermonizer) mixed up with an actual *murder* made their various peccadilloes seem relatively minor.

The rest of the country found the whole thing fascinating. Jay Leno devoted up to half his routine for a week to Jack Redfield jokes. David Letterman did a "Top Ten List" of upcoming sermon topics for Jack Redfield. A prominent tabloid psychic claimed to have predicted the whole thing, and to have helped the Tulsa police in their investigations. Geraldo Rivera—well, actually, Geraldo Rivera acted about the same as usual.

The thrust of most newspaper and TV editorials was, roughly: well, it had to happen sooner or later. These characters have come up in the middle of scandals involving sex, tax evasion, and fraud; what was left but murder?

Everybody, of course, used plenty of qualifiers and disclaimers—"alleged" being the favorite, with such weasel clauses as "reputedly under investigation in connection with" getting plenty of mileage too. Nobody actually came out and said, or wrote, "But of course we all know the bastard is guilty, so fuck him"—but the message got across.

Polls indicated the regular watchers of "The Jack Redfield Hour" were about evenly split between those who believed him to be an innocent man, unfairly persecuted, and those who were ready to set up the stake and start piling on the firewood. The fringe elements, naturally, came out in force; "48 Hours" ran a brief interview with a tall, burr-cut man with weird close-set blue eyes who claimed the whole thing was a conspiracy of the "devil worshipers" to discredit a man of God.

During all this time, Jack Redfield himself made no public statements, submitted to no interviews, and generally stayed in his citadel out of sight. The World Faith Tabernacle was closed and the TV show went over to tape from earlier services, as did the radio hour. The media people set up camp outside the gate of the Jack Redfield Ministries complex, like a medieval army laying siege to a walled city, and made life hell for anybody who went in or came out. There was a nasty incident, quickly smoothed over, when Mad Mel Rains demolished a camcorder and attempted to do the same to the cameraperson.

The first police interviews took place at Redfield's office and his home, and, from what Wiley Harmon told me, they were extremely polite, even deferential. "Redfield's ass is covered with little round marks from being touched with ten-foot poles," was Harmon's summation. Then, when the publicity became intense, it was necessary for credibility that the Reverend be taken downtown for a couple of hours, past the waiting cameras. Still nobody talked arrest. This, it was emphasized, was still an ongoing investigation.

Like everybody else, I had often heard the phrase "media circus." Any circus I've ever seen, however, was a model of taste, decorum, and intellectual content compared with what went on in Tulsa that summer. And I would include in the comparison a certain "circus" I once attended, as a young serviceman, in Tijuana, which was billed as Carmelita's Dog and Pony Show.

Much of this was told to me later, by people who took a close interest in the affair. I watched a few TV news programs and read the *Courier* occasionally—mostly following Rita's stories, which were excellent—and Rita told me things. And Wiley Harmon called me up now and then, primarily to accuse me of such things as fellatio, coprophilia, and first-degree incest; apparently the intrusive and intensive media presence was playing hell with the bribery-and-corruption business.

But I didn't really pay very close attention to the details at the time. I was heavily into the novel-in-progress by then; twentieth-century Tulsa seemed unreal to me. There were days when I got up and grabbed a cup of coffee and went straight to the typewriter and didn't leave it—except to snatch a rare bite of food, which was usually eaten at the desk while typing one-handed—until three or four in the morning. There is a point during the writing of any novel when it all comes together and suddenly you know what you're doing and how you're going to do it and the only question is whether you can get the words down on paper as fast as they come into your head. At least there is such a point if you're lucky . . . and this was it, this time around, for me.

Rita came over now and then, not as often as I'd have preferred under other circumstances; she was as busy as I was. There were nights when we just went to bed and to sleep, too exhausted to do anything but cling to each other like worn-out children. We were both, I imagine, drinking more than was good for us just then.

One morning there was a check in the mail from Mr. Brandon, he of the runaway daughter. I had to think for a few seconds before I could place the name; I'd completely forgotten the entire affair. And it had only been a couple of weeks. . . .

The days went by. Other news began to catch the attention of the media: a riot between gays and skinheads in Chicago, a serial killer in a small town in the Missouri bootheel, a leading Republican senator accused of sexually harassing a Senate page. The American public, as usual, displayed the attention span of so many autistic gerbils; Jack Redfield began to be Old Stuff. The media presence at the gates began to thin out and drift away.

There were still plenty of them around, though, the day I went out to meet Jack Redfield.

The phone call came at nine in the evening. The guy at the other end said, "Mr. Roper? Mr. Taggart Roper?" and when I admitted it he said, "This is Reverend Jack Redfield."

I suppose my initial reaction was a little extreme, but I'd been in the middle of a difficult and important love scene in which the hero had been about to learn the real identity of the woman he'd rescued from the Kiowas. A bad time, in other words, for an interruption.

I said, "All right, you cocksucker, did Wiley Harmon put you up to this? You tell the son of a bitch I'm going to kick his fucking ass, cop or no cop—"

"Mr. Roper," the voice said a little stiffly, "please believe me. This *is* Jack Redfield."

83

And, before I could make an even bigger ass of myself, he went on: "If you'd like to verify my identity, you can call the switchboard at the Ministries complex, and I will instruct them to give you my home number—"

I cleared my throat. I didn't really need to clear it; it just seemed the safest thing to do with my vocal equipment at the moment.

"No," I said weakly, "no, that's okay. Uh, that is, um. You, uh, wanted . . . ?"

"I need to speak with you," he said. "In person, not over the telephone."

I came within about a molecule's thickness of saying, "Well, fuck me," but I managed to get the brakes on in time.

"Could you come to my office," he went on, "tomorrow morning, say at ten o'clock? Or would some other time be more convenient?"

"Ten's fine," I said. Or croaked.

"Come to the main gate," he said. "The security people will have instructions to let you in. Do you know how to get to the complex?"

"I'll find it."

"Good. Ten, then. Good evening, Mr. Roper."

When I had hung up the phone I suddenly had a flash of insight: I knew now why people like Richard Nixon made all those secret tapes of their dealings. Despite the risks, there are times when your life gets so bizarre, when you find yourself involved with so many weird people and events, that you need to be able to play your conversations back to yourself just to make sure they really took place.

As it was, I printed myself a note: REDFIELD—TEN A.M., and taped it to the front of the refrigerator. Otherwise, it was even money I'd wake up in the morning and say to Harry, "You know, I had the most remarkable dream. I dreamed Jack Redfield called here, and . . ."

I found the place all right. You could hardly have missed it.

The Jack Redfield Ministries complex was spread out over a

number of acres of flat southern-Tulsa real estate. The whole thing was, by my estimate, as big as the campus of a small college—which, I later learned, was what it had once been, though the buildings were all new now. All the structures were the sprawling one-story kind, made of yellowish brick. The grounds were nicely landscaped, with plenty of bushes and trees and even a few flowerbeds. Sprinklers flashed in the midmorning sun, fighting their endless round-and-round battle with the dry heat of a Tulsa summer.

The entire complex was surrounded by a high chain-link fence. I had to drive around a little to find the main gate, but I knew I was getting there when I saw the cars and TV trucks parked up ahead.

The mob besieging the main gate had indeed thinned, as I'd heard; at least it was possible to *see* the gate now, and the harried-looking man in the little guardhouse beside it. Most of the media people, in fact, were sitting in their parked vehicles on the other side of the road, looking tired and bored, like cops on a stakeout. There were a couple of real cops sitting in a parked cruiser drinking something out of plastic cups. All in all, it was a pretty quiet scene compared to the madhouse I'd seen on TV the first few days. The only real action consisted of a tall, gray-haired man who paced back and forth in front of the gate, carrying a sign in one hand and a Bible in the other and wearing an utterly demented expression. The sign read WOE UNTO THE FALSE PROPHETS! Nobody seemed to be paying him any mind.

When I drove up to the gate there was a distinct stir all around. No doubt there were some hurried and worried conferences in the parked mediamobiles: Who the hell is this guy? Is he somebody we need to get on camera? Is he somebody we need to interview? Is he *anybody?*

I identified myself to the gate guard and he said immediately, "Oh, sure, Mr. Roper. They told me to let you in." He was a big, rangy young guy with short spiky hair and a bent nose. One of Mad Mel's born-again ring colleagues, maybe. "Just a minute," he said. "I'll call, have somebody take you up to the admin building."

I said, "I'm sure I can find my way."

He shook his head decisively. "Sorry. Nobody inside without an escort until further notice, that's my orders."

In the mirror I saw a number of doors opening across the road. "Let me inside the gate anyway," I said, "before those assholes get here. I think they've decided to find out who I am."

"Sure." He hesitated. "But you'll have to watch about using language like that when you're on the grounds."

"Sorry," I said.

"It's okay," he said, reaching for the gate release lever. "I catch myself cussing sometimes, these days."

I got the Camaro through the gate and he got the gate locked just in time to stop a sudden massed charge by the news brigade, who had obviously decided anybody who was getting admitted had to be worth checking out. "Praise the Lord," I said, and he nodded, not smiling at all.

TEN

Jack Redfield's office wasn't quite what I'd expected. I'd had a mental picture of a kind of oversized version of a pastor's study—walls lined with tall bookshelves, leather-covered chairs, desk cluttered with church bulletins and sermon notes. I guess I was remembering childhood visits to my uncle, who'd been a Presbyterian minister.

Redfield, however, had a big spacious office you could have roller-skated in. The furniture was modern and severely efficient; the bookshelves were recessed into the wall and seemed to contain as much computer software as actual books. The desk was enormous and much of its surface was occupied by a computer setup, three telephones, and several rows of buttons and switches. It could have been the office of a top-level executive of a successful corporation—and, of course, it was.

The Reverend got up and came out from behind the desk when I entered. "Mr. Roper," he said, sticking out his hand. "Glad you could come."

He was a bit bigger than I'd expected; the photos and the TV hadn't properly shown the broad, powerful-looking shoulders. His grip was impressive. It occurred to me that this guy was physically capable of throwing a very hard punch. To the mid-section, say.

"Have a seat," he said, indicating a chair in front of the desk. "If you'd care for some refreshment? Naturally we're alcohol-free, but I could have a Coke brought, or coffee—"

"No, thanks," I said, sitting down.

"You're sure? It would be no trouble at all."

I had a sudden vision of that weird scene from *Blind Ambition,* where Nixon, played by Rip Torn, keeps bugging John Dean to let him send for a Coke. I said, "No, really, I'm fine."

"Well, let me know if you change your mind." While I admired his suit—it probably cost more than my last book advance—he went back behind the desk and sat down and folded his hands and looked at me. "Taggart Roper," he said. He had that gift of saying your name and making it sound like a fanfare of trumpets; his tone of voice said that he couldn't believe he was actually having the pleasure of meeting me. I mean, he was *good.*

"I read your book *Steps of the Sun,"* he said. "You know, I've always felt that the Western novel embodies such values as truth, courage, and personal integrity, at a time when most so-called serious fiction ignores or even derides these concepts. I found your work very impressive."

It was like getting laid by a really top-notch whore: you know you're being faked out by a pro, but it feels so good you don't care. I guessed his staff had been up all night, finding out who I was and what I did for a living and the title of my most recent book.

"Well," he said, "of course I didn't ask you here to talk about your work." He leaned slightly forward. "Mr. Roper, I believe you know a young woman named Amy Matson."

A kind of spasm passed over his face, and he added in a lower, tighter voice, "My daughter."

"Yes," I said, a little warily. "At least I'm acquainted with her. I don't think you could say I know her, really."

He blinked slowly. Little lines appeared at the corners of his eyes and mouth. "Mr. Roper," he said, "you certainly know her better than I do. God forgive me."

Just like that, the slick façade turned transparent, revealing a man stressed almost to the breaking point. Behind the rimless glasses, the pale eyes registered excruciating pain.

"She called here yesterday," he went on, his voice almost back to normal. "I'm afraid she had quite a hard time reaching me—naturally the incoming calls are screened very closely, especially during these recent days—but she persisted, and finally she managed to get through to me."

He bowed his head and stared down at his desk. "It was a strange sensation," he said, "talking for the first time with my own daughter, and her a grown woman. I had dreamed for years of one day getting to speak with her, but not like this—" He shook his head violently. "She was quite hostile at first, you know."

"She's having trouble handling this," I said. "The shock—"

"Oh, of course, I understand that," he said. "When she realized that I wanted to help her, she calmed down and we were able to talk, after a fashion."

It must have been, I thought, one of the awkwardest, most painful telephone conversations in history.

"She told me that she was in serious straits. That she had no money and no job, and that she was living with a young man, a kind of delinquent, who bullied and terrorized her. That was why she called me, you see," he went on. "She wanted money. As I say, she was very belligerent until I made her understand that I would be only too pleased to assist her. The least I could do, surely."

He sighed. "But she refuses to come here, or to my home, or to meet me in person at all. Which I suppose is understandable," he said, "and, really, I suppose a meeting would be unwise at this time. It would be terrible for Amy if those news people should find out about it, and begin hounding her. For that matter, I don't need the extra publicity myself."

He grimaced. "My attorney insists I should not give her anything, or have any conversations or contact with her. Says it might be interpreted as the sign of a guilty conscience. As if I didn't have one already."

I wondered where all this was going. But I kept quiet and let him do it his way. He had the ball. Hell, he owned the stadium.

"Her request," he said, "was that you, Mr. Roper, should act as—um—courier. She has great faith in your integrity. She said, in fact, that you were the only person in this area whom she trusted."

He picked up a long unmarked envelope from his desk. It looked pretty thick. "Here," he said, "is the money I want to send her. It should be enough to take care of her needs for a little while, until this affair can be straightened out. In any event, it is the amount we agreed on. In cash, as she requested."

I took the envelope. It was pretty heavy. "Sure," I told him. "If you're sure."

"Amy is sure. That's all that matters." He picked up a second envelope and held it out. "This is a little compensation for your trouble."

"That's not necessary—"

"Yes it is," he said very firmly. "Amy insisted that you should be paid. If you don't take it, I will have broken a promise to my daughter."

I took the envelope and stuck it in my pocket without looking inside. He seemed relieved.

"Tell me something, Mr. Roper." His face took on a sad, wistful expression. "What is she like? I haven't seen her since she was a baby. Lorene wouldn't allow it. I'd like to know about her."

I shrugged. "I'm afraid I can't help you. She seems to be an intelligent and decent person, but—" The disappointment on his face was a cruel thing to see. "I've only met her twice," I said. "I don't really know anything about her, that you don't already know."

His forehead corrugated itself in a deep frown. "Then how is it that she places so much trust in you? I hope you won't be offended, Mr. Roper, but I'm a trifle concerned here."

I thought about it for a couple of seconds. "You're an ordained minister," I said. "Anything I tell you, if I say it's in confidence, it has to stay here, right? Like making a confession to a priest?"

He nodded slowly, still frowning. I said. "Okay. I met your daughter the last week in June—"

And sat there and told him the whole story, how I'd black-bagged Lorene Matson's house and what I'd found and how I'd finally turned it over to the cops. He listened with a close attention that reminded me of Wiley Harmon; I realized his job description included listening to confessions too. At the end he sat back and nodded. "Yes," he said, "that explains a number of things. I was wondering how the police got some of those items."

He gave me a slight smile. "I must admit I was wondering about you, too. After all, you are a writer and a former journalist. It crossed my mind that you might be some opportunist pretending to befriend Amy in the hope of getting an inside story you could exploit. I see now why she puts such faith in you."

I said, "If you don't want to employ me, now that you know I was the one who fingered you—"

His smile actually got wider. "Mr. Roper, I don't blame you in any way for my present troubles. It was God's will that my sins be exposed. *'Be not deceived, God is not mocked; for whatsoever a man soweth, that shall he also reap.'* For twenty years I lived a lie and accepted the praise of men in His name, and at last He has chosen to bring me down. Don't feel guilty, Mr. Roper," he said gently. "You were merely the instrument of the Lord's justice."

It was a new one on me. Waylon Jennings used to sing that the Devil made him do it the first time but the second time he done it on his own. This was the first chance I'd ever had to lay my mistakes off on God. It would have been a real comfort, if I could have believed it for a damn second.

Redfield was looking at me very intensely. "I didn't kill Lorene," he said. "I wish I could somehow make you believe that. Then perhaps you could make Amy believe it. . . . It's true I knew Lorene, fathered her child, made secret payments to her. And as I've told the police, I was there that night. She'd called me, asked me to meet her, she wouldn't say why. It was very rare that we met face to face—I assumed some emergency had come up. When I arrived she was lying dead on the floor."

He closed his eyes and shuddered. "I should have known then that it was God's will that my sins should find me out. Instead I ran shamefully away. I called the police from a pay phone, but it took me half an hour of aimless driving around the city to get up the courage to do even that."

He stood up suddenly and began to pace back and forth before the big plate-glass window. "I knew Lorene for a very long time," he said. "We were childhood friends, playmates. We went to school together until my father moved the family to Tulsa."

He was getting into his preacher voice now, just a little bit, turning on the big pipes. It was quite something to hear in that low-ceilinged room. I don't think he knew he was doing it.

"I met her by accident here in the city," he said. "I was a young man fresh out of seminary. My wife had been ill—she has never been strong—and had gone to Chicago for specialized treatments. Lorene and I got together to talk about old times, and. . . ." His face spasmed again. "She was a beautiful young woman. I was a lonely young man and a weak one. You can fill in the details."

After a pause he went on: "My wife returned from Chicago. I went to Amarillo as pastor of my first church. I didn't know what had happened until over a year later, when Lorene tracked me down and told me about the child. She demanded money. Naturally I agreed, and we made the necessary arrangements. You saw the records."

He stopped pacing and faced me. "It was some time after that before I learned that she had taken to prostitution. I did everything I could think of to make her stop—offered to pay for her training in some good-paying job, even to support her as well as the child—but she refused. She seemed to take a perverse pleasure in causing me pain, and even in degrading herself."

He raised his hands. "I stand before you, before God and mankind, a liar and an adulterer. My poor wife has suffered so—she can't have children, you know, and learning that another woman did bear me a child. . . ." His voice trailed off for a moment and then came back strong. "But I swear to you I did not kill Lorene Matson. I could never kill anyone. I have even lost support among religious conservatives," he said, "for my public opposition to the death penalty."

His face took on the ghastliest grin I had ever seen on a living human. "Of course," he said, "at the time I didn't know I would one day have a personal stake in the issue—"

He made a strange choking sound in his throat. "Forgive me," he said. "You'll get the money to Amy right away?"

"As soon as I leave here." I stood up and put out my hand. "If you need me again for anything like this—"

"Never fear," he said, taking my hand. "This business will not go on much longer, Mr. Roper. You'll see. The Lord will bring it all to a close, sooner than you think."

But Amy Matson wasn't at the motel when I went looking for her. The fat Pakistani behind the desk said she'd left a couple of days ago. He didn't know where she'd gone, and the sight of a study in green of a deceased U.S. president didn't do his memory any good.

"Thee young man," he said, looking bored, "is still occupying thee room. He was threatening me to answer him thee same question. I am telling him as I am telling you, I do not know where thee young lady is going."

Baffled, I went home, wondering what the hell I ought to do next. While I was making myself lunch, the phone rang, and it was Amy.

"I didn't tell Redfield where I was," she said. "I was afraid he might try to come see me. I moved out day before yesterday. Larry just got too bad to take."

She laughed. "I took some money from his wallet and left while he was asleep and took a cab. Had the driver take me to this other dump, I'm not even sure where it is. I'll give you the address."

I wrote down the address. I knew the place. It struck me that Amy was exhibiting a pretty fair talent for intrigue; she'd done a very professional job of covering her tracks.

"Can you come on over, like, right away?" she said. "I really need the money."

"Soon as I finish lunch," I said.

She laughed again. "Hey, just come, we'll have lunch together. If my dear old daddy came through," she said, "I'm buying."

"All *right,*" she said, a little while later, looking at the contents of the envelope. All I could see was hundreds. "Now I'll be okay for a while. I wondered if he'd actually do it."

We were sitting in my Camaro beside a Burger King, which had turned out to be her idea of lunch. Well, it would still be better than anything I'd have produced for myself.

I said, "He seemed to be genuinely concerned about you, Amy. I don't think he's necessarily a bad person."

She put the envelope in her purse. "You don't think he did it, do you?"

"I'll be damned if I know what I think," I said honestly. "But one thing doesn't always prove another. Good people sometimes do incredibly bad things." Christ, listen to me. Spend the morning with a preacher, start sounding like a sermonette myself.

She said, "I guess you're right. When I talked to him, he was actually pretty nice, in a stuffy sort of holy-Joe way. I guess he's having a rough time too."

"Think you might get together with him, one of these days? Get acquainted, at least?"

"I've thought about it. Maybe I should. Give him a chance to tell his side of things," she said. "But right now I'm just not ready, you know? This is going to take some time."

She reached for the door handle and stopped. "Hey," she said, "did he pay you? For bringing me this?"

I nodded. She said, "Good, because I made him promise he would. Since you wouldn't take that two-fifty from me, I figured I'd set it up for you to get it from him."

"Thanks."

"Hey," she said, "I don't forget. I take care of my debts."

She got a funny look on her face. "I guess that's one way I

kind of take after my old man, huh?" And while I was considering that, "Come on. Let's go in and get a burger."

On the way home I stopped at a music store and bought myself a new harmonica. When I took out the envelope Jack Redfield had given me, it turned out to contain five hundred dollars. I said, "Jesus Christ."

The salesman said, "Something wrong, sir?"

"No," I said. "Only—let me see that expensive chromatic job again, will you?"

The telephone rang a little after midnight. I got up from the typewriter and picked up the receiver and it was Rita.

"I'm calling from a pay phone," she said, "and I've got to get back to the scene, but I thought you'd want to know."

"Scene?" I said stupidly. "Know?"

"It's Jack Redfield," she said. "He hanged himself this evening. They just found the body."

ELEVEN

T hey buried the Reverend Jack Redfield on a Friday. Traditionally it always rains the day of a funeral, but this was Tulsa and getting into high summer, and it would have taken more than a funeral to coax rain out of that beaten-brass sky.

The service was held at the World Faith Tabernacle and was closed to the public, but a considerable crowd showed up at the cemetery; a mixture, no doubt, of the still-faithful, the still-angry—wanting to make sure he was good and dead—and the merely curious. The press and TV people at least had the decency to stay outside the gates, but all the channels that evening carried shots of the family and associates leaving the grounds. I recognized the mother, Amanda Redfield; her face was partly obscured by a veil, but there was no mistaking that stiff, upright form. She walked beside Mad Mel Rains, who wore a suit and tie with the grotesque elephantine dignity of a Mafia body-guard, and she held his arm, but she did not appear to be in real need of support.

The widow was having more trouble; she leaned on the arm of a well-dressed middle-aged man I thought must be a relative of hers. Later I learned he was her brother and had flown up from San Antonio for the funeral. There were various other black-clad characters, most of them wearing expressions of sorrow mixed with embarrassment, whom I took to be members of the Ministries staff. The camera shot was too long to see who was crying and who wasn't.

And, by Christ, there was Amy Matson. She walked along by herself, off to one side of the family formation and to the rear—I couldn't help remembering my father's expression, "Welcome as a bastard at a family reunion"—but her head was up and her carriage said that she was damn well here and the hell with anybody who didn't like it. From the commentary, none of the media people knew who she was.

I didn't go. There was never even a question about that. Even watching the TV coverage—and they repeated the story on both evening and late-night news, and then the national networks beat it to death—took a certain amount of effort on my part. For one thing, by then I was pretty drunk. And had been for a while, and was for a good many days to come. In fact when I say the funeral was on Friday I'm only repeating what I learned much later from back-edition newspapers. At the time, my sense of dates and times had begun to deteriorate badly.

I didn't stay wasted the whole time; I sobered up enough, now and then, to take care of Harry, and eat a little something, and otherwise keep the life-support systems running. And I never got really falling-down, toilet-hugging, shoe-pissing drunk, either. I suppose you could say it was a pretty half-assed binge, by the standards of such things; any genuine alcoholic would have found my efforts pathetically amateurish.

But hell, it worked for me.

Rita came over at last, looking for me. When she walked in I was sitting on the floor—Harry had the couch and it seemed rude to make him move—ballocky-bare-assed naked, trying to play "Nearer My God to Thee" on my new mouth harp. There was a half-empty Jim Beam bottle beside me and the floor was littered with empty Michelob bottles; I'd been drinking boilermakers.

She said, "Oh, Tag. Look at you, for God's sake."

I waved the Hohner at her with one hand and the Jim bottle

with the other. "Enter, my sister," I said, "join us in worship, say hallelujah. Let the congregation rise and sing the dirty words to 'Pretty Redwing.' "

She shook her head and spat a few smoky-sounding Cherokee syllables. The books say Cherokee doesn't have any curses or obscenities but according to Rita that's severely untrue. "You asshole," she added in English.

"Thank you, sister, for that living testimonial. Take up a collection. Dear beloved," I said, getting louder, "are you living in *sin*—"

"Shit. I don't need this," she said, kicking a Michelob bottle out of her way as she started back toward the door. "Call me when you get through feeling sorry for yourself. Assuming, of course, this doesn't represent a permanent lifestyle change."

She stopped at the door and looked back at me. "Christ, Tag," she said, "so maybe you fucked up. You think you're the only one who ever made a bad judgment call? The rest of us do it too, all the time, and we damn well have to live with it."

She waved a hand at the typewriter on the desk, untouched since the night Redfield had hanged himself. One thing at least, I knew better than to try to write drunk.

"You sit there," she said, "constructing these worlds, creating these people and moving them around, and it's fantastic that you can do that. I guess it makes you a kind of God. And everything always works out right in the worlds you create, because if you find out you fucked up, you just have to go back and retype a few pages.

"This is the real world," she said, "where life isn't written by you and Louis L'Amour. In the world us real people live in, the hero doesn't always make everything right by stepping out onto the main drag and outdrawing the bad guy. Often as not, the silly son of a bitch shoots his own God-damned foot off."

The door slammed behind her. I looked at Harry. "Say amen," I suggested, but he snorted wetly and shoved his head between the couch cushions, not even looking at me. "Yea, verily," I said after a minute, and started working on "Bye-Bye, Blackbird," getting badly hung up on the sharps and flats but hanging in there to the end anyway.

*　*　*

But Rita's sermon must have soaked through, all the same, because next morning when I woke up—all right, it was around eleven-thirty, that's still *morning,* damn it—I didn't immediately reach for my old buddy Jim. Instead I got up and lurched into the can and took a very long, very hot shower, and then I went into the kitchen alcove and made a fresh pot of coffee and drank a couple of cups of it and fixed myself some soft-boiled eggs and toast and washed that down with more coffee. Then I got a trash bag and picked up the empties from the living room floor, while Harry crunched up the eggshells, and after that, by God, I even shaved.

I put on a clean pair of jeans and a clean T-shirt with one of Tommy Ninekiller's designs on the chest, and my old jungle boots, and called Harry, and the two of us ran—well, trotted — up to the main road and back, both of us wheezing a bit by the time we returned. After that I sat down at the desk and reread the last chapter I'd written and, with hardly any regret at all, threw the whole thing away, because what Rita had said had also told me, indirectly, what I'd been doing wrong on paper too.

I was about a page and a half into the new draft when I heard a car pull up next to the trailer. I started toward the door, thinking it might be Rita, but then I remembered Larry and had a look out the window first.

It wasn't Rita, or Larry either. It wasn't anybody I knew, in fact. Not, at least, unless somebody among my acquaintances had just acquired a white Lincoln Continental. Sitting there next to my tin-can trailer, with my old Camaro in the background, the damn thing looked as out of place as a *New Jersey*-class battleship at a canoe-rental dock, and nearly as long.

The door opened and a woman got out. I couldn't see her very clearly through the dusty glass, but I didn't recognize her. She moved out of my line of sight and a moment later there was a knock on my door. I opened it and the woman said, "Taggart Roper?" and when I nodded she said, "I'm Mrs. Martha Redfield."

I suppose I stood there looking not unlike a damn idiot.

——
99

She said, "I believe you met my late husband. Reverend Jack Redfield." And when I still didn't speak she added, "May I come in?"

Earth to Roper. Come in, Roper. "Oh. Oh, sure. Of course. I'm sorry." I stepped back away from the doorway and made a sort of headwaiterish gesture with one hand. "I was working," I said by way of explanation. "Sometimes I get, you know, preoccupied."

She came in and stood looking about while I cleared the latest accumulation of junk off the chair. The cardboard box was still sitting there with its collection of Redfield publications. I kicked it surreptitiously out of sight behind the couch. "Take the chair," I said. "My dog sheds on the couch." I remembered Harry, then, but he was back in the bedroom asleep on my bed, worn out from the run. I went and gently closed the bedroom door without waking him. When I got back Martha Redfield was sitting there in the chair, her hands folded in her lap, looking at me.

She said, "I'm sorry if I interrupted your work, Mr. Roper. I could come back another time—"

"No, that's fine." I hesitated. "Coffee? That's all I've got to drink." The Jim Beam bottle on the end table testified that that was a lie, but it didn't seem relevant.

"Yes," she said politely, "coffee would be nice. Cream and sugar."

Shit. "I don't have any cream," I said.

"Then never mind. I'm not supposed to drink coffee anyway." She sounded apologetic. There was no reason for that, but I had an impression there didn't have to be. She had the manner of a person for whom unnecessary apologies had long been a way of life.

I sat down on the couch and looked her over. She was, I estimated, a few years older than me, and wearing it well; her long light-brown hair held a few streaks of gray, and little birds had been walking at the corners of her eyes, but her skin was clear and her shape was trim and her legs were good. Or so it seemed from what I could make out; with the long loose cut of that black dress, she could have been built like Jack Palance for all that really showed.

She sat in a very prim, careful sort of way, knees together, hands in lap, back not quite touching the chair. Clearly she was nervous; I guessed it wouldn't take much to send her running back out the door.

"Mr. Roper," she began formally, "Amy Matson has told me about you."

I said meaninglessly, "Oh?" and she nodded. "Amy and I," she continued, "have talked a great deal since the funeral. I don't know that you'd say we've become *close,* but we've spent time together. She wanted to know more about her father, and I wanted to get to know her."

She looked directly at me for the first time since entering the trailer. "That may sound strange to you, but I'd be a poor Christian indeed if I blamed that child for the mistakes of my husband. Or her mother," she added. "I don't hold any resentment against anyone."

She paused and seemed to reflect. "No, that's not true. I do hold a great deal of resentment against some of the news people for the way they behaved. You know, even Our Lord Himself didn't have to put up with having cameras shoved into His face while He was being crucified."

She stopped; she'd shocked herself. "I'm sorry," she said. "It's sinful of me to harbor such feelings. And they weren't all bad. There was a young Indian woman from the *Courier* who was very kind."

She sighed. I figured she did that a lot too. "I couldn't give Jack children," she said, "and it did hurt terribly to learn that he had fathered a child by another woman, under sordid circumstances at that. But still, Amy is his child, and I'd like to become—not a mother to her, perhaps, but at least a friend. Sister Amanda," she added, "is not happy about our relationship."

"Sister Amanda? Your mother-in-law?"

"Yes. Those people all call her Sister Amanda. She has never been happy about anything I have done in my entire life." She smiled very faintly without using her eyes to do it. "Her feelings have not gotten warmer since the will was read. Did you know what my husband did, that last day, after you left? He called in his attorney and changed his will. Amy will inherit a very considerable share of his estate. Sister Amanda is trying to contest the will. She regards it as the worst kind of treachery that I refuse to join in her suit."

The air conditioner chose this moment to start making a loud metallic clatter. I went over and hit it hard with the heel of my hand and it quieted down. "Go on," I said, sitting back down.

"Amy," Martha Redfield said, "told me that you don't believe Jack murdered that woman. Or at least that you aren't convinced of his guilt, as everyone else seems to be."

Oh oh. Should have seen this one coming. I said carefully, "I don't see that the evidence was all that strong, no. You could say I've had my doubts."

Her face lit up. I know that's a corny expression, but in this case it was what happened; you could have read a book in a dark room by her face just then.

"Please," she said all in a rush, "if there's anything you know, if you've got any ideas at all to point to his innocence—"

I held up both hands. "Wait, wait. Please," I said, "I didn't mean to raise false hopes. I only mean that the case against your husband didn't look particularly solid to me. The motive wasn't as credible as everybody made out—I still don't see why a man would pay someone off for nearly two decades and then suddenly decide to kill her. And Jack Redfield impressed me as an intelligent man, capable of figuring out that she'd have the proof of their relationship stashed away somewhere, and that it would eventually turn up and point to him." I saw her wince a little when I said "their relationship" but she only nodded without speaking.

"As for his being there the night of the murder," I went on, "his explanation sounded at least reasonable to me. Anyway, the police themselves were never satisfied enough to place him under arrest or bring charges. I understand the case is still officially considered open, unsolved."

"Officially," she said bitterly. "Tell that to the television reporters and the print journalists. Tell it to the entire American public. As far as they're concerned, his suicide amounted to a plea of guilty."

She reached up and dabbed at the corners of her eyes. "I was the one who found him, you know," she said. "He'd gone into his study at home, immediately upon coming in from the complex. He hadn't eaten dinner or responded when I called. Finally I got worried enough to open the door."

Her voice and face said that opening the door to his study without an invitation had been an unprecedented, almost desperate act. That told me more about their marriage than anything else I'd heard, but I don't suppose she realized it.

"He left a note," she said. "It was in his shirt pocket. Just a slip of paper, and all it said was 'Ezekiel 21:24.' "

Her eyes went out of focus and she recited, " *'Therefore thus saith the Lord God: Because ye have made your iniquity to be remembered, in that your transgressions are discovered, so that in all your doings your sins do appear; because, I say, that ye are come to remembrance, ye shall be taken with the hand.'* " She looked at me again. "But he had talked to me about the whole affair—the night after the police first came to interview him, he told me the story in great detail—and I know that what he meant was the sin of adultery, and of deceit and hypocrisy, not murder."

I said, "He said as much to me. More or less."

There was a short silence. She seemed to be collecting herself. "Mr. Roper," she said, "I came here hoping you could tell me something that might help prove my husband's innocence of murder. Failing that—" She touched the purse on her lap. "I would like to pay you to look for such evidence. I would pay a great deal for anything that would clear his name and memory."

I leaned back and looked at her for a minute or so. I might not be able to interest the publishing industry in my literary work, but I certainly was getting a lot of interesting job offers locally these days.

I said at last, "I'm not a detective, Mrs. Redfield. I could recommend a very good private investigator—"

She was shaking her head. "Amy Matson says you can do it if anybody can." Her voice had grown stronger, her phrasing less hesitant. "Mr. Roper," she said, "you managed to find the evidence that made my husband appear guilty. Can you not at least try to find something to clear him?"

And, of course, that was it. She'd played her hole card with flawless timing; she'd said the one thing to which I could not reply.

I said, "I'll look around, ask around. See what I can turn up. I can't make any promises." I stood up. "I hope you won't get your hopes up."

She stood up too. "I understand."

"I don't know if you do. If Jack Redfield didn't kill Lorene Matson, the obvious way to prove it is to find out who did. That's what you might call the Perry Mason solution," I said. "But in view of Lorene Matson's profession, and the world she lived and worked in, the possibilities are almost endless. That's why the police made only a token attempt to solve the case, before—" Before I dropped that package into their laps; I couldn't quite get myself to say it. "I'll see what I can do," I said instead.

"That's all I ask." She started to open her purse. "Let me give you something in advance, for expenses—"

"It won't be necessary. If I run into any serious expenses, I'll get in touch."

She moved toward the door. "Thank you," she said. She stopped and turned suddenly to face me. "Mr. Roper, I don't expect miracles. I know you're not really likely to find anything. I just had to feel I was doing *something,* you know?"

"I know what you mean," I said. "Maybe it's what I needed too."

When Martha Redfield was gone—getting that Lincoln turned around in my yard was quite an operation; I thought for a while she was going to have to call Houston Mission Control for help—I went to the phone and called the *Courier* and asked for Rita's extension.

"Want to come over tonight?" I said when she came on the phone.

"Are you back?" she asked instantly, "I mean, are you *back?*"

"I'm back," I told her. "For whatever it's worth."

"I'll be there," she said.

TWELVE

When I woke up the next morning Rita was gone and the sun was shining in the trailer's windows. I went through my getting-up-and-getting-dressed routine with a feeling of real purpose for the first time in a lot of days. Today, by God, I was going to start digging, see what I could find out for Martha Redfield. . . .

But before I could do anything, while I was still on my second cup of coffee, I had another visitor. I was getting to be the most popular author in Yuchi Park; I might, I thought as I went to the door, have to hire myself a social secretary.

Standing on the steps was Mad Mel Rains. His weight seemed to be making the trailer tilt slightly, but that was probably just my imagination.

"Taggart Roper," he said. When he said it it wasn't a question; it was more like an accusation. "Like you to come with me," he went on. "Somebody wants to see you."

I looked him over. I had to look all over the doorway to see all of him, too. He wasn't particularly tall—he seemed to be about my height, five-eight or so—but he was one of the most massive-looking men I'd ever seen. Biceps like loaves of bread bulged out of the sleeves of his white T-shirt. The T-shirt bore the emblem of a cross and a stylized crown and the legend JESUS IS THE ONLY KING. The thin material was stretched so tight over his pectorals that the letters were distorted. If he possessed a neck you couldn't have proved it by me.

Up close, in person, his face was even lumpier than it had appeared on the screen. He had blond hair cut nearly skinhead short, and eyes of a blue so pale they were almost white.

I said, "You want to try that again? Maybe with a few more details?"

He sighed impatiently. "Somebody wants to talk to you," he repeated. "I'm here to bring you. Please," he added with some effort.

There was something in his voice that brought back memories of my reporter days. After a second I realized what it was: that peculiar strained quality that you hear in the voice of a man who is being very careful to speak politely and formally, when all his instincts and habits are urging him to drop the crap and start kicking ass. I'd heard it at many a crime scene when a cop was reciting the Miranda rights to a suspect. In the case of the cop, the constraining force had been the presence of reporters and cameras. Here and now, I figured Mad Mel had been given orders. By whom, though?

I said in a carefully neutral tone, "Do I get to know who wants to see me?"

He scowled. At least I thought it was a scowl; with a face like that, it was hard to tell. "Mrs. Redfield," he said reluctantly. "Okay? Now you gonna come?"

"Mrs. Redfield?" I said, puzzled. "But she was here only yesterday, and I told her—"

"Not Mizz Martha," he said. His voice held a distinct edge of scorn. "Sister Amanda Redfield. You know, Reverend Jack's mother."

"Oh, the *real* Mrs. Redfield," I said dryly.

"Yeah," he agreed. "So, you coming or what?"

"Oh, I'll come," I said. "Wouldn't miss this for the world. Let me get my keys."

"You can ride with me." I saw a big white pickup truck parked in the yard. The door bore the logo of the Jack Redfield

Ministries. "I'm supposed to bring you," he explained. "That's what she said to do."

I shrugged. "Right with you," I said. "I'll just lock up."

Mad Mel didn't talk for most of the ride. As we crossed the river, though, he said suddenly, "Are you a Christian, Roper?"

There were several possible responses, most of which would have required more discussion than I felt like having with Mad Mel Rains. I said at last, "By your terms, probably not."

"Not my terms," he said seriously, "God's terms. Like, you're born again or you're not. I know what I'm talking about," he went on. "I used to be a sinner, man—drugs, women, gambling, you wouldn't believe it. Then I heard Reverend Jack on TV and it changed my whole life around."

His enormous hands tightened visibly on the wheel. "I know what they're saying about him now, but nobody better say it to my face. Maybe he did wrong a long time ago, but he made up for it, helping people get Jesus into their hearts. Seven years, now, I've watched over him and his family, making sure nobody hurts them."

He glanced sideways at me. "See, I figure that's why God gave me my strength and my speed, so I could protect Reverend Jack and Sister Amanda and the others. And, Jesus willing, I aim to keep on doing that. Anybody messes with them, they're messing with me."

He seemed to be waiting for some kind of answer. When I didn't offer one, though, he said, "Huh," in a curiously satisfied way, and that was all the conversation for the rest of the ride.

I'd expected we'd be going to the Ministries complex. Instead, we rolled through an area of big new-looking estates, down where Tulsa and Broken Arrow had gradually spread into mutual and pricey contact over the last decade or so. I'd never been in this part of town before. In actual straight-line miles, it wasn't all that far from my place in Yuchi Park, on the other side of the river. Even in driving minutes, the distance wasn't too great. Measured in dollars, though, it would have taken

Carl Sagan to express just how far it was. Millions and millions, that's for sure.

The Redfield home was actually relatively modest by the standards of the neighborhood, though it was still plenty big and expensive-looking. Mad Mel turned the pickup down a long paved semicircular drive, lined with flower beds and ornamental bushes, and stopped in front of a large, rather rambling two-story house faced in rough brownish stone. You could have parked my trailer on the front porch and still had room for the afternoon bridge party. A neatly-groomed lawn stretched off into the distance on either side. I'd been expecting a certain level of *nouveau-riche* tackiness—some of the big-time electronic preachers in the Tulsa area were notorious for putting up fantastically expensive eyesores—but this place, to my untrained eye at least, had a nice, pleasing appearance, and fit in well with the general landscape.

"Here we are," Mad Mel announced, unnecessarily, and we got out and went up the walk. A tiny black woman opened the door and Mad Mel took her aside for a brief low-voiced conference. "This way," he said to me, gesturing with a hand the size of a bunch of bananas. "She's out on the sun porch."

The sun porch was a long, spacious, sun-bright space enclosed by seeming acres of gleaming plate glass. Tropical looking plants grew in stone jars and redwood tubs. Several small birds—finches, I thought—twittered nervously in an elaborate bamboo cage as we passed. Well, Mad Mel would have had that effect on anybody.

Amanda Redfield was sitting at the far end of the sun porch, in a big fancy wickerwork chair that rose up in back to make a kind of frame or backdrop for her face. It was a face worth framing. She'd looked forbidding in photos and TV shots, but the real thing was exponentially more impressive. Suddenly Mad Mel was only the second most intimidating figure on the scene.

"Mr. Roper," she said in a dry cold voice, like someone breaking handfuls of glass rods. "Sit down."

I sat; it wouldn't have occurred to me to disobey just then.

She looked at me for a long time without evident pleasure. But then I suspected it had been a long time since much pleasure had registered on that long, severe, oddly aristocratic face. She still wore that black bat-out-of-hell dress she'd had on at the funeral, or one just like it. Her white hair was done up on top of her head in a sort of bun. She wore no makeup and no jewelry except for a plain gold band on her left hand.

"Mr. Roper," she said at last, "my daughter-in-law went to see you yesterday." My face must have registered something because she made a small dry snorting sound. "Oh, she told me, last night. She didn't intend to tell me, but in the end she did. As she always does. She can't keep anything from me, you know."

Her speech was a bit of a surprise. Considering her background and general appearance, I'd have expected her to sound like, oh, a slightly classier version of Granny Clampett. The Dust Bowl accent was there, all right, but only if you listened for it. Amanda Redfield spoke in a crisp, precise manner that reminded me a little of Katharine Hepburn. Say in that scene in *The African Queen* where she pours Bogie's booze over the side. I could just picture this one doing it, too.

"Martha isn't here this morning, if you were wondering," she continued. "She went into the city, shopping, with my son's bastard daughter." The pinch of her lips said clearly what she thought of *that*. "I took advantage of their absence to have Mel bring you here, so I can explain things to you."

She tapped the armrests of the chair with bony, restless fingers. "Mr. Roper, this family has been through a great deal in recent days. Much of it, I might add, has been inflicted by persons of your trade, but that's neither here nor there. My son is dead by his own hand and everything he worked to build is in ruins. The name of this family has been permanently soiled," she said, "and there are other troubles we still have to deal with, concerning my son's estate."

Mad Mel had moved to stand beside her chair and a little to the rear, arms folded. He was watching the old woman but I had the feeling he was somehow watching me at the same time.

"My point," she said, "is simply this. We do not need to have you, or anyone else, prying into the sordid details of my son's life, keeping the wretched affair alive in everyone's memory. We need to withdraw now, and put this business behind us, and above all we need to pray for the Lord to show us what to do next."

She pointed suddenly at me. I could damn near feel the energy hitting me in the chest. "You will leave us alone," she said. "You will forget my daughter-in-law's foolish proposal. You will in fact forget you ever heard of any of us."

I said, "Is that a request or an order?"

"It is neither, Mr. Roper," she said calmly. "It is a statement."

She sat back and watched me. When I didn't speak she said, "Do you have nothing at all to say?"

I shrugged. "I'm trying to think how to say it, is all. I'm trying to think," I said, "of a polite way to say what we used to say when I was a boy: 'Or you'll do what?' "

Mad Mel's arms unfolded very fast. His face began to darken. "Listen," he said, "you don't talk like that to Sister Amanda—"

"Be quiet, Mel," she said, still in that placid chilly voice, not looking at him. "Don't be childish, Mr. Roper. I don't mean to threaten you. I don't see that it's necessary. Tell me what my daughter-in-law was supposed to pay you, and I'll give you that myself." And when I didn't immediately react, "Oh, very well, I'll double it. Right now, and you won't have had to do anything to earn it, except go away and forget about my son."

I said, "You're pretty sure I'm for sale."

"I have never known a man of your sort who wasn't," she said baldly. "I know your kind very well, always working some sort of deal, some hustle. My late husband was like that."

Mad Mel had refolded his arms. I took this to mean he wasn't going to rip my head off immediately after all.

"So," she said, "how much is it going to cost me to be rid of you?"

I shook my head. "Sorry," I said. "It doesn't work that way."

The funny thing was, she'd have had at least a fifty-fifty chance of getting her way if she'd simply asked me nicely. After all, I didn't seriously expect to find anything that would make a difference; I'd only taken the job as a half-assed gesture of appeasement to my own lingering sense of guilt. All she'd have had to do would have been to make me feel guiltier about snooping around in her family's affairs than I did about letting things lie. That wouldn't have been hard.

She made an impatient gesture. "Which I suppose means you've got grander plans. No doubt you think you'll find something you can sell to the sensational press. Or perhaps you intend to write a book and make yourself famous as well as rich. I've seen what you do," she said scornfully. "My son was reading a book by you last summer, on this very porch. I picked it up and looked at it. Lurid, trashy fiction, full of violence and sex."

Son of a bitch. So the Reverend actually *had* been a reader. Sister Amanda didn't know it, but she'd just blown any shot she might have had at getting me to forget about him.

"Well," she went on, "I'd hoped we could handle this as a simple, if sordid, business transaction. You compel me to remind you that I can make life very difficult for you, Mr. Roper."

"For example?"

"You are not a licensed private investigator. You are operating outside the law," she said. "I believe a complaint to the authorities might be very effective."

"Forget it. I'm also a working professional writer. Try and prove I'm not simply researching a projected book. First Amendment, remember?"

I wasn't at all sure the First Amendment would do me much good in this part of the country. Rita and I used to say that on the East Coast a writer got respect but no money, on the West Coast a writer could make money but got no respect, and in Oklahoma you had to explain to people what a writer did.

"But don't let that stop you," I added. "You go right ahead and file a complaint. We'll go into court and I'll call up all my contacts in the news media. They'll have a wonderful time telling the country how the late Reverend's mother is trying to prevent me from clearing his name. I can hardly wait."

I wouldn't have thought it possible for her face to get any meaner, but it did. "Mr. Roper," she said in a kind of python hiss, "you're making a serious mistake in trifling with me."

She pointed that laser-beam finger again. "You have been warned." It would have been a corny, melodramatic line if anybody else had said it. When she said it, it wasn't corny at all. "I suggest you think about these things before you do anything you'll come to regret."

She made an imperious gesture. "Mel, take Mr. Roper home."

I said, "Under the circumstances, maybe I'd better just call a cab."

Mad Mel looked me over and grinned. The grin made his face look even more brutal than before. "If you're afraid to ride with me," he said, "I'll get one of the niggers from the house staff to drive you."

"Nonsense," Amanda Redfield said crisply. "Mel, you will drive this man home, and nothing else, you understand? You will not harm or threaten him on the way, or when you arrive. There," she said, looking at me. "Does that satisfy you?"

"Satisfy" wasn't really the word, but I said, "All right." Mad Mel was clearly one who followed his orders precisely, like it or not. At least when they came from her. That wasn't really to his discredit; the old woman could have housebroken a rhinoceros or attack-trained a butterfly.

"This way," Mel said to me. "We'll take the pickup again."

Despite Amanda Redfield's orders, I was halfway expecting Mel to lean on me at least a little on the way home. But he didn't say a word, didn't even acknowledge that there was anyone in the cab with him, all the way back down the highway and across the river to Yuchi Park.

When he had stopped the pickup in front of the trailer, though, he turned to face me and said, "You got a VCR?"

I stopped yanking at the door handle and looked at him, too surprised to reply. "You got a VCR, man?" he repeated, a little louder. "You know, play videotapes with?"

"Oh. Yes," I said, blank-headed. "Why?"

"Reach in the glove compartment," he said.

The glove compartment was full of black videotape cassettes, unboxed and unlabeled. "Take one," Mad Mel said, "they're all alike."

I pulled a cassette from the stack and he said, "This is something we produced this spring, me and the other guys from Black Belts for Christ. Reverend Jack wouldn't let me show it on the program, but some of the Christian cable shows are interested in running it. Anyway," he said, "reason I'm giving you a copy, I want you to watch it."

His voice was reasonable, almost friendly. He might have been advising me to get a bet down on the next Drillers game.

"I want you to watch it all the way through," he said, "and while you do I want you to think about what Sister Amanda told you."

"I'll do that," I said, opening the door and getting down. He nodded, once, as if satisfied, and a moment later he was roaring off down the drive toward the main road. I watched him go and then I turned back toward the trailer, where a barrage of hysterical barking from inside told me Harry had finally woken up.

I watched the tape that evening, while I dined on canned chili and crackers and Michelob. It was, all in all, a memorable cultural experience.

There were no titles or credits or lead-ins. There was just a brief bit of hissing leader tape and then all at once the screen lit up and this enormous foot was coming right toward the camera, so fast it seemed about to come clear out of the TV and into the room. Involuntarily I jumped back slightly in my chair.

Then the foot dropped away and was replaced by a head-and-shoulders of Mad Mel. "Hi," he said, "I'm Mel Rains. Some of you may remember me from my days in the ring and in films as Mad Mel."

There followed a very professionally-assembled montage of scenes from what appeared to have been a fairly impressive career. Mad Mel was shown grappling with Hulk Hogan, with Rowdy Roddy Piper, with a host of various lesser figures from the pro wrestling world. In a white karate *gi,* he faced and demolished a series of opponents in kick-boxing and full-contact karate matches. Dressed in biker rig, obviously playing a heavy in some forgettable action movie, he squared off against Chuck Norris. It was all very fast and colorful and exciting, even if you didn't normally care for that sort of thing.

At the end of the montage Mad Mel appeared again on the screen, wearing a JESUS IS THE ONLY KING T-shirt like the one I'd seen him in today. Maybe the same one, for all I knew. "That was what I used to do," he said seriously, "before I learned about Christ."

He spoke, then, for ten or fifteen minutes, not moving around or gesturing, just facing the camera and talking. To my surprise, he was a pretty fair speaker; no doubt the lines had been written for him, but he delivered them with conviction and good timing, and he used his gravel-down-a-chute voice to real effect. His big rough face and his weird pale eyes glowed with an almost hypnotic intensity.

His message seemed to be aimed mostly at teenage boys— "young men" he called them, but the target age was clearly pre-voter range—and Mad Mel wanted them to know that you could be a real macho man and still follow Christ. "Jesus Christ was no wimp," he bellowed. "The Romans, the toughest soldiers the world has ever seen, tried to kill Him and they couldn't!" And later he assured his audience that "Satan is a loser! He can run from the Lord but he can't hide!"

At the end the camera followed Mel as he strode over to a heavily-constructed table, where a number of bricks were piled in no particular pattern. A couple of short lengths of two-by-four had been placed crosswise on the table, four or five inches apart.

"I want to show you something," Mel said. He picked up a brick and held it up with a decisive gesture. "This," he said dramatically, "is drugs."

He laid the brick carefully across the two boards, so that it was supported by its ends. "This," he said in the same way, picking up another brick, "is alcohol." He laid it on top of the first brick.

He went through the pile of bricks like that, naming what

115

each one stood for: gambling, stealing, promiscuity—he had a little trouble pronouncing that one—and so on. At the end he had quite a stack. The camera zoomed in for a close-up as Mad Mel held up his right hand and slowly, impressively, closed the fingers into a huge fist.

"And this," he said, holding the fist up to the camera, "is the power of Jesus Christ."

Voom, the camera pulled back to a full-length shot. And BOOM, that big fist came down in a vertical punch so fast that there was nothing but a blur and then a kind of explosion of brick fragments. An instant later Mad Mel was standing there folding his arms and the table and floor were covered with chunks of brick. Not a brick had survived intact.

The camera closed in once more on Mad Mel's face. In a slow throaty rasp he said into the camera, *"Get the message?"*

The phone rang a couple of hours later. It was Mad Mel. The conversation was very short.

"Did you watch the video like I said?" he asked.

"Yes," I said.

"Do you understand what I'm trying to tell you?"

"I think so."

"Good," he said, and hung up.

THIRTEEN

Wiley Harmon glanced casually about the parking lot and then quickly opened the door of my Camaro and slid in beside me. "Here," he said, and handed me a big thick manila envelope, the kind I use for manuscripts. From the weight and bulk, it contained at least as much paper as a full-length book manuscript, too.

"Heavy son of a bitch," Wiley commented. "You wanted it all, though, it's all there."

I hefted the parcel experimentally. "You know," I said, "I'm surprised the environmental movement hasn't gotten after the police departments. You guys must be responsible for a lot of trees getting cut down, the amount of paper you go through."

"Fuck the trees," Harmon grunted. "How can you respect anything that big that'll let a dog piss on it? Speaking of paper, I think you got some for me."

I handed over the paper in question. Several oblong slips of it, in fact, green in color, bearing the likeness of one of the more evil bastards ever to occupy the White House. I wondered sometimes what Rita's people felt when they looked at a twenty—although for most of them that didn't happen often enough to be a major problem. Wiley Harmon, uninterested in social and historic implications, merely counted the bills and stuck them in his wallet.

"Sorry the nut ran higher than expected," he said, "but there's people I got to pay off, like the file room asshole who made the copies for me, and a couple of them decided to raise their prices." He looked at the file on the seat between us. "You really think you're gonna find anything in all that shit?"

"Probably not," I said, "but I don't have that many options. I thought maybe something in the file would suggest a line I could follow."

He gave me a sardonic look. "Hey, I'll give you a suggestion, only you ain't gonna wanta follow it. It ever occur to you," he said, "there's one person on the scene, had a hell of a fine motive to pop Lorene? Somebody nobody's even mentioned yet?"

"Go ahead."

"Your latest, I guess you'd say client. The preacher's old lady. What's her name? Martha Redfield. Think about it," he said. "Not only has she got the basic pissed-off-wife motive— which has been plenty good enough for hundreds of wives over the years to put a hole in their old man's other broad—but Lorene represented a real threat to the family's finances. Shit, in her position you bet your ass *I'd* have done it. Or had it done."

"But if she did it, she'd hardly be trying to get me or anybody else to investigate the killing. She'd want the whole thing to stay where it lies right now."

"Only if she knows she did it." Harmon's face wore an unusually thoughtful expression, for him. "I've known of a couple of cases where the perp blanked out, genuinely didn't remember killing anyone or even being there. And I'm not talking about drunks or dopers, either, or nut cases. Just straight citizens whose brains shorted out for a while, you know? Both of them," he added pointedly, "were nice respectable women who'd killed their husbands."

"It sounds far-fetched."

"Tell me one thing about this fucking case that isn't far-fetched," Harmon snorted. "Christ, it's something out of a supermarket tabloid."

He grinned suddenly. "Or maybe she figures, hey, hire this guy Roper to dig around, that'll make me look better if somebody ever does get suspicious. No danger of *him* ever actually finding anything."

"You son of a bitch," I said, while he guffawed. "Get your ass out of my car."

"Sure." He opened the door, still laughing. "Happy reading."

Driving home, I told myself you could really get crazy if you started letting Wiley Harmon play with your head. But I wished he hadn't said that about Martha Redfield. Now it was there, it wouldn't quite go away.

The file on the Lorene Matson case was even more voluminous than it had seemed at first glance. Any homicide generates a staggering amount of paperwork; but when you've got a high-profile case that gets a lot of publicity, and may be heading toward a major trial, then everybody concerned starts cranking out the paper by the ream, the better to cover their asses in case things turn rancid.

I plowed doggedly through the whole mess, forcing myself to read page after page of bad typing and clumsy, stilted cop prose. None of it told me anything I didn't already know, except for odds and ends that meant nothing in any context I could assemble.

Time of death was put at around ten o'clock. Two bullets had penetrated the thoracic cavity, one striking the heart, the other the left lung. Both bullets had remained inside the body and had been recovered, as had two ejected cartridge cases found near the front door. The murder weapon had been a .32-caliber automatic pistol, make unknown, and the ammunition had been manufactured by the Remington-Peters company. The weapon had not been found and, unless the killer was a complete idiot, was somewhere on the bottom of the Arkansas River. By now it would be covered by inches of silt.

The scene had been checked for fingerprints. All those found had been those of the victim except for a partial and badly smeared palm print on the outside front doorknob, which might or might not have belonged to Reverend Jack Redfield. No unusual fibers, stains, or particles had turned up.

There was a very detailed and carefully worked-up study by a forensics expert, full of technical terms and hard to read. What it boiled down to, though, was what Wiley Harmon had already told me: somebody had walked in the front door, shot the victim in the living room, and left. Jack Redfield had claimed, in his statement, that the door had been closed when he got there but the latch had not caught; there was, of course, no way whatever of proving or disproving this.

Around eight that evening, I pushed the whole heap of paper aside and sat for a moment staring blankly at the photographic evidence Wiley Harmon had also copied. That was the other thing you did when you had a trash case and needed something to make the investigation look good, I thought: take lots of pictures. I picked up the stack of photocopied black-and-whites and leafed through them. The copier had destroyed most of the detail; with few exceptions, it was impossible to tell what I was looking at without checking the typed information at the bottom. A couple of shots, for example, supposedly showed the entry wounds in close-up detail, but they looked more like telephotos of the lunar surface.

There was one fairly clear morgue head-and-shoulders of the victim, though, and I tossed the other stuff aside and studied that while I finished my current beer. Lorene Matson, everyone had said, had been a good-looking woman even pushing forty; I saw that she'd even managed to look fairly good dead, considering.

Remembering something, I went over and rooted around in the cardboard box of Redfieldiana until I found the little framed photograph I'd taken from the dead woman's dresser. Somehow I'd failed to put it in with the material I'd given Amy Matson, as I'd intended to do; and I'd made a point of not mentioning it to Wiley Harmon, since taking it at all had gone well beyond the bounds of even a blackbag toss. I'd been meaning to get in touch with Amy and ask if she wanted it, but one thing or another had always gotten in the way.

I carried it back to my chair and compared the two faces, the child and the dead woman. No question, they were the same. The effect, looking at them side by side, was pretty depressing. I turned the morgue shot face down and started to put the framed snapshot back, and then something nudged the back of my mind, just the least bit, and I stopped and looked at it again.

It took a minute or so for the memory to register. When it did I laid the little photo aside and started rummaging in the box again, and a moment later I had the Redfield biography open on my lap, going through the illustrations.

There they were again, just as I'd remembered them: Sister Amanda and the infant Reverend, in front of that big King-fisher County farmhouse. I picked up the snapshot and studied it again, ignoring now the figures in the foreground, concentrating on the lines of the house some distance behind them. The house was far enough away, in fact, that it was slightly out of focus, but the shape of the roof was clear enough. I looked back at the picture in the Redfield book and then I laid everything down on the couch and picked up the phone. The number I called was unlisted but Martha Redfield had already given it to me.

The voice that answered wasn't anyone I knew; I thought it must be the black maid I'd seen the preceding morning. Whoever it was, she wasn't enthusiastic about getting Martha Redfield, but finally she did it.

After several minutes of dead-phone waiting, there was a click and Martha Redfield's voice said, "Yes? Hello?"

"This is Taggart Roper—"

"Oh, yes." There was an almost pathetic eagerness in her voice; it made me wish for something, anything to give her. "Have you found anything?"

"Not yet. Not really. What I wanted to know," I said, "did your husband happen to tell you the details of how he came to know Lorene Matson in the first place? He said something to me about their being childhood friends."

"Yes," she said, sounding puzzled. "They grew up together.

Her parents worked for his father on the farm. Since Mr. Redfield was gone so much, working on his oil deals—I've heard my mother-in-law talk about that often enough—he hired Mr. Matson to do the heavy work and more or less run the farm. I think the wife helped Amanda with housework and cooking. They lived on the farm, Jack said, in a house near the Redfield home."

Her voice took on a soft, curiously wistful tone. "Jack was an only child," she said, "and you know that terrible empty country out on the Plains. Lorene was the only playmate he had. I suppose it was only natural, when they ran into each other years later in the city, that—" She stopped suddenly, her voice breaking up. "Why?" she asked after a moment's pause. "Does that mean anything?"

"I can't see how it does," I said honestly. "It just answers a question that was bothering me."

"Oh," she said, disappointed.

There was a soft clicking sound and a slight change in the background tone. Somebody else had picked up a phone in that house and was listening in.

"I suppose I was expecting too much," Martha Redfield went on, evidently not noticing. "Have you considered looking into the records of—"

"Martha." The voice that crackled through the receiver was unmistakable; there was no one else on the planet, let alone in the Redfield house, who sounded like that. "Martha," Sister Amanda said again, "who is that you're talking to?"

"I'd better hang up," Martha said instantly. And did, before I could say anything. There was a click but the dial tone didn't come on. Instead I heard Amanda's cold dry voice, speaking louder now: "Who is that? Who is that? Taggart Roper, is that you?"

I wanted badly to invite her to perform a supreme act of self-esteem, but it would have made even more trouble for Martha Redfield. I hung up the phone without saying a word, and sat there for a few minutes expecting it to ring, but it didn't.

Finally I went back and gathered up all my various papers and literature—the Redfield Archives, I was beginning to call them in my mind—and stacked them in something approximating order, down by the end of the couch. The little framed picture, after a moment's reflection, I set on the end table by the phone; maybe if I saw it all the time I'd remember to give it to Amy.

And, for the moment, I couldn't think of anything else to do. Getting those bootleg copies of the police files seemed to have been a waste of time and money. I couldn't even justify asking Martha Redfield to compensate me for the bribe I'd paid to Wiley Harmon.

I went to the desk, finally, and tried to do some work on the novel in progress, but I didn't have much luck. Too many of my brain cells were still worrying at the Redfield affair; too much of me wouldn't let it go. Staring at the paper in the typewriter, I couldn't see buffalo herds and Indians and cavalrymen, as I needed to. Instead I kept seeing two little kids, a boy and a girl, wandering across that dusty, windswept yard out on the Oklahoma plains. . . .

Next morning, though, I woke up with a clear picture of where I wanted to go with the chapter I'd been fighting. By midafternoon I had more work done than I'd managed to complete in the last couple of weeks. I don't know why it happens that way sometimes; maybe there's part of the mind that works these things out while the rest of the brain is sleeping.

I got so involved in the writing, in fact, that I barely remembered in time that I was supposed to have dinner at Rita's. Walking away from the typewriter took a real effort at that; anybody but Rita, I might not have made it.

It was nearly dark by the time I got to Rita's place. She had dinner on the table already: something with rice and strange little dark beans and other things I couldn't identify, not my usual sort of fare but pretty damn good just the same. We ate and talked and then we went into the living room and talked a little longer. Then I got up and walked over to her and picked her up and carried her into the bedroom and laid her on the bed and, well, laid her on the bed. That was even better than dinner.

"Yeah," she said afterward, lying beside me on the bed,

"you're back, all right. I thought we'd lost you for a while there."

It was after midnight when I finally drove away from Rita's. Traffic on I-44 was still heavy, though, everybody roaring along in close-packed clumps with great empty stretches between them, changing lanes at random and without signaling, burning the next guy's retinas in the mirrors with headlights on high beam, and all the other little quirks that make driving in Tulsa such a sphincter-exercising experience. Oklahoma drivers, on the average, are among the worst in the United States—which is saying a lot to begin with—and Tulsa drivers aren't even average Oklahoma drivers. On top of all that, statistics indicate that after midnight more than half the drivers on the road in *any* urban area are legally drunk. In the interests of safety, then, I followed my usual rule: drive just as by-God fast as you can, so you don't spend any more time than you can help on the same road as those crazy bastards.

It wasn't till I was off the expressway and heading down the old two-lane toward Yuchi Park that I started noticing the headlights behind me. They'd been back there for some time, I guessed, but I hadn't noticed them in the freeway traffic. They were high off the ground and pretty big; a small truck or a big van, I thought. The driver was staying right on my ass and he had those lights up all the way; the glare was starting to get on my nerves, in fact, and I sped up to get clear of him.

He sped up too.

I cursed and speeded up some more. He stayed right with me. The interval remained too constant for this to be chance. Some drunk, I decided, or a teenager—or, most likely, a drunk teenager—having primitive fun tormenting the handiest stranger. Well, the hell with this asshole, whoever he was. I didn't feel like playing these jackoff games in the middle of the night. At the next intersection, I turned off down a narrow two-lane side road that, as far as I knew, didn't go anywhere in particular. Let the clown go on his way and find somebody else to annoy.

Except he didn't go on his way. In my mirror I saw the headlights swing around the corner and come right down the side road after me.

Well, shit. I'd made a bad move; this was a deserted stretch of road, no traffic this time of night, no houses for miles, just empty Arkansas River floodplain stretching off into the dark on either side of the road. Not a good place to get into confrontations with manic good ol' boys, let alone bad ones.

The headlights were so close behind me now that they lit up the interior of the Camaro. I could see my own hands white-knuckling the wheel. Then suddenly the lights swung hard to the left, into the other lane. I could hear the sound of a big mill dropping into a lower gear and starting to wind up.

For a moment instinct said to stand on it; old as she was, my Camaro could probably outrun whatever this bozo was driving. The problem word was "probably." If he did have something with serious muscle—and you get quite a few awesomely hopped-up pickup trucks on eastern Oklahoma roads—this would be a bad place and time to get into a high-speed contest. The narrow old blacktop was gnarled and potholed and the Camaro's shocks were no longer up to specs.

Much as it galled me, I'd ease off and let the wiggy bastard pass. Having proved, by the rules of his world, that his penis was longer than mine, he'd roar happily off into the night—

It was only when he came abreast of me and then began drifting toward me that I realized what was happening. Well, I'm slow to catch on sometimes.

There was nothing fancy or tricky in it. He just ran me the hell off the road. I didn't fight him; he had the mass and the power and resisting would only cost me a lot of bodywork. Metal scraped metal briefly and then the Camaro was off the pavement. There was no shoulder, just a sharply-sloping strip, not quite an embankment, covered in scraggly weeds and gravel and cut with deep little gullies. I got an instant's glimpse of a big dark-colored pickup truck charging past and then I was fighting for control as the Camaro tried to stick its nose into the ditch. When I wouldn't let it do that it wanted to turn over. The tires slid and spun and gravel rattled against the underworks. The wheel almost got away from me. I was cursing steadily, more or less automatically; I think some irrational part of my mind had decided that the instant I stopped screaming curses it would all be over.

When I finally got the Camaro stopped she was still right side up and she hadn't quite made it into the ditch, but it was damn close. Only the prolonged spell of dry hot weather had saved me; if the dirt had been just the least bit moist, if I'd had the slightest bit less traction, that would have been it.

I sat for a second or two, not moving, catching my breath before beginning the job of getting back onto the road. That was when I became aware that the pickup truck had stopped, a little way down the road. Its big taillights cast a bright red glow over the blacktop.

As I watched, the lights blinked and dipped and then began swinging to the side; the driver was turning around. I glanced around briefly, trying to think if there was anything in the car I could use as a weapon, but there was nothing except the jack handle in the trunk, and I'd never get at that in time. Maybe I ought to get out of the car and take cover in the ditch, in case this maniac had a gun. It was more than possible, in this part of the country.

But I stayed put, I'm not sure why; and then the big pickup was rushing back up the road, engine screaming in bottom gear, and sliding to a noisy stop on the blacktop next to me. There was a grinding sound as a window was cranked down. I saw a pale oval appear. It looked like a face; that was all I could tell about it.

A voice called, "Hey, Roper!"

It was a high, redneck-nasal voice; it sounded fairly young, but it wasn't quite a teenager's voice. It was the kind of voice that used to ask you how many gallons you wanted, back when gas stations had people who pumped gas.

"Hey, Roper!" it said again. "You all right down there?"

There was a pause—maybe he actually expected me to reply—and then a high, loony laugh. "You better watch your ass, Roper," he yelled. "You better start listening when people tell you things. Something liable to happen to you, you keep fucking around."

The big tires screeched suddenly as the driver hit the gas. A few seconds later the taillights had vanished up the road, back the way we'd come.

FOURTEEN

The first thing I did when I got home, naturally, was to get my old shotgun out of the closet and stuff the magazine tube full of number-one buckshot shells. The brass was a little green; it had been a long time since I'd bought that box of twelve-gauge shells, and they'd been sitting on a shelf in my closet, unopened, ever since. But that wouldn't make any difference at all if I started pumping them into the chamber and pulling the trigger. As, by that time, I was very much in the mood to do.

Next morning, though, I had cooled down enough to think things through more rationally, and I realized that the shotgun wasn't really the solution to my problems.

I mean, it was a good well-made weapon, but it was just too long and clumsy to use from inside a car, and there was no way of carrying it on me when I had to move around on foot. I could have taken a hacksaw to the barrel and a handsaw to the stock, but that would have put me in violation of some pretty Draconian federal laws; and anyway, I didn't want to mutilate the old Winchester, which had belonged to my father. What I needed was a pistol.

And, as it happened, I owned one. It was just kind of weird, that's all.

Back when I'd started writing my first novel, I'd set great value on acquiring the kind of firsthand knowledge that would, I hoped, give my narration authenticity. I'd gone over the terrain where the historic events had happened; I'd even taken a few lessons in horseback riding—acquiring in the process a deep and abiding hatred for horses, but never mind that.

And, still in the interests of authorial expertise, I'd bought a black-powder cap-and-ball pistol of the type commonly used during the period I was writing about. Not an antique, of course—I'd found out very fast what astronomical prices genuine Civil War weapons brought—but a modern replica, made in New England, of a Colt .36 revolver, the kind known to its contemporaries as a "Navy Six." Truthfully, I couldn't say whether it ever did my writing any good, but I'd had a lot of fun down by the river banging away at beer cans and floating driftwood with the old-fashioned weapon. I'd even had a dust-jacket photo taken, holding the Navy in a kind of Inspection Arms pose and looking bad-assed into the camera, but the publisher had decided not to use it.

I dug the flat wooden case out of the bottom drawer of my dresser and took the long-barreled revolver out and looked it over. I hadn't even had it in my hands in almost a year, and the last time I'd fired it had been two New Year's Eves ago. It seemed to be all right, though; at least there were no signs of rust, and the bore and chambers were shiny and clean. Which was a relief, because black-powder residue absorbs water right out of the air, and if you don't get the weapon absolutely clean after you use it—and the process is easily as much fun as cleaning a very dirty oven—you wind up, very quickly, with an inefficiently-shaped tack hammer, or an interesting paperweight.

I hefted the Navy thoughtfully and aimed it at my reflection in the bedroom mirror. It balanced and pointed as naturally as I'd remembered; it wasn't nearly as clumsy as it looked. Ballistically, according to the figures I'd read, it was roughly equivalent to a modern .38. Not exactly a cannon, but hell, plenty of people had managed to fight a war with guns just like it, to say nothing of various private-sector shootists such as Wild Bill Hickok.

At the very least it would beat the hell out of a jack handle.

Loading it was a big pain in the ass, a complex ritual involving loose black powder, little shiny copper percussion caps, and round cast-lead balls. I'd gotten rid of the powder and the caps when I'd quit shooting, seeing no point in keeping explosives around the place, but the case did contain a little cloth bag of .36-caliber balls. I put everything back in the case, stowed the case back in the drawer, and drove into Broken Arrow, where the gun shop that had sold me the Navy proved still to be in business. I bought a can of FFFG black powder and a little flat can of caps, stowed them in the trunk—God help anybody who tail-ended me; we'd both go up together—and drove back home, keeping a wary eye on every big pickup truck that came near me.

At least, I thought as I carried my purchases inside, I hadn't had to buy bullets too. That had been one of the main reasons I'd given up shooting the Navy in the first place. For some reason, most of the black-powder shooters in the Tulsa area had favored the heavier .44-caliber models, and it had proved hard to find balls to fit my .36.

Which isn't as minor a problem as it may sound. Try going into a windowless concrete-block bunker named BIG BUBBA'S GUN HEAVEN and walking up to a six-foot-five, two-hundred-seventy-five-pound, no-neck humanoid with a Marine Corps tattoo on one arm and a Harley-Davidson tattoo on the other and a .357 Magnum Python in a speed-raked holster on his belt and a black T-shirt that says BORN TO KILL LONG-HAIRED COMMIE FAGGOTS WHO BURN THE FLAG AND SAY WRESTLING'S FAKED . . . *you* go up to that guy and say:

"Pardon me, do you have small balls?"

Luckily, as I say, I still had an adequate supply of slugs left from my shooting days; at least it was adequate considering I didn't expect to fire very many shots, if I had to fire any at all. I *better* not have to fire very many, I thought as I thumbed a ball into the first chamber on top of a measured charge of black powder and rammed it home with the loading lever mounted under the barrel. Once I shot this thing empty, any bad guys left standing would have time to inflict whatever they chose to inflict, up to and including the Death of a Thousand Cuts, before I got it reloaded.

And—in one of those bits of real-life timing that you'd never buy if you saw it in a movie—it was just when I'd finished loading up that the phone rang and, surprise surprise, it was Mad Mel.

He said, "Hear you had a little accident last night, Roper. You want to be careful. Man can have some pretty bad accidents if he isn't careful, you know?"

"Mel," I sighed, "quit trying to do gangster-movie lines. You aren't very good at it."

"Sorry that had to happen," he went on, apparently unoffended. "But sometimes, somebody won't listen, you have to find a way to get his attention, you know what I mean?"

I said, "Mel, God ruined a perfectly good penis when He gave you ears and a nose, didn't He?"

"Don't blaspheme," Mel said calmly. "Don't use the Lord's name in vain. I don't like people to do that."

I wanted to scream at him, but it wouldn't have done any good. "If it makes you feel better, Mel, you succeeded in getting my attention."

"Good," he said. "And we're not gonna have any more trouble with you, are we?"

"Goodbye, Mel," I said, and put the receiver gently back in its cradle.

Cleaning up the mess on the kitchen table, I picked up one of the lead balls and bounced it in my palm, thinking about Mad Mel and how he'd looked close up. Suddenly the bullet in my hand seemed very small and trivial. I wondered if I'd started, in Wiley Harmon's phrase, writing checks with my mouth that my ass couldn't cover.

At the county medical examiner's office, a little later that day, I discovered that there was actually an established and perfectly legal procedure by which I could get a look at the file on Jack

Redfield's death without having to pay anybody off. I nearly went into shock. True, the "fee" they soaked me with came to more than the average bribe, but still, it's nice to see the freedom-of-information principle at work.

The money didn't buy me any help, though. The coroner's report told me nothing except that the Reverend had definitely committed suicide by hanging, with no evidence whatever that he'd had any help doing it. Well, I hadn't really expected anything to turn up in that direction; it had just struck me as a base I ought to cover, since I wasn't exactly ass-deep in ideas at the moment.

Amy Matson had moved out of the second motel too, but this time, when I came around asking, the desk clerk had a message for me. And for me only; I actually had to show him my driver's license before he'd give me the note Amy had left. He wouldn't even take the gratuity I offered. The young lady, he informed me in one of the plummiest Bombay accents I'd ever heard, had already compensated him.

She'd moved to a good hotel downtown, one considerably above my usual price range. When I telephoned her room from the lobby she picked up the phone almost immediately. "Oh, wow," she said when I identified myself. I hadn't known they still said that. "Hey, listen," she went on quickly, "Martha Redfield's here with me. Got here just ten or fifteen minutes ago, in fact. Is it—" Her voice dropped to a kind of nervous murmur. "Is it, like, all right? If that's a problem—"

"No, that's okay." Might even be a minor bonus, getting to talk with my more-or-less client without the Ayatolless listening in. "Shall I come up?"

"Just a minute." There were muffled conversational sounds and then Amy came back on. "Why don't we meet you in the coffee shop? We were just about to go down for coffee anyway."

"Fine," I said, and hung up and went looking for the coffee shop.

By the time my two dates showed up, I was halfway through a pretentiously heavy mug of the worst coffee I'd tasted in years. Not that that had surprised me; there is an almost inviolable rule, in the public dining institutions of this country, that the quality of the coffee is in inverse proportion to the fanciness of the cup times the square of the price. You could probably express it as a mathematical formula.

Amy was wearing a smart little white summer dress that showed a lot of leg; a couple of the men at the tables were sneaking looks as she went by, and getting glared at for it by the women they were with. She was looking considerably better than when I'd seen her last. So was Martha Redfield, come to that; she was still in black, but she'd done something with her hair, and her face was a little happier.

"Oh, wow," Amy said again when I handed her the little framed photograph. "Thanks. I remember Lorene showing me this once. I didn't have any pictures of my grandparents."

She studied the snapshot with a mixture of curiosity and sadness. "I don't know anything about them, really. I think she's still alive, the way Lorene talked last time it came up. In a nursing home out in Arizona."

"Perhaps when this is all over," Martha Redfield suggested, "you might want to go out and visit your grandmother."

There was something in her voice when she spoke to Amy, and in her eyes when she looked at her; a kind of tenderness, I suppose you'd call it. I remembered what she'd told me the other night at the trailer. Well, Amy was the closest thing to a daughter that Martha Redfield was ever likely to have. I wondered how Amy felt about the relationship. Of course she'd been shorted in the mother department too.

Amy said, "Grandmothers, oh boy, like I didn't have one right here in Tulsa," and they both winced. I probably did too. "God," Amy went on, "what an *evil* old bat. She's got this lawyer trying to contest Redfield's—my father's will, cut me out of it. Tried to have me thrown out of the house when Martha took me out there last week, but Martha stood up to her." She glanced at the older woman, who was wearing a faint look of pride. "Said the house belonged to her according to the will and she could bring anybody in she wanted, even though she has to let the old lady live there."

Martha took the little picture from Amy. "That's the old

Redfield house, all right," she said, pointing. "I've seen it enough times in the family photo album." She looked up at me. "You know, Mr. Roper, I went out there once. With Jack, I mean. He wanted me to see the old home place. Of course the house was no longer standing, but he said the country was still unchanged." She shivered slightly. "I don't think anything ever changes in that part of Oklahoma. Just wind and dust and tumbleweeds and that great big awful sky pressing down on you. . . ."

She gave a self-conscious little laugh. "My prejudices are showing, aren't they? But I grew up in mountain country, in southern Missouri, and all that empty flat land out there makes me nervous."

"I'm not crazy about it myself," I told her, "and I'm from Kansas."

Amy took the picture back and put it in her purse. A fat waitress drifted over and asked if anyone wanted to order, sounding as if she hoped not. The two women ordered coffee. I said I was okay. When she was gone Amy said, "I don't know why I ordered coffee. I bet it's terrible in here, huh?"

Her voice was high and a little tense; her hands moved nervously on the table as she spoke. I realized suddenly that she hadn't lit a cigarette since she'd arrived. And we weren't in the nonsmoking section, either. With all that was going on in her life, it didn't seem like a good time to add nicotine withdrawal as well; but maybe she just didn't want to smoke in front of Martha Redfield.

"I don't suppose," Martha said to me, "you've found anything yet? I hate to seem to be pressuring you—"

"Oh, hey, right," Amy put in excitedly, "you're doing some sort of detective stuff, aren't you? Trying to find out who really killed Lorene?" Her voice, as much as the phrasing, said that she'd definitely abandoned her own belief in her father's guilt. "I told you this guy was good, didn't I?" she said to Martha.

"I'm afraid I haven't had any luck yet," I admitted. "Tried a few ideas, but nothing that took me anywhere."

Amy laughed suddenly. "Hey," she said, "if *I* had to pick a prime suspect, I'd go for the old lady."

We stared at her. "Really," she said, grinning. "Sister Amanda. My dear grandma. Think about it. She had the motive—her son was getting shaken down—and if there's anybody around here capable of cold-blooded murder, it's her. Christ, just *look* at her."

The waitress reappeared with the coffee and we all sat in awkward silence until she was gone. Finally Martha Redfield said, "Actually, I'm not sure she *isn't* capable of murder, or anything else. Or having that brute Mel do it for her. He'd kill the President if she gave him the order."

I said, "Are you seriously suggesting—"

"Oh, no, no." That embarrassed little laugh again. "It's ridiculous, of course. For one thing, she had no motive. You see," she said, "Sister Amanda didn't know about any of this—about Jack's relationship with Lorene Matson, the payments and so on—until everyone else did. He'd kept it secret from her all those years." Her lips twisted slightly. "Believe me, Mr. Roper, that in itself is an amazing fact. You never saw the relationship between Jack and his mother from the inside, so to speak, as I did," she said, "so you can't imagine how amazing it is."

"Hm. There's no doubt about it, though?" I said. "I mean, that she didn't know?"

"As it happens, I was in the next room when he told her," Martha Redfield said. "The door was slightly open and I heard the entire conversation. This was right after the story came out, after the first visit by the police. It was right after he'd told me the whole story for the first time." Her voice broke up a little, but then she recovered. "No question about it, Mr. Roper. The whole thing obviously came as a tremendous shock to Sister Amanda. In fact it almost seemed that she was as upset to learn that he'd kept a secret from her—"

She shook her head and sipped at her coffee. "I may not get along with my mother-in-law, Mr. Roper, but I've lived under that roof with her for many years, and I know her all too well. Trust me, she didn't know. She didn't even know that Jack had seen Lorene since childhood."

It was interesting information, and it answered some questions I hadn't even thought to ask; but I didn't see that it did me any good, except for eliminating a suspect I hadn't taken seriously to begin with. For one thing, whoever had punched me out in that darkened house, it hadn't been an old lady.

Amy was putting the little picture in her purse. "I'll have them put this stuff on my room bill," she said.

I didn't argue with her. I try not to be too hopelessly old-fashioned about these things; and anyway, I didn't particularly want to pick up the tab for three cups of horrible coffee, not at the prices in here. Judging by the price, the stuff had been made with human blood. Of a rare type.

"I'm going to take care of you, too," Amy told me. "Soon as they straighten out all this shi— uh, all this business with the will. I know you feel kind of bad because of all the trouble that went down with that stuff you found, but hey, you were just doing a job I hired you for, right? And you took a lot of chances and this has been a lot of trouble for you, you ought to get something out of it. Besides," she added, "if you hadn't found that stuff, I'd still be in that motel with Larry. I don't think I could stand it."

"Good old Larry. Heard from him?"

"Yeah, he turned up at that other motel, don't know how he found me, tried to give me a hard time. Figures he's going to get his hands on some of that money, after all I took off him. I told him no way. Here, the doorman and the desk clerks and all, they've got instructions not to let him in."

"He sounds like a dreadful person," Martha Redfield said faintly.

"He is. Watch out for Larry," Amy said to me. "He blames you for his getting shut out of the big money. He might come looking for you again."

I thought about Mad Mel and his friends. If only Larry were all I had to worry about. But I said, "Thanks, I'll watch out." It made her happy and it didn't cost me anything extra.

FIFTEEN

They picked me up going away from the hotel. No doubt they'd been sitting in the hotel parking area waiting for me to come out. Some hotel employee had perhaps been paid, or otherwise influenced, to call in reports on Amy Matson's visitors; that might have been a little too devious for Mad Mel, but it was the sort of thing Sister Amanda would have thought up. Or maybe they'd just been following Martha Redfield to see if she was going to meet me.

There was a big blue pickup truck hanging on my tail a couple of vehicles back as I got onto the expressway; if it wasn't the same one that had run me off the road last night, it was damn similar. I couldn't see it clearly enough to get a look at the driver, or even to tell whether anyone else was on board. He didn't crowd my tail this time; maybe because it was broad daylight and there were plenty of witnesses around, he stayed back there and played it with elephantine caginess.

And he had help along today, though it was a little while before I realized it. A bright red Jeep was working along through the traffic, staying roughly at seven or eight o'clock, and after a few miles it became obvious that the driver didn't just happen to be going our way. The Jeep was the stripped-down, military sort, no upper bodywork except a heavy roll-over bar, and the driver sat fully exposed, so it was easy for me to see that he was watching my car—and, occasionally, glancing toward the dark-blue pickup, maybe for signals, maybe just to make sure the other bastard was there.

We crossed the river on the Redfork Expressway, hanging together in our weird little triangular formation, and I got off onto 75—the Okmulgee road—and headed south. Sure enough, they stayed right with me. There was less traffic now, but the blue pickup still hung well back. When I finally turned off onto the Yuchi Park road, which is two-lane, the Jeep dropped back and fell in behind the pickup.

Decision time again. I could cut the odds at least in half, just by lowering my right foot; old or not, the Camaro would outrun any Jeep ever made, and if she wouldn't outrun the pickup maybe I could outdrive the son of a bitch. In the daylight, on a good road that I knew better than my own living room, I felt a lot more confident about the outcome of such a contest. Hell, it would even be fun. It had been a while since I'd done any serious high-speed driving.

But then what? They knew where I lived, surely; if I burned them on the road, they'd just go wait for me to come home, and maybe tear up the trailer or even do something to Harry while they were waiting. Or they might pick me up another place, another time, some ugly scene like last night. Better to get this business settled—or run this particular play, at any rate—right away. . . .

About halfway between the Highway 75 intersection and the borders of Yuchi Park, a side road runs south for a couple of miles, crossing empty weed-grown fields, and dead ends in an expanse of raw-scraped dirt and weathered wooden stakes. The sign beside the road claims this is going to be a major industrial park. In the years since the sign went up and the stakes went down, nobody has even attempted to build anything there. I've never known the story; but then the area around Tulsa is dotted with failed enterprises like that.

I turned down the side road, tooling along as slow as I could drive without making my intentions too obvious. Of course, any intelligent person would wonder why I was turning off here to begin with, but I didn't figure that included these guys. Anyway, if they did start wondering, they'd just assume I was trying to get away from them. Unless they were from around here, they wouldn't know that the road went nowhere.

And sure enough, they made their move just where I'd expected, maybe a mile from the turnoff, where a slight rise of ground hid the scene from the main road. They did it so quickly and neatly that they must have worked out the moves in advance. Or maybe they'd done this before, to other people.

Suddenly the pickup truck swung into the other lane and came roaring up alongside. I could see it clearly now, a big, powerful-looking job riding high on heavy-duty suspension and fat go-anywhere tires. The dark blue paint job looked like custom work and the note of the engine said there were things under the hood that never came from the factory. Through the glass I could make out the heads and shoulders of the driver and another man. Both of them were looking at me.

I thought they'd try to run me off the road again, and I braced myself for the experience, though here there was a broad gravel shoulder and no real ditch to worry about. But the pickup just kept going, shooting on past me, and then suddenly it swung hard to the right and slid to a violent stop, blocking the road. I barely got the Camaro stopped in time.

In the mirror, I saw the Jeep come up behind me and wheel to the side in the same way. Now they had me boxed in. Or thought they did; I was fairly sure I could get past either vehicle if I didn't mind chewing up a little dirt—but that wasn't what I had in mind.

I sat and watched as they dismounted and deployed. The pickup's license plate, I noticed, had been conveniently splattered with mud, making the number unreadable. The bumper bore a couple of plastic stickers. The one on the left read OLIVER NORTH—AMERICAN HERO. The one on the right said AS A MATTER OF FACT I DO OWN THE ROAD. The rear window of the cab wore an American flag decal.

The two guys who got out of the pickup weren't as big as

Mad Mel, but they were sure-God big enough. The one who got out on the right side wore a black T-shirt with some sort of orange and yellow logo, and tight jeans faded nearly white. He had longish yellow hair and a bushy Buffalo Bill mustache and his face was partly hidden by wraparound shades. His upper arms were so big I couldn't figure how he got his shirts on and off.

The other one, the driver, was taller and rangier in build, with long ropy-muscled arms and a lean, predatory face. He wore a ragged pale-blue tank top, showing off a deep brick-red tan, and jeans hacked off to make shorts. His hair was cropped so close to his head I couldn't tell what color it was. There was no facial shrubbery. He didn't even appear to have any eyebrows.

I didn't have time to get a really good look at the Jeep driver before he came up into the Camaro's blind spot, and I didn't want to turn my head far enough to lose sight of the two coming up in front. All I could tell was that he was short and built like a fire plug and he was carrying something in his right hand.

I stayed put and let them move in. When they were half a dozen paces away, I slid suddenly across the Camaro's seat, popped open the right-side door, and jumped out onto the shoulder. Before they could react I had the Navy revolver in a two-hand grip, arms extended, elbows supported by the Camaro's roof, the long barrel covering the two gorillas from the pickup truck.

I said, not particularly loud, "Far enough, assholes."

They stopped. Stopped walking, stopped moving, I think even stopped breathing for a minute there. Buffalo Bill said, "Hey, he's got a gun!" His voice was high and rather childish. "Sonny, he's got a gun!"

There was a faint sound off to my left. I swung the Navy's muzzle to cover the Jeep driver, who was still moving toward me. "You too," I said. "Back off!"

He stopped even more abruptly than his buddies had done. I saw now that he was holding an aluminum baseball bat. He had massive shoulders and arms and a lumpy, mashed-in face; in fact he looked like Sluggo, only bigger. Much, much bigger.

He stared at the gun in my hands for a moment. "Yeah, Sonny," he said without turning his head, "what's this shit? Wasn't nothing said about the son of a bitch having a gun."

The pickup driver was studying the Navy too. "Shit," he said after a minute, "that ain't a real gun."

"Fuck it ain't," Sluggo said emphatically. "I'm closer to it than you are. That ain't no cap pistol."

"Yeah," Sonny said, "but I mean it's like an antique. My grandpa had one like that, his daddy had it in the Civil War. That thing don't *work.*"

I turned through a few degrees and thumbed back the big old-fashioned hammer and fired. There was a big loud bang—the Camaro's roof helped amplify the sound—and a cloud of smoke. The blue pickup's right rear tire suddenly began making a loud whistling sound. The pickup began to settle earthward at that corner. Buffalo Bill said, "Holy shit!"

Sluggo was glaring at Sonny. "Antique, huh? You silly son of a bitch."

Sonny was still staring at the tire, which was assuming a very lopsided shape by now. "Damn," he said, seemingly to himself, "that's a brand-new tire. The hell. . . ." I had his voice pegged now; he was definitely the one who'd run me off the road last night.

Sluggo turned around with a decisive movement and started walking back toward the Jeep. "Fuck this shit," he said flatly. "I didn't sign on to get my ass shot off." He tossed the baseball bat into the weeds beyond the shoulder. "I'm outta here," he added.

"Hey," Sonny said, "you can't just quit like that—"

"Watch me, motherfucker," Sluggo said without looking back. "You ain't big enough to stop me. Mel don't like it, tell Mel he can come see me about it."

He climbed into the Jeep and started the engine and gunned it, spraying gravel, wheeling the Jeep around in a tight half-circle and accelerating briskly back toward the main road. All three of us stood and watched till he was out of sight.

I looked at Sonny and his anthropoid friend. "Everybody's

been quoting the Bible at me lately," I said. "I'll give you a quote now: *'Go, and do likewise.'* "

Sonny and Buffalo Bill looked at each other. "Think he'll shoot?" Buffalo Bill said dubiously.

"Nah," Sonny said after a second. He sounded really tense, as if he was working himself up to something. "Can't shoot us," he added, looking back at me. "We're unarmed."

"Yeah," Buffalo Bill said, brightening. "That's right, ain't it?"

And, for God's sake, they both began walking toward me again, hands dangling down at their sides, heads down a little, starting to move faster now, their rubber-soled running shoes slapping the blacktop with explosive little *whap* sounds. "You better put that thing down," Sonny shouted. "We have to take it away from you, it's just gonna be worse on you."

"Huh," Buffalo Bill added. "We gonna stomp your ass—"

I said, "Wrong, steroid-breath," and shot him.

I was aiming for his leg, but I'd forgotten the Navy's tendency to shoot high and to the right. The ball caught him in the flank instead. He screamed "JESUS!" and fell down on the pavement, clutching the check of his ass.

I swung the Navy's muzzle to cover Sonny, earing back the hammer again. Sonny, though, had slammed on his brakes so hard his shoe soles skidded on the blacktop. "Jesus," he said, a hoarse echo of his wounded partner.

"You know," I said, "you boys need to watch out about your language. Mad Mel doesn't like that sort of talk at all."

"Jesus," Sonny said again. He was staring at Buffalo Bill, who was lying on the roadway, still clutching his hip and screaming. Blood was starting to ooze between the huge fingers. "You *shot* him," Sonny said incredulously.

"Yep," I said. "Sure did. Not much gets by you, does it?"

"Just shot him," Sonny said in a thin wondering voice. "Wasn't even armed."

"When they get that big," I said, "they count as permanently armed in my book. Anyway, aren't you clowns always telling us your hands are deadly weapons?"

141

I gestured with the Navy. "You better get him to a doctor. I don't guess he's going to bleed to death, shot in the ass like that, but there might be brain damage."

"YAAAAAAAAAAAAAHHHHHH," Buffalo Bill commented.

"Hope you've got a spare," I said, "but you can stand to run on that flat till you get to a phone. I'd try to come up with a good story about a gun going off accidentally or something. I don't think Mad Mel would like it if you guys said anything to get the police into this thing. In fact maybe you better call him before you do anything else."

Sonny looked down at his writing partner and then at the pickup truck. I said, "Oh, and just in case you've got a gun in that pickup, if I see you moving toward it before I'm out of here, I'll kill you. Okay?"

I got back in the Camaro and turned it around. I kept the Navy on the seat beside me, ready to hand, and I watched Sonny & Co. closely all the while, but nobody made any threatening moves. Nobody made any moves at all, except for Buffalo Bill's spasmodic thrashing. Sonny seemed almost paralyzed. His eyes were huge and fixed on me; he looked like a stoned owl.

"Say hallelujah," I called out the window. And drove off, back up the road, feeling an urge to hum some sort of tune. The last I saw of them, Sonny seemed to be trying to help Buffalo Bill to his feet. I hoped he didn't get a hernia. Or rather I hoped he did.

I thought I'd get another call from Mad Mel that night, but none came. But I don't suppose we had anything left to say to each other anyway.

SIXTEEN

Wiley Harmon said, "Shot
him in the ass with *what?*"
I reached over and opened the Camaro's glove compartment
and took the Navy revolver out and handed it to him. He
turned it over in his hands a minute or so, studying it, his face
working. Finally he laid the piece in his lap and looked at me
and broke up. "Jesus Christ," he said, when he was finally able
to talk again. He wiped tears from his eyes with his knuckles.
"Oh, Jesus Christ."

"His name came up a couple of times," I said, "but not in
what you'd call a reverent context. I was shocked."

"Shit." Harmon shook his head, still wiping his eyes. "Those
assholes weren't from Mel Rains's Judo for Jesus Club or whatever the fuck he calls it. He wouldn't mix his holy-Joe brick-
busters up in a low-grade muscle job like that. Bad publicity if
it ever came out, and anyway most of them are real straight-
arrow types, wouldn't go for it. I'd guess he called in a few
markers among the local punks. He still maintains his contacts
from the days before he got religion, or so I hear." He rubbed
his head. "Anyway, this Sonny, I'm pretty sure I know him. A
real bad piece of shit, got a couple of assault busts. And about
as much religion as a tarantula."

He picked up the Navy and looked at it again. "Man, you're something else, you know that? Running around with this fucking Civil War horse pistol, bigger'n shit. Hang on just a minute."

He got out of the car and walked across the gravel parking area toward his Honda Accord. We were out back of the Tulsa Expo stadium at the fairgrounds, where a bunch of Indians were getting ready for a powwow. It was Friday, still midday, and none of the people walking by had gotten into dance outfits yet, but a couple of burly young guys walked past my car, headed toward the stadium, carrying a big hide-headed drum. The nearer one, with shoulder-length black hair and a face out of a Catlin painting, wore an Iron Maiden T-shirt.

Wiley Harmon came back after a couple of minutes, clambering in beside me again, his hand in his outside jacket pocket. "Fucking Indians," he said. His voice held no particular rancor; he would, I knew, have said "Fucking Czechs" in exactly the same way if a polka band had been passing. "Here," he said, and passed something over, keeping his hand low, out of sight from outside the car. I looked down and he was handing me a pistol.

"Take it," he said, and when I still hesitated, "For Christ sake, Roper, take the fucking thing. It ain't hot."

I took the pistol from his hand and looked at it. It was a medium-frame double-action revolver with a short barrel and worn, chipped wooden grips. The finish was almost completely worn away, exposing grayish metal.

"No big deal," Harmon said. "Cheap-ass copy of a Smith and Wesson thirty-eight, made in Brazil. Shoots okay, though. Better than what you got, anyway."

He grinned at me. "Took it in trade, so to speak. This pimp was behind on his payments, gave me this instead. I ran the numbers through and it's clean. I was hanging on to it just in case, you know what I mean?"

I knew. In case Wiley shot a suspect who proved to be unarmed, he would have planted the .38 on the body. Or in case he wanted to pull someone in and had no legitimate charge he could bring, the gun would be "found" in the suspect's pocket, good at least for a concealed-weapons charge.

I said, "The budget's a little tight right now, Wiley."

"No sweat. You're bound to make a serious payday sooner or later. Just remember your friendly neighborhood bad cop when it happens." He grinned again. "If you don't get your ass killed first, of course."

I hefted the .38 experimentally. "Keep the fucker out of sight, will you?" Harmon said irritably. "Bad enough somebody might see me with you, these days." He reached in his other jacket pocket and passed me a handful of shiny brass cartridges. "Stoke that piece with half a dozen of these. Hollow-point handloads, make a hole you could drive a fucking eighteen-wheeler through. Dude in Skiatook makes them up for some of us. You're gonna be stressing that piece of greaseball iron right to the limits, though, so save the hot loads for serious shit, no popping beer cans with them."

I stowed the .38 and the cartridges in the glove compartment and put the Navy in with them. "You get busted packing," Harmon said, "I don't know your ass from a hole in the ground, right?"

He looked out the side window, watching a couple of amazingly fat teenage Indian girls waddling past in identical black bicycle shorts. "All *right,*" he said approvingly. The sight of their big rolling buttocks seemed to put him in a good mood. "Hey," he said, "I'll even throw in a little favor, no charge. I'll see to it Sonny doesn't bother you any more. I got a way I can put some pressure on him to leave the area."

"Probation?"

Harmon chuckled. "Fuck, no. There's these three bad-ass Seminole brothers down in Jenks, going to be really interested to find out who it was got their sister pregnant last year. Sonny fucks around about getting out of town, he just might disappear permanently." The thought seemed to please him. "I shoulda done it long ago. I always did hate that son of a bitch."

"Thanks," I said.

"Hell," he said, "you been a good steady customer over the

years. Not a big spender, but steady. I try to look after my regulars."

He tilted his head, still grinning. "Got any new angles on the Redfield business?"

I shrugged. "No," I said. "I'm just about out of gas."

A pickup truck rolled past, towing a horse trailer, heading toward the horse-show pavilions. "Fucking cowboys," Wiley Harmon said.

The hell of it was, Sister Amanda and Mad Mel were leaning on me for nothing. I'd told Wiley Harmon the truth; I'd just about exhausted my small stock of ideas on the Jack Redfield affair. Even the straws I'd clutched at had proved to be illusory. It was possible that I'd have packed the whole thing in by now, told Martha Redfield to forget it, if I hadn't gotten pissed off from all the harassment.

I sat in the parking area for a while after Harmon had left, watching a bunch of people putting up a teepee in the grassy area across the drive. Most of them looked pretty light to me, but that didn't mean anything; lots of the smaller tribes in eastern Oklahoma are more white than Indian, genetically, and there are even tribes that have no surviving fullblood members at all. I could hear them talking among themselves, though, and it definitely wasn't in any European language.

Finally, for want of anything else to do, I drove across town to Lorene Matson's neighborhood.

The house at 6833 Minkolusa Drive looked as it had when I'd been there last, except that the yard had been trampled to dust by cops and news people and, no doubt, the idle and nosy. There were a few fragments of yellow police-line tape fluttering in the wind, tied around the porch stanchions. This kind of yellow ribbon, the person it was tied for wasn't ever coming back. . . .

I parked in front of the house, this time, and got out and walked up to the little front porch. The door was locked, of course. I could have opened it easily, but I thought about it and decided not to bother. My luck these days, some neighbor would see me going in and call the cops; I could talk my way out of a roust, maybe, but it would be a lot of trouble and I wasn't in the mood.

I stood on the porch a few minutes, trying to visualize what had happened here that night. Nothing came to me, though, except a growing conviction that I didn't know what the hell I was doing.

Idly, for no particular reason, I glanced into the cheap metal mailbox that hung beside the door. Empty, of course; that would have been one of the first things checked, and one of the most common things rechecked later on. Without any better reason, I stuck my fingers down inside the box and felt around.

And went catatonic for an instant, then, because there was something under my fingertips that wasn't metal.

I groped and scrabbled and scratched, not getting anywhere; there was definitely something in there, but it didn't want to come out. Finally, glancing guiltily over my shoulder—I was undoubtedly committing a federal offense as well as a local one—I unhitched the mailbox from its nail, turned it upside down, and gave it a sharp whack.

A rectangular green card fell out. I picked it up and hung the mailbox back in place, turned and walked briskly back to the car, and got in and drove away, the card lying on the seat beside me. Some blocks away, I pulled over and had a look at my discovery.

It didn't look like much. It was the size of a standard postcard, and in fact it seemed to be just that, some sort of postal card, addressed to Lorene Matson, 6833 Minkolusa Drive, Tulsa OK 74135. Instead of a stamp there was one of those little postage-paid marks. I flipped it over and then I saw what it was. I don't know why it didn't register sooner; I'd had occasion to fill out more than one of the damn things in my business.

It was simply a postal return receipt. If you've got a package or letter to send and you want to make sure it gets there, but you don't want to go to the expense of registered mail, you can fill out a little card which, for a modest fee, is attached to the item being sent. Eventually, barring the occasional screwup, the card will come back to the sender, establishing that the letter or package did get where it was supposed to go. I used to send manuscripts that way, when I was starting out, until I learned that the pongids who staff the average publishing-house mailroom don't like to have to bother signing for packages or doing anything else they don't absolutely have to do, and often as not they'll retaliate by losing or trashing the manuscript.

There's really quite a bit of information on a return receipt by the time it completes its travels. This one had been mailed from Tulsa on May 19. It had reached its destination on May 23, which meant, unless the return trip had been ridiculously slow, that the card had been in the mailbox for several days before the murder. So not only had a lot of cops missed it, Lorene Matson herself had failed to find it in the mailbox. Remembering how I'd only located it by feel, and how much trouble it had been to get it out, I wasn't surprised. I had a mailbox similar to Lorene Matson's, and I'd had the same thing happen to me. Once my utilities had almost been cut off because a bill had gotten stuck up against the front of the box in exactly the same way.

The item—the card, unfortunately, didn't tell me whether it had been a parcel or just a letter—had been sent to:

ROSE MATSON
GOLDEN SUNSET NURSING HOME
4570 MCDOWELL ROAD
PHOENIX, ARIZONA
85065

I drove home, thinking, glancing occasionally at the little green card lying on the seat beside me. Just before I got onto the expressway, I remembered old business and pulled over again, this time to take Wiley Harmon's snub-nosed .38 out of the glove compartment and slip half a dozen hollow-point loads into the chambers. I laid the gun on the seat, on top of the green card, and drove on my way, looking carefully around me all the way. But if anybody was following me, I never spotted him, and nobody bothered me all the way home.

* * *

I looked at that green card a lot of times that evening. I knew what it said, of course; by the time I'd finished supper I could have recited every word on it from memory. It just seemed that looking at it might trigger some sort of mental chain reaction that would make everything add up.

Clearly, I'd found something; just as clearly, I didn't know what the hell it was, let alone what to do with it.

Still, life has to go on. Harry's dewclaws were starting to get long; they had a tendency to grow in a kind of semicircle and cause sores and infections if I didn't cut them regularly. The trimming job was a simple business in itself, involving nothing more than a few whacks with a pair of overpriced clippers the vet had sold me—later on I'd realized I could have done the job just as well with my wire cutters—and no more dangerous or painful than an ordinary manicure. But Harry had decided long ago that this was a fiendish torture intended to mutilate and cripple and maybe even kill him, and he invariably made such a scene that I tended to put the business off as long as possible.

That evening, though, I noticed that the dewclaws had grown out to the point that I could no longer neglect them. I got the clippers and dragged Harry out from under the bed, where he'd dived as soon as he'd seen me getting the clippers out, and got him in a kind of half-nelson on the kitchen floor and went to work. He thrashed and struggled and snuffled and whined and occasionally let off dreadful high-pitched yaps that probably convinced the people up the road that I was performing un-speakable experiments on him. As always, he made the whole thing take about ten times as long as it would have if he'd simply held still.

I got the last dewclaw trimmed, finally, and let Harry go, and he ran frantically into the bedroom and back under the bed. I stood up, remembered the damn clippers, and bent down to pick them up.

I heard the whacking impact against the trailer wall, and the flat bang from somewhere outside, but somehow they didn't register. I started to straighten up and then there was another bang and another, and the kitchen window shattered a foot from my head. I hit the floor without stopping to comb the glass out of my hair. Two more shots punched through the aluminum wall, while I tried to tunnel through the floor.

The shooting stopped. An engine roared, out by the end of the drive, and tires spun briefly and threw gravel. I ran and got the shotgun, but it was a pointless, ritualized response; I knew the son of a bitch would be long gone before I got the door open, and I was right.

I stood there a minute or so, staring out into the dark—making a hell of a fine target, I realized finally, but there was nobody out there now to do anything about it—and then I went back inside and put the shotgun down, handy to reach, and poured myself a big slug of Jim Beam and drank it down without a pause. I started to pour myself a second, decided the glass was slowing me down, and stuck the bottle into my face instead.

When my hands had stopped shaking—well, more or less—I got the broom and the dustpan and cleaned the glass up off the kitchen floor. After that I checked out the bullet holes. Two slugs had gone through the window; the others had punched through the trailer wall right below the window opening, and there were holes in the opposite wall where they'd struck. The bullets didn't appear to have been of very large caliber: .22s, maybe, possibly .32s, no bigger. I tried poking a .38 cartridge nose-first into one of the holes and the bullet wouldn't fit.

I thought about calling Wiley Harmon, but there was no real point in it; officially, this was far outside his jurisdiction, and unofficially, I didn't see what he could do. I sipped a little more bourbon and looked at the bullet holes, and at last I went on into the living room and sat down. The green return-receipt card was lying in my chair and I picked it up and started to set it aside, when finally something clicked very softly into place inside my head, like the cylinder latch of a well-oiled revolver locking home.

Amy Matson sounded pleased to hear my voice on the phone, but a little confused by my questions. No, she didn't know her grandmother's first name; if her mother had ever mentioned it,

150

she'd forgotten it. Yes, she still had the little photograph. Sure, I could borrow it back. "What's going on?" she asked. "You onto something or what?"

"I don't know yet," I said. "I'll let you know if I find out anything."

I told her I'd come by in the morning and pick up the photo. She said that would be fine. I hung up and got out the phone book and began calling airport numbers, asking about flights to Phoenix.

SEVENTEEN

unday I flew to Phoenix. That was one of my bigger mistakes of that summer, right there.

A good deal has been written and said, and even played with in film, about the possibility of the United States some day turning into a full-fledged storm-trooper police state. If you ever wonder whether it could actually happen, don't waste your time and energy watching videotapes of cops beating the shit out of unarmed traffic offenders, or news reports of citizen rallies in support of those same cops, or interviews with jurors arguing that the poor officers were just defending themselves against this vicious brute who kept hitting them on their nightsticks with his kidneys. Ignore the Supreme Court's recent fuck-the-citizen decisions and even the polls that show a majority of American citizens don't know what the Bill of Rights is, don't believe the rights it guarantees are really a good idea, and think the police ought to have more power.

No, if you really want to determine for yourself whether the people of the United States would hold still for a totalitarian dictatorship, just go down to the nearest air terminal and watch the docility with which they tolerate the blatant overbooking fraud, the outrageous and unexplained delays, the lost or smashed luggage, the snotty attitudes of the reservation clerks, the incredible prices and shitty service in the coffee shops, the cramped waiting areas with the furniture that fits no human ass ever known, and the cabs waiting to rip off the unwary even more. . . .

And observe with particular attention the meekness with which they submit to the Gestapo bullying by metal-detector operators and roving security guards who still don't seem to be able to prevent the operations of an army of purse snatchers, pickpockets, and luggage thieves; and then, if you like, get on a plane and check out the accommodations—legroom to fit Japanese midgets, elbowroom for approximately half a passenger per seat—and reflect that not once in the history of our time has a mob of passengers sacked and burned a terminal, or hijacked a plane, or even lynched a metal-detector guard or stomped a baggage handler to death; and if that doesn't move you to despair for the future of human dignity in America, there's just no getting through to you.

I arrived in Phoenix filled with a profound and overriding resolve that, once this trip was finished, I would never again fly *anywhere*—barring genuine and extreme emergencies—if it was geographically possible to drive there instead. A thousand-mile cross-country drive would have been fun by comparison.

Head bursting, stomach churning, bowels blocked, and eyes slightly crossed, I shambled through the Phoenix terminal, surrounded by fellow passengers whose faces bore expressions much like those I'd seen long ago during the fall of Saigon. At least I'd avoided the lost-luggage nightmare, by bringing nothing with me but a few essentials in a nylon carry-on shoulder bag. I wasn't the only one who'd had that idea, there were people lurching grimly past lugging carry-on bags so enormous I wondered if they were sneaking the kids and the dog along.

The auto rental agency was easily the most efficient operation in the terminal, and its employees actually seemed to have some concept of courtesy and respect. That almost compensated for the shortcomings of the car they rented me, a small, utterly gutless Japanese import with not much more legroom than I'd had on the plane. The engine made strange sounds and delivered so little power that I could barely keep up with the traffic on the Maricopa Freeway. I had a feeling that if I stopped and raised the hood, instead of an internal-combustion engine I'd find a team of hamsters treadmilling frantically inside a wire wheel. The shocks had been made by Chef Boyardee, and the bodywork had such lousy aerodynamics that the damn car tried to change lanes with every gust of crosswind.

Next time, I swore, I'm taking the Camaro. Better yet, next time I'm staying home.

It was late afternoon by the time I got into Phoenix. I didn't even slow down for the big hotels; I knew better than that. After a great deal of driving around and asking questions, I found a small, faintly shabby motel with rates I could stand. The trick is to find out where the main highway used to run before they put in the freeway; there you find the bypassed, near-derelict motels with peeling paint and signs hopefully advertising weekly and monthly rates. In Arizona in tourist season, that was all I could afford.

The desk clerk was Indian—the other kind; she even wore a sari and a red dot on her forehead—and more than happy to rent me a room. She walked with me to the door and showed me where the knobs and switches were, and wished me a pleasant stay. When she was gone I tossed the shoulder bag onto the bed and considered what to do next. It was getting on to supper time but my insides were going to have to recover a little more before I'd feel like eating.

Instead I went back out and walked about a block to a liquor store, where I picked up a bottle of Jim Beam. Back in the motel room, I considered getting some ice from the machine down the walk, said the hell with it, and stretched out on the bed and drank bourbon straight from the bottle until my nerves began to settle down. After a while I got out my current harmonica— it had caused a hell of a row, going through the metal detector; the surly black woman at the gate had examined it suspiciously for several minutes before grudgingly letting me keep it—and played "Blue Spanish Eyes" over the rattle of the air conditioner, while outside the windows Phoenix began to get dark.

* * *

The last time I'd been in Phoenix had been almost twenty years ago, back in the summer following my sophomore year in college. We'd gone in together and bought an old VW van, three of my buddies and me, and decided to drive it out to California for the summer. My chief memory of Phoenix was of getting pulled over on the edge of town, apparently for altogether whimsical reasons, and questioned, bullied, insulted, and generally harassed for half an hour or so by a couple of shitheads with badges. But hell, that was standard procedure for cops all over the United States that summer. Later, we realized we'd been damn lucky we hadn't had a bag of cheap grass planted on us so they could really have some fun.

Driving through the city Monday morning, I could see that it had grown enormously since that long-ago visit. In fact Phoenix seemed to have turned into a kind of monstrous concrete-and-asphalt melanoma, spreading at an exponential rate out over acres and acres of what must have been perfectly valid desert. It had once been the material of jokes, I remembered, that people from the East would sink their savings into real estate in southern Arizona only to find it consisted of nothing but sand and cactus; but if they'd hung on to their purchases, some of those people would be having a laugh of their own by now. What Ed Abbey used to call the Californication process was under way with a vengeance, turning what had been a boring minor city into a smaller edition of Los Angeles. The air was so bad it even made me miss Tulsa. I hoped to God—any God, even Sister Amanda's God—this wouldn't take long.

Part of the growth of the region, obviously, had come in the form of mass migrations of old people. I'd never seen so many nursing homes, retirement villages, and geriatric clinics. Maybe the idea was to move somewhere so depressing you wouldn't mind dying.

The Golden Sunset Nursing Home was out on the eastern side of Phoenix. It was almost noon by the time I got there; I'd taken my time about starting out, figuring visiting hours wouldn't be until the afternoon anyway. The place was a little unusual in being a two-story building—in the Southwest, with space and labor cheaper than materials, they tend to build horizontally rather than upwards—of dark brick. It looked a little on the old side, but solidly built; I guessed it had once been a smallish hotel. A couple of very old women sat in wheelchairs on the front porch, staring out across McDowell Road, where there was nothing to see but traffic and dust and fumes. They weren't looking at each other and they didn't look at me as I walked by.

Sweating inside my best lightweight suit, I went in the entrance and across the lobby to the front desk. A fat, dark young woman in white said, "Yes?" Actually she said, "Jes?"

I said I'd come to see Rose Matson. She said, "Bisiting hours twel' thirty." The clock behind her said five minutes till twelve. I told her I'd come all the way from Oklahoma to see Rose Matson with information about the death of her daughter. She said, "Bisiting hours twel' thirty."

After another couple of tries I realized she wasn't stonewalling me, she was merely exhausting the possibilities of her English vocabulary. The various old people sitting around the lobby were taking in the exchange with a certain amount of amusement; I heard a few snickers. An old man in a chair by the front windows called out, "Get Don. Tell her to get Don."

She nodded, then, looking relieved. "Joo wait," she said to me, and disappeared off down the hall toward the rear of the building. I leaned on the desk, waiting, and looked around the lobby. At least the place looked clean. In fact it was scrubbed to hospital standards. I'd been afraid this was going to turn out to be one of those terrible concentration-camp places you hear about.

The fat orderly, or whatever she was, came back after a few minutes with a big, blond-haired, pleasant-faced young man in a long white coat. "Hi," he said, shaking hands with me, "I'm Don, the head nurse. Can I help you?"

I told him I wanted to see Rose Matson. His face took on a curious expression. "Are you family?" he asked.

"No." I'd thought it over, considered lying, and decided on at least part of the truth. "My name's Taggart Roper. I live in Tulsa, Oklahoma. I'm a writer."

His eyebrows went up. "Writing one of those exposés of the

nursing-home business? Don't tell me you're writing a book about Rose."

"Her daughter was murdered back in May," I said. "The case received national publicity. A famous television evangelist—"

"Oh," he said, and then, *"Oh.* I'll be damned. You mean *that* was Rose's . . . well, I'll be damned." He shook his head. "As many times as I heard the story on the news, read about it in the papers and magazines, it never occurred to me to match the last names. And I even met the daughter once, back earlier this year, when she came out for a visit. Though I don't know if I ever caught her first name."

I said, "I take it, then, since you didn't know, that Rose Matson hasn't ever learned about her daughter's death."

Inside I was saying, *oh shit, oh shit.* It had just occurred to me that I might be expected to be the one to break the news. That wasn't going to be any fun at all. I wasn't even sure I could do it.

But Don had that funny look on his face again. "Come with me," he said. "I'll let you see Rose. You'll understand then."

He took me down the corridor, past rows of doors—some of them open, revealing the interiors of small dormlike rooms—and up to the second floor in a new-looking elevator. At the top we waited, holding the doors, while an old woman, hunched over like Quasimodo, got into the elevator. She was leaning on a metal walker and she muttered steadily to herself the whole time.

Down another corridor, and we stopped at a door that bore a white card marked ROSE MATSON. "She has a private room," Don said. "The daughter was very insistent on that, even though the cost is quite a bit more."

Don didn't knock, which surprised me. He just turned the knob and eased the door quietly open. "Go on in," he said to me.

The room was even smaller than the others I'd seen, but the small bed and the single chair left a good deal of space all the same. The walls were a gleaming antiseptic white; the paint looked pretty fresh. There were shelves along all the inside walls, three or four feet above the floor. The shelves seemed to be completely filled with stuffed animals. Stuffed dogs, to be exact, in every imaginable shape and color and style. I'd never seen so many stuffed dogs in my life.

A very thin, birdlike woman stood near the windows. She wore a long white garment, a gown I suppose you'd call it, and rubber sandals. Her hair was completely white and hung down past her shoulders. Her face was as lined and wizened as some sort of dried fruit.

She was holding a stuffed dog in her arms, a little brown plush puppy with long floppy ears and a sad expression. She was petting it with one hand and she seemed to be talking to it under her breath, though I couldn't make out any words.

Don said, "Rose. Rose, you've got a visitor. Look."

She glanced around very briefly, with a look of total uninterest. "Mm," she murmured vaguely, and went back to petting the stuffed dog.

"This is Mr. Roper, Rose," Don said. "He's come to talk to you about Lorene. You know, your daughter, Lorene."

He might as well have been reciting the multiplication table in Swahili for all the comprehension, or interest, she showed. She continued to pet the dog; now she seemed to be holding it so it could look out the windows.

On a sudden impulse I reached into my jacket pocket and pulled out the framed photograph from Lorene Matson's dresser. Stepping forward, holding it up, I said, "I've got a picture here you might like to see. It's you and your husband and your little girl. Remember?"

She turned around again and looked at the picture. For just an instant a kind of dim recognition seemed to rise in the dark eyes, but then it was gone. "This is my dog," she said to me. Her voice was surprisingly clear. "His name is Floppy."

She went over to the shelves and began pointing. "That's Daisy, Toby, Ralph, Nosy—"

Don had me by the arm. "Come on," he said, pulling gently, and when we were out in the corridor, "Once she starts, she doesn't stop till she's named them all. You don't want to stick around. Now and then she can't remember one and then she goes back and starts all over again."

I nodded, too shaken to speak. From inside the room I could still hear Rose Matson's voice, calling off the names of her dogs. She was starting to get louder.

"Come on," Don said again. "Want a cup of coffee?"

Coffee wasn't what I wanted just then, but I didn't figure this place served what I needed. I nodded again and followed him, back down the long shining corridors.

"She's not as old as you might think, either," Don said a little later, over a cup of moderately bad coffee. "Early seventies, I don't remember exactly. She's aged so much—I mean physically, too—these last few months."

"Has she always been like that? Since coming here, that is?"

He rubbed his jawline. "No, that's the sad part. Oh, she's been a little childish all along—she already had most of those damn dogs when she came here—but she was lucid enough, pretty intelligent in fact, didn't forget things the way so many of them do. She talked clearly and expressively about life in Oklahoma during the Dust Bowl years, for example."

He stirred sugar into his coffee with a plastic spoon. We were sitting at a table in the nursing home's dining room; he'd gotten us the coffee himself. All around us, old people were eating. One glance around had convinced me to keep my eyes to myself; some of the sights were less than attractive.

"This particular home," he said, "takes mainly people who are able to take care of themselves to some extent. We aren't set up to handle the really helpless cases. When Rose Matson came here, she was one of the more self-sufficient ones. Then—" He spread his hands helplessly. "Earlier this year, back around the first of March as I recall, the daughter came for a visit. She stayed in town for several days, in fact, and took her mother out for dinner a couple of times, and so on— they seemed to be having some long discussions. I was really pleased to see that. So many of our people here, you know, their families don't come to see them, they just don't want to be bothered, it seems. . . ."

He looked around the dining room and sighed deeply. "Anyway, very shortly after the visit, Rose began to take a sharp turn for the worse. We haven't been able to determine what happened. Maybe there was something they talked about that upset her, maybe it was just the stress and excitement of an extended visit. There's so much we don't know about the aging process, especially the psychological aspects. At any rate, Rose has been as you saw her for several months."

"Did Lorene know?"

"I couldn't say. Possibly not." His voice got lower. "Our esteemed director doesn't believe in worrying the families unduly with such information, unless it relates to increased care costs. She should have worked for the CIA, our director I mean. She's very good at observing the 'need to know' principle."

I reached in my jacket pocket again and took out the green return-receipt card and handed it to him. "Do you happen to know," I said, "what this was all about? A package, maybe? Did Rose actually get it?"

But Don shook his head. "That's outside my jurisdiction, Mr. Roper. You'll have to see the director." He grinned faintly. "Good luck."

I should have known the director of the Golden Sunset Nursing Home wouldn't be what I'd anticipated. Not a single person or thing had turned out as I'd expected from the start of this business. I had a feeling it was going to be that way right up to the end. If, of course, there ever *was* an end; by now I was starting to wonder about that too.

From Don's remarks, I had somehow formed a mental picture of a grim, forbidding older woman, sort of an institutional version of Sister Amanda. Wanted for war crimes, maybe, Germanic accent and a funny-looking lampshade on the desk and a Doberman crouching on the office floor. . . .

Victoria Gambillon was in fact a handsome woman about my age, with curly black hair and large dark eyes and a good shape that the tailored white uniform didn't conceal. She might have been called attractive, if the adjective "sterile" hadn't kept forcing its way in there. She looked at me with a precisely metered little smile, one with as much warmth as the dark side of the moon, and eyes that took my measure and found me lacking in any valuable qualities whatever. And after I'd gone and worn my good suit, too, on a day when the heat was enough to make you want to take off your body and sit around in your bones.

She said, "I don't quite understand your connection with Rose Matson, Mr. er Roper."

Nice little touch, that, hesitating just a little to let me know I was so unimportant she was already having trouble remembering my name. I gave her another dose of creative candor:

"As you know, Rose's daughter was murdered in May, in Tulsa. She had a daughter of her own, by a minister named Redfield—I'm sure you've heard about the scandal."

She nodded impatiently. I said, "The daughter, and later the minister's widow, asked me to look into the facts of the case. I'm not a lawyer or even an investigator, just, um, a friend of the family." Sister Amanda would shit sanctified bricks to hear me say *that*. "Doing a favor, that's all."

The director's face said that she couldn't imagine why any of this should interest her. But she said, "You came here thinking Rose might be able to tell you something? What a wasted journey you've had. You should have called first."

She frowned suddenly. "I'm glad, though, that someone has finally informed us of Lorene Matson's death. She is, you see, the person who pays Rose's bills here. The situation may get awkward."

"Is Rose, well, overdue?"

"No, no. Lorene Matson paid a full year's fees in advance, at the start of this year. She did that at her own initiative and even insistence. I must say, I wish more of our clientele would show that kind of forethought." She made a very faint little sigh, perhaps of regret for having lost such a solid customer. "At the end of the year, however—"

"I'm sure the daughter—well, granddaughter, since we're talking about Rose—will want to continue. Her father left her quite a bit of money," I said. "I don't think you'll have a problem."

"Good." At last I'd succeeded in pleasing her. "Please have the granddaughter get in touch with us, then. Even now, we will need her name and address for our records, as next of kin."

"Rose Matson has no other surviving family?"

"Not as far as we know." Her elegantly lipsticked mouth turned crooked in a grimace of distaste. "Except, of course, for her husband. For our purposes, though, he hardly counts."

"Husband?" I hadn't even considered the possibility. "Matson is still alive too?"

"Homer Matson," Ms. Gambillon said, biting her words off with even white teeth, "is alive, God knows why. At least he was last month, when he showed up here, drunk as usual, and demanded once again to see Rose. He does that every now and then. When he is refused admittance, he usually tries to get money from me. I have no idea why he expects to succeed in that."

"Know where he lives?" I said casually. "I suppose I ought to at least look in on him, since I'm out here."

"Homer Matson is what people nowadays call a 'homeless person.' When I was younger we called them 'bums' and I don't see why the word was abandoned. Occasionally a few of them manage to get themselves an apartment in some slum building and share it until they're evicted, or until they burn it down, but generally they live where they can. He could be living in an excellent home, too," she added. "The state of Arizona would make arrangements, since he is of retirement age. But he would have to give up his drinking and carrying on, and apparently he'd rather live in some hobo jungle out in the desert than like a civilized man."

After a moment's pause I said, "There's one other thing I need to ask you about." I took out the return-receipt card and passed it over. "Apparently Lorene Matson sent her mother some sort of package or other item shortly before she was killed. It's possible it contained evidence that would point to the identity of her killer."

She looked at the card briefly and handed it back. "Mr. Roper," she said, "see that door? It opens into a large closet, which is full of things that come in the mail for these people.

Things that for one reason or another are inappropriate for them to have. For example, you'd be surprised how many people see nothing wrong with mailing a box of candy to a diabetic. Or cigarettes, when we do not allow smoking here, or cash, even though any personal funds are supposed to be sent through this office and disbursed only under supervision."

I said, "You intercept and impound their mail? Isn't that illegal?"

"They, or their families, sign a release when they come here," she said frostily. "The administration has full authority to make decisions and take actions in the patients' interests."

She gestured toward the closet door. "Of course nothing is actually destroyed—that *would* be illegal—although, if too much material builds up, we contact the family and ask them to take it away. And normal mail, harmless gifts, are not interfered with. The stuffed dogs Rose Matson occasionally received from her daughter," she said, "were given immediately to her. The package you refer to was full of some sort of legal forms or papers which she could not possibly have understood, so it went into the closet."

I said, "You didn't happen to take any note of the content—"

"Certainly not. I don't *read* their mail." Her eyes said the nerve of me to suggest it. "I merely glanced inside, saw the nature of the contents, and put the package in the closet. Where it will stay," she added pointedly. "Unless you have some sort of authorization, such as a court order, entitling you to take it."

"I could get Amy Matson on the phone," I suggested. "Let you talk with her."

She shook her head, a slight, measured movement. "A voice on the telephone, which could belong to anyone, is not proper or adequate authority." She frowned. "In fact I have no real proof that you are who you say you are. On reflection, I've already talked with you more than I should have."

I stood up. "Is the air conditioning turned up too high in here," I said, "or is it just you?"

She gave me that tight little smile again. "I believe you can find your way out, Mr. Roper. Please do so."

EIGHTEEN

Nobody at the Phoenix cop headquarters knew anything about Homer Matson or had any interest in talking with an out-of-town civilian about some homeless old drunk. The Maricopa County sheriff's office wasn't any better, but a deputy did suggest I try some of the organizations that worked with the homeless.

It was a good suggestion, even though it did result in my spending much of the afternoon in depressing surroundings. There are plenty of indigent types on the streets of Tulsa, God knows, and I'd seen the poor bastards on the sidewalks of New York the last time I'd been there. But nothing had prepared me for the army of homeless men and women who, it seemed, had thronged to the Southwest, where rain was rare and the winters mild.

"Once they're here," the worker at the storefront mission told me, "it's nearly impossible for them to raise enough money to get off the streets, or to move on. They can't clean up or dress up enough for anything but menial jobs, and around here those are all taken by Mexican illegals."

He was a nice young guy, in his mid-twenties I judged, with the speech of an educated person and good clothes that fit him well. But he looked out at the men and women who sat in the folding chairs in the front room—just sat, staring into space or dozing, waiting for dinner even though it was hours away, because there was nowhere else to go and nothing else to do—and his eyes were those of an infantry platoon leader too long on the line.

"More than half of the men are veterans," he said tiredly, "mostly Vietnam vets, a few older ones who served in Korea or even World War Two, but we're starting to get a few young men who served in Arabia too." He looked at me with those terrible burned-out eyes. "What's happened to this country? What kind of nation are we turning into?"

I didn't have an answer for him, but he didn't look as if he expected one. He held the framed photograph of the Matson family and studied it a little longer. "I think I know this man," he said. "Of course he's much older now, but I think they call him Homer, and this looks a little like him."

He handed me back the picture. "He represents a different group from those people out front," he said. "Men like him—they've spent years wandering around, working at various jobs or just hoboing, long before the present economic holocaust. They know all the tricks of survival on the street and on the road. It's been rough on them, too, because the flood of the new homeless has swamped the support facilities they used to depend on, but still they tend to take care of themselves pretty well."

"Know where I can find him?"

"If this is the man I remember," he said, "he was living out on the edge of the desert, last I heard. Out past Apache Junction, there's an area of federal land where camping is permitted—the authorities had backpackers and such in mind, of course, but a good many transient and homeless types wind up there, and some of them have semi-permanent camps. The rangers come and chase them off now and then, in a half-hearted sort of way, but they always come back."

He laughed, rather sadly. "Quite a few of them own cars, strange as that may seem, and live in them. That's another bizarre thing about life in the United States, you know—there are homeless people who own automobiles. I spent a hitch in the Peace Corps in Africa, and there were very few people, even the middle classes, who had cars. Yet even the poorest of the poor there at least had some sort of shanty or hut to call home."

I stood up and took out my wallet. "Could you use a small contribution?"

"Anything at all," he said. "Anything at all."

When my friends and I had driven through the area, back during the reign of King Richard the Furtive, Apache Junction had been a tiny crossroads community out on the desert east of Mesa. Now, I learned, it was merely the easternmost point of a continuous and graceless urban smear: Mesa, Tempe, Scottsdale, Phoenix itself, all ran together without a break all the way to the edge of the mountains. Make that suburban rather than urban; none of these alleged cities, Phoenix included, seemed to have any center, any real downtown. Just miles and miles of gas stations and fast-food joints and motels and tacky housing developments and shopping malls as big as Third World countries, all of it baking in its own ugliness under a brutal afternoon sun.

It was getting fairly late by the time I got out to Apache Junction; the sun was still a good way from down, but the hard-edged shadows were getting long. The narrow blacktop road that ran northward toward the mountains was in good condition and I had it mostly to myself, but I took it easy anyway, since I didn't know exactly what I was looking for. A sign announced that I was passing the Lost Dutchman State Park. I'd read about the Lost Dutchman legend, one of the more enduring bullshit stories of the West; people used to wander off into these mountains looking for it, and get fatally lost. Nowadays a man lost in the Superstitions could simply wait till dark and see the lights of Apache Junction spread out virtually at his feet.

More signs along the road marked the borders of various other patches of public land: Bureau of Land Management, National Forest Service. Forest? The biggest things growing anywhere in sight were the tall saguaro cactuses that rose like giant fuck-you fingers from thickets of lesser cactus and patches of low dry bushes. Here and there, along washes and dry streambeds, clumps of stunted willows appeared, their leaves yellow with drought and dust.

I saw a flash of metal or glass off through the brush. I pulled over for a look and saw that some sort of vehicle was definitely parked out there, but that was all I could tell from the road.

I got out and walked slowly through the brush, trying to avoid the clumps of prickly pear and other knife-packing vege-tables, stopping now and then to disentangle my pants legs from various grabby little shrubs. I wished I'd changed out of my suit before coming out here. Sand crunched under the soles of my dress shoes. I didn't want to think what I was doing to them. Or what might be crawling around out here, waiting to bite visiting authors. The heat was incredible; the air burned my lungs every breath I took. It was like being inside an enormous oven, turned clear up to BROIL.

Suddenly I came around a clump of cactus and almost walked into the shiny metal side of a big blue pickup truck. Christ, I thought crazily, they've followed me here too . . . but this one was fitted with a white camper bed, and had Illinois plates. A man came around the rear and said, "Hi."

He was a tall, well-built young guy with short reddish-brown hair and bright, friendly blue eyes. He wore expensive-looking twill shorts and a clean white T-shirt and high-topped running shoes. He had a beard but it was trimmed short and neat.

"Looking for something?" he said affably. "Or somebody?"

I told him, not really expecting any help from this quarter. But he nodded vigorously and said, "Oh, sure, old Homer, I know him. Wait and I'll take you to him."

He climbed into the camper bed and I heard him rummaging around. I noticed, now, the stuff spread out in the cleared space next to the truck: a Coleman pressure stove with a couple of pots on the rack, a folding lawn chair, a big plastic insulated water keg. The ground was free of litter, though.

"Here we go," he said, pulling on a floppy cloth hat. "You shouldn't walk around outdoors bareheaded in this country," he added. "Very dangerous."

He led the way down a kind of trail through the brush, heading roughly eastward, away from the road. I said, "Kind of hot weather for camping out, isn't it?"

He glanced back and laughed. "Camping out my ass," he said. "That's my home back there."

"Sorry."

"Don't be. I'm not. I came out here last year to do some hiking," he said. "Went back home and found that my company had been taken over by a big outfit and my job had been eliminated, along with the jobs of over a hundred other people. My wife reacted by filing for divorce. Got the kids and the house and damn near everything else. I got to keep the truck and my ulcer. Couldn't find another job in my field, nobody'd hire me for anything else, they said I was overqualified for regular labor. I said screw it, remembered this place, and came back out here for a while."

"What did you do?"

"Electrical engineer."

"Jesus."

"Hell," he said, "I'm as happy as I ever was in Peoria. The ulcer's gone and I've lost a lot of flab. I guess I'll rejoin the mainstream one of these days, but I'm in no rush. What's your line?"

"Freelance writer."

"Oh?" he said. "Want me to save you a campsite?"

The camp was back in the brush a quarter mile or so from the paved road, at the edge of a very dry streambed. There were two old cars—a green Ford and a brown Oldsmobile—and a decrepit VW van, parked in a kind of loose semicircle in the thin shade of a patch of desperate-looking willows. All the doors were open. Several cheap folding chairs stood here and there in the little clear area enclosed by the junkers. The chair closest to me bore the stenciled words PROPERTY OF PHOENIX FULL GOSPEL MISSION. The sand was littered with empty bottles and cans.

A man sat in one of the folding chairs, drinking from a bottle of Ripple. All he had on was a pair of hacked-off khaki shorts and a mesh-back gimme cap with a Poulan chainsaw logo on the front. He was skinny as a spider, his exposed skin was burned brick red, and his straggling hair was nearly white. Another man, a squat dark type in T-shirt and jeans, sat on the ground nearby, fiddling with the knobs of a pocket-sized radio. He didn't seem to be getting any sound out of it. A pair of bare feet stuck out the back door of the Oldsmobile. My guide pointed. "That'll be Homer. The feet. Good luck waking him up, if he's sleeping off a drunk."

"Thanks," I said.

"Thanks, my ass," he said, and held out his hand.

I got out a five and handed it to him. "All right," he said, and grinned. "Economic realities of our times, friend. Nothing's free."

He turned and disappeared back into the brush. I started across the clear space toward the Oldsmobile. Neither of the men paid me the least attention as I walked past. Probably thought I'd come to join the community.

Homer Matson was a sunburned, dried-up streak of muscle and wrinkled hide, like a strip of beef jerky wearing jeans and a straw hat. He had no teeth and didn't seem to have any hair, but his eyes were alert and, despite the traces of cheap wine on his breath, he seemed lucid.

He cried, quietly and with a certain dignity, when I told him about Lorene. "So my little girl's dead," he said at last. "Sounds like hell to say it, stranger, but I knowed for years something like that was bound to happen. She was always wild. Run off, you know, back when she was just a kid, sixteen or so. After the Redfields moved to the city, that was." He wiped his eyes with the backs of skinny, spotted hands like a lizard's. "Broke her mama's heart when she did that. That's when we moved out to Arizona and I took to drinking."

He looked at me with wet speculative eyes. "Don't suppose you happened to bring . . . ?"

I took the pint of Jim Beam from my jacket pocket and passed it over. "Oh, my, son," he said, and uncapped it and took a long pull straight from the bottle, his hands shaking slightly. "Needed that," he said frankly, and held the bottle out. "Have a drop with me?"

I shook my head. "Keep it."

"Why, thank you, son." He took another drink and shuddered. "And I'm a grandpaw," he mused. "You know, we heard Lorene had a baby, but I never knew anything about it. She just turned into a regular hoor, you know," he said, looking at me a little defensively. "Lord knows a man tries, but sometimes they just go wild on you."

He stared off across the dry wash. We were sitting on the hood of his sixty-some-odd Olds. The other men were still ignoring us.

"Rose may of known more than me," he said. "About Lorene and the baby and all. Her and Lorene stayed in touch some. See, Rose and me, we hadn't lived together for a lot of years even before she had to go into the nursing home. Lorene come out here a few times, paid for the nursing home—well, the Social Security paid for some of it, and there's Medicaid and all, but hell, that's just a fart in a windstorm, mostly it was Lorene. She come to see me, too, last time."

"Lorene did?"

"Yeah. I was in the VA hospital for a few weeks. Lorene come to see Rose, she come over and visited with me too. Had us a real long talk." A curious, almost sly expression crossed his face. "I told her a thing or two," he added cryptically. "She found out she didn't know as much about the old man as she thought she did."

He looked sad again. "They won't let me in to see Rose," he said. "I try ever now and then, but that froze-faced bitch that runs the place won't let me in. Last time, she called the law, I spent the night in the can. Had to fight off this queer nigger all night long."

I got out the little photograph and showed it to him. "Hey," he said, looking pleased, "I remember when this was took. Mr. Eugene Redfield hisself took this, give us the picture. I wondered what happened to it. Lorene must of took it with her when she run off. How about that." He raised the bottle again, his Adam's apple bobbing briefly. His eyes stayed on the picture.

"That was a nice place," he said after a minute. "Best job I ever had. Mr. Redfield didn't give me no shit, paid me good, always made sure our house was fixed up. They hadn't moved off, I guess we'd be living there yet."

Again that odd sneaky expression flickered across his face. "That Amanda Redfield, now," he said, "boy, she was pretty hot stuff back then." He snickered softly. "I seen her on television once, while I was at the VA. That little boy of hers growed up to be a big preacher. He had her on the show, man, she was just a dried-up old prune. Sure not like she was back when I worked for her husband."

I took the photograph back from him. He said, "Lorene and little Jacky was good friends, you know?"

"Yes," I said, "I know. He told me."

"You know him? That's right, you said you come from Oklahoma yourself. How's he doing?" Homer said, uncapping the Jim Beam again. His hands were no longer shaking but his voice was starting to fuzz at the edges. "He still preaching on television?"

"He's dead too," I said. "You didn't hear?"

"Hell, son, I don't hear a damn thing out here. Dead, huh?" he said, and shook his head in wonder. "Don't tell me somebody shot him too."

"He committed suicide," I said.

"Son of a bitch." He washed this latest information down with yet another slug of bourbon. "Son," he said, "you bring good whisky but bad news, you know that?"

He stared down into the neck of the Jim Beam bottle, as if seeing some sort of explanation there. "Hard luck all over," he muttered.

I got out my wallet and handed him a twenty. He gave me a suspicious look. "What's this for?" he asked.

"I told your granddaughter I'd look you up," I said. "She asked me to be sure you were all right." What the hell, one more lie wouldn't make any difference.

"Well, thank you, then." He stowed the twenty carefully in

his jeans pocket. "Heading back to Oklahoma soon?" he said as I slid down off the Oldsmobile's fender.

"Yes," I said. "Soon as I take care of one more piece of business."

I walked back across the clearing and started down the trail toward the road. When I looked back, just before the willows hid the camp from view, Homer Matson was still sitting on the fender of the old car, holding the Jim Beam bottle, staring out across the desert at some vision of his past. He didn't wave goodbye.

I went into the Golden Sunset Nursing Home at four in the morning. It was a little earlier than my usual hour for a job like that but the light comes early in desert country in the summer.

I parked the rental car in an alley a block away and made my way cautiously on foot across the parking lot that took up most of the block in back of the nursing home. There were enough cars still there—night-shift employees, I guessed—to give me cover, and the lot wasn't very brightly lit.

A uniformed security guard was leaning against the building beside the rear entrance, having himself a smoke. I waited in the shadow of somebody's Isuzu while he finished his cigarette and when he walked on around the building toward the front, I tried the back door. It was locked but not very well; a half-bright three-year-old could have opened it.

The rear entrance opened onto a small vestibule, where brooms and mops hung in racks, and then a long, narrow, poorly-lit corridor led past storage rooms and closets to the dining room. There was nobody in the dining room and only a couple of lights were burning. I crossed the big dim space at a fast walk and started down the main corridor, then ducked into a handy closet just as a couple of nurses or orderlies came down the hall, talking low and fast in Spanish. The closet contained, among other things, several freshly-laundered white linen uniform jackets still in plastic wrappings. I took one and put it on, just on general principles of camouflage, and went on down the corridor, but the masquerade was wasted; nobody else was around to see me.

The night duty nurse was sitting at the front desk, her back to me, reading a slick-paper magazine. She didn't hear me as I crossed behind her and moved down the little side hallway to the door of the director's office.

To my surprise, Ms. Gambillon's office door was unlocked. Maybe the cleaning staff had forgotten to lock it; I didn't think she'd be prone to oversights. I got inside quickly, locked the door myself from the inside, and took out my pocket flashlight; it wasn't really likely that anyone would notice light coming from under the door if I switched on the overhead lights, but there was no use taking chances.

The closet had a better lock than the outside door. It still wasn't much of a barrier, though. It was a damn big closet, nearly as big as Rose Matson's living quarters. I looked at the shelves that lined the walls, all full of boxes and parcels and envelopes, and despaired. It would take a month to go through all this junk. The damn woman must have had a couple of years' worth of impounded mail in there.

But it was all right; her basic obsessive-compulsive neatness saved me from having to paw through it all. She had the stuff organized in alphabetical order. It still took me a few minutes, because there were a lot of M's, but then there it was, a big fat manila envelope, the heavy-duty kind that I used to mail manuscripts, addressed in big black-marker letters to Rose Matson.

I tucked it under my arm and stepped back out of the closet—I had a momentary impulse to rifle through some of the other packages, just to find out what Victoria Gambillon considered contraband, but there was no time for being silly—and pocketed the flashlight and eased the office door open. Down the little side corridor, I could see the night duty nurse still bent over her magazine.

She didn't even look up as I walked past. Maybe she saw me out of the corner of her eye, picked up the white of the uniform jacket, and assumed I was all right. Or maybe she just didn't give a damn. Not many people do at four-thirty in the morning. I walked on across the lobby and out the front door. The security guard was nowhere in sight. A few minutes later I was tooling westward along McDowell Road, the package lying on the seat beside me. The streets were almost totally deserted. In the darkness, Phoenix didn't look quite so bad.

Back at the motel, I sat on the bed and dumped the envelope's contents out onto the bedspread beside me. It had already been opened, but the contents, held together with large rubber bands, didn't seem to have been disturbed.

I took the rubber bands off and began thumbing through the stack of papers. And felt an instantaneous kick-in-the-crotch rush of disappointment: I'd come all this way, gone through all this crap, for this?

The papers in my lap were far from new to me. In fact I could have recited parts of their contents from memory by now. What I had was simply another set of copies of the more important documents from Lorene Matson's secret stash—Jack Redfield's signed acknowledgment of paternity, a couple of the letters, some hospital papers, Amy's birth certificate, a few sample pages from the ledgers, that sort of thing. I'd seen it all before; for a while there I'd seen it in my dreams.

I said, *"Shit,"* or something of an equally original nature. For a second I was ready to hurl the whole packet across the room. Instead I tossed it across the bed, papers scattering every which way, and got up to go take a shower. Maybe I could get a few hours of sleep before I had to make the plane.

But then, stepping over the scattered photostats, I glanced down and saw something that didn't look familiar.

I bent down and picked up a little sheaf of official-looking forms, not more than four or five sheets, held together with paper clips. Attached to the back was a single sheet of yellow paper from a legal pad, covered in longhand writing. The hand looked like Lorene Matson's; I'd seen enough examples of her writing by now to be a near-expert.

I sat back down on the bed and flipped through the sheets of my new discovery. It was material I hadn't seen before, all right, but I couldn't see that it did me any good. I couldn't see how it could have done *anybody* any good; and yet, by its nature, it was something that somebody had gone to considerable trouble to get.

I had a copy of a page from the records of a Tulsa diagnostic clinic, giving the results of a series of tests on Amanda Redfield. I couldn't tell what she'd been suffering from, if anything. I had a sheet from the Army service record of Eugene Redfield, who had served from 1942 to 1946. There was also a form from a Veterans' Administration hospital, dated this year, giving the basic data on Homer Matson. And there was a copy of a physical examination form from a Tulsa doctor, apparently relating to the renewal of an insurance policy on Reverend Jack Redfield.

I said aloud, "What the *hell?*"

The yellow legal sheet read:

Dear Mama,

This is the papers proving the things I told you about when I was out there. I want somebody else to have a copy and you are the only one I trust. I do not think Jack would ever do anything to hurt me but Mama, you know the life I am in, there is lots of things can happen. You always said that to me your self.

If anything should happen to me you get a hold of a lawyer and show him all this stuff and tell him what I told you and he will know what to do so you and Amy are taken care of.

Mama, I am sorry you got upsett when I told you about all this, but *I have to do this.* If I work it right I can quit you-know-what like you always wanted me to do. And put Amy through the rest of her school and get you out of that place and into one you like better. Maybe I can even come out there and we can get a nice place and live together.

If Daddy comes around don't talk to him about any of this because he drinks and can't keep his mouth shut.

I will write you very soon explanning everything. Love,

Lorene

I wished to God she'd explained it right then; I didn't have a clue what was going on. I should, I realized, have searched through the impounded-mail collection a little more and checked for further communications from Lorene that might at least have provided clues.

I sat there on the bed, staring at those forms and rereading that short pathetic letter, until the sun began to shine through the flimsy curtains. And at last I stood up, said shit a couple more times, and began gathering and packing everything for the flight back to Tulsa.

NINETEEN

I drove home from Tulsa International late Tuesday afternoon, enjoying the sensation of driving a real car again. On the way I stopped at a mall toy shop, bought a big black-and-white-spotted stuffed dog, had them wrap it for mailing, and drove to the nearest post office and sent it to Rose Matson.

There was another dog waiting for me at home, and I opened the trailer door expecting Harry's usual manic welcome-home routine, but his manner was distinctly reserved; he didn't seem at all thrilled to see me again. Oh, he leaped up on me as I came in the door, nearly knocked me back down the steps, licked my hands, ran around and around me several times, and tried to hump my leg; but hell, for Harry that was *nothing*.

I found the explanation on the shelf above the sink, in the form of several cans of an expensive brand of dog food that I never bought. Beside them, the box containing Harry's usual dry mix was obviously untouched. I looked at Harry, who was banging his tail hopefully on the floor. "Spoiled you already, has she?" I said. "Gone a couple of days, I come home to a damn overprivileged overweight canine slob."

Harry whacked the floor some more with his tail, letting his tongue hang out appealingly, really getting into his patented sickening cute-doggy act. "Stuffed dogs," I said, "I got a stuffed dog right here. Should have mailed your hairy ass to Phoenix. You'd fit right in."

Harry made a whining two-tone sound, ready to agree to anything if there was a chance of getting fed more of the pricey stuff. I said, "Oh, all right," and reached for the can opener. "You realize this is what they feed those high-class dogs, the ones with pedigrees. You don't even know who your daddy was. You ought to move up into northeast Oklahoma where they've got all those weird little mixedblood tribes, you're a 'breed if I ever saw one—"

It hit me then, just like that. I said, "Son of a bitch."

Harry whined some more, probably saying there was no need to bring his mother into this. I said, "Son of a bitch," again, louder, and started toward the living room, where I'd left the nylon shoulder bag that held the papers I'd stolen from the nursing home.

But I made myself stop and go back and open the can and give Harry the contents. After all, indirectly or not, he'd just handed me the combination to the whole Redfield affair.

Late that night, in the bedroom, I said, "You spoiled my dog while I was gone. Shaggy bastard's been eating better than I have."

"I got your mail and brought it in too," she said. "Put it on your desk. Did you find it all right?"

"Uh huh." A notice the insurance on the Camaro was about to expire, a badly-typed solicitation to get in on a chain-letter scheme, a form letter from my college alumni association wanting me to contribute generously toward the new football stadium, a notice from the library wanting me to return my overdue books, a Wal-Mart summer sale circular without even any good lingerie pictures, and a seed catalog addressed to old Mr. Berryhill up at the corner. Be still my beating heart. "Thanks," I said.

"So," Rita said, laying her head on my upper arm and cutting off most of the circulation, "what happened in Phoenix? Did you find what you went for?"

I hesitated. I'd known this was coming, but I'd still been hoping she wouldn't ask.

"I better not tell you about it yet," I said finally. "I did find out something, and it looks important—but that's just it, it's too important for me to talk about until I've made sure I've got it figured right. Also there's one other person I have to tell first."

Most women I've known would at this point have begun either whining or ripping me a new set of body orifices. But Rita was a pro. "Okay," she said. "If it's something I can't use yet, there's no point in telling me and making me sit on it anyway. Of course as soon as you *can* talk—"

"You'll be the first one to get the story, same as always. I ought to know pretty soon."

"I just hope this is going to come out all right for you," she said. "I mean, I hope you're not about to put yourself through something like that last business. I hope you're not setting yourself up for another case of the horrors. These people aren't worth it."

"It'll be okay," I told her, almost believing it myself.

"Yeah, right. I saw that cardboard over that broken window, and that duct tape over the little holes in the wall. And since when do you keep a shotgun sticking out from under the bed? You must think I'm blind as well as stupid, Tag Roper."

"It'll be okay," I repeated. "It's all going to be over pretty soon, if I'm right." Then, remembering something, "Hey, do you know a doctor I can talk with? One who really knows his bananas?"

"A *doctor?*" She rolled over and stared at me. "What the hell do you want with a doctor? You're really starting to worry me."

"Relax. I don't need medical attention, just information. Preferably without having to pay for it," I said. "Everything's been too damn expensive already."

"Hm." She thought for a moment. "There's a guy I know, used to work at the Indian hospital in Tahlequah. Has his own practice here in town now, I'll leave you his name, he's in the book. I can give him a call in the morning, if you want."

"Thanks."

"Glad to be of help," she said a little acidly, "considering I still don't even know what I'm helping with. You sure you're all right? Everything in place?" She began running her hands over my body. "Nothing got bit off by the coyotes out there in the desert? You didn't go fooling around, catch something I ought to know about?"

Her hands quit groping and went to work. "We better make sure everything's still all right. Little test here, see if it's working," she said, the last few words with a little difficulty. "Oh, yes, it's working all right. Working just fine," she said, rising up, straddling me, "just *fine*—"

Dr. Jonas Morton was tall, thin, and midthirtyish, with thick glasses and a soft diffident voice. He was one of the blackest men I'd ever seen; his skin was almost blue.

He pushed the papers back across the desk to me and said, "Oh, yes, Mr. Roper, your surmise is correct. No doubt about it."

"And there's no other possible explanation?" I said. "Forgive me, but it's really very important."

"Unless one or more of the persons who filled out these forms made a mistake," he said. "Which I suppose is possible, but it seems rather far-fetched. And it's not a mistake that would be particularly easy to make."

He watched me pick up the papers. They weren't the ones I'd taken from the nursing home; I'd made copies on a coin-operated machine, and blanked all the names out with typewriter correction fluid.

"I don't suppose I want to know where you got those forms," he said, pushing his glasses up on the bridge of his nose. "All of them represent records that are theoretically confidential."

I said, "My father used to say that a man has nipples because theoretically he might have a baby."

Dr. Morton chuckled. "Your point is taken," he said. "I am very aware that people do obtain access to such things, rules or no rules. I've had a few problems myself, relating to credit ratings and the like. I don't know how it's done."

"Generally in the same way everything else gets done in this society," I said. "Somebody pays somebody off."

He nodded, as if that confirmed what he'd always suspected. He ran his palm over his short hair. I wondered how he'd gotten along at the Indian Health Service hospital. Unfortunately, Indians can be just as prejudiced as anybody else.

"Actually," I added, "sometimes it's easier and quicker to get access to confidential information than to get the public agencies to show you things you're legally entitled to see. In my experience bribery is a lot more effective than the Freedom of Information Act."

"Yes. . . . In any case," he said, "you didn't really need a doctor, you know. Any first-year medical student, or even a registered nurse, could have answered your question. Or for that matter a high-school biology teacher, or you could even have dug up the basics yourself at the library. The principles are quite simple."

"Rita recommended you."

He smiled broadly. "That pleases me. She was one of my favorite patients. Well." He stood up and stuck out his hand. "Give her my best, won't you?"

I shook his hand and thanked him and went out to the street and got into the Camaro. About to start the engine, I thought of something and instead reached over and unlocked the glove compartment.

The .38 Wiley Harmon had given me lay there among the road maps and tollgate receipts and Kleenexes. I took it out and dropped it into the inside pocket of my suit jacket. I didn't know whether I'd be needing it any time soon, but if I did, it wasn't going to do me much good locked in the glove compartment. The weight felt funny against my chest, and the jacket didn't hang quite right now, but then it hadn't been all that great a fit to begin with. My good suit was already in the cleaners, getting rehabilitated from its desert adventures.

When I looked up, a small, serious-faced black boy was standing on the sidewalk, looking in the window of the car at me. I said, "Hi."

"You got a gun," he said thoughtfully. "You the po-lice?"
"Detective." I narrowed my eyes at him. "You know, like on TV."

He studied me briefly. "Bullshit," he said decisively, and roller-skated away.

Home again, I opened a beer and considered what to do next and how to do it. Obviously, before I did anything else, I ought to talk to Martha Redfield. But how the hell was I going to get in touch with her? If I called at her home, it was odds-on Sister Amanda would be eavesdropping, or Mel. I could go out to the house in person, but I didn't know how much luck I'd have getting in the door, and if Mel was around there was an excellent chance I'd get my ass stomped into the bargain.

I thought up several plans, most of them impracticable. I was still chewing on the problem when Martha Redfield solved it for me by calling me.

"I'm sorry," she said. After everything, she was still doing that. "But my mother-in-law is taking a nap upstairs, and Mel is outside working on his pickup truck, so I thought it would be a chance to call you. Have you learned anything yet?"

"As a matter of fact, I need to talk with you," I said. "Face to face, though, not on the phone. There's something I have to show you."

"I'll come there," she said immediately. "To your place. I remember the way. I'll say I'm going to see Amy, so Sister Amanda won't insist on coming along."

There was a note of excitement in her voice that worried me. She wasn't very experienced at deception and subterfuge. I hoped she didn't blow it. "Be careful," I said. "Don't give yourself away. When did you figure on coming?"

"Seven this evening?"

"Sure," I said.

"I'll be there," she said.

She showed up early, in the event, a little after six-thirty. It was still daylight outside. She parked the Lincoln awkwardly beside my Camaro and got out and came up to the door, where I was waiting. I already had Harry locked in the bedroom. This was going to be difficult enough without his contributions.

I stuck out my hand as she came in the door but to my amazement she grabbed me around the waist and clutched me for a moment, pressing herself against me. It was a childlike move rather than an erotic one, but it still took me off balance. "I'm sorry," she said after a second, not letting go. "I'm just so confused. You're the only one who's really trying to help me."

She pulled back, then, looking flustered. "I'm sorry," she said again.

"It's all right," I said, and put my arms around her and held her a little longer.

She moved against me suddenly. Her hand came up and groped over my chest. More exactly, it groped at the lump under my suit jacket. "Why," she said, pulling away and staring at me, "you're carrying a gun. Have I gotten you into something—"

"No, no." I took her elbow and led her over to the sagging chair. "Something to drink?" I said without thinking.

She shook her head. "No." She smiled self-consciously and sat down. "Actually I think I'd like something, right now. But I've never had a drink in my life, and if I start now I'll probably get silly. And you did say you had something important to tell me, to show me."

I sat on the couch facing her. "I went to Phoenix a couple of days ago." The manila envelope from the nursing home closet lay on the couch beside me and I picked it up and hefted it, showing it to her. "It's a complicated story, and I suppose I'd better begin by—"

There was a sudden enormous booming crash. The trailer door flew violently open, so hard it banged against the inside wall.

Mad Mel Rains said, "Everybody hold real still, all right?"

He came through the doorway, his shoulders almost touching the frame. He had on a dark-blue warmup suit. In his right hand was what I took at first to be a little pocket pistol, a .25 or a .32, but then I realized it was a full-sized Army .45 automatic. His gigantic hand almost swallowed it.

"Keep your hands where I can see them," he added, closing the door with his free hand. "You too, Mizz Martha."

She was staring at him, white-faced. "My God."

"No," I said, "just the hired help. Mel, didn't anybody ever teach you to knock?"

He wasn't listening. His eyes were scanning the room, while the .45 in his hand covered me. "Huh," he grunted, and stepped over and lifted the Navy revolver from the end table. I'd unloaded and cleaned it but I'd never gotten around to putting it up. "This the gun you shot Buddy with?" he asked.

"One and the same," I said. "Want me to shoot him again so you guys can compare holes?"

He turned the old-fashioned weapon in his left hand, his forehead creased in wonder. "Huh," he said again. Shrugging, he lobbed the Navy into the farthest corner of the room, where it clattered out of sight behind a stack of books. If it had been loaded it might well have discharged, but either Mad Mel didn't think of that or he didn't care. "You got anything else?"

"Shotgun in the bedroom. Shall I go get it?"

"Stay put. That's all?"

I stood up and opened my jacket and held it out away from my body by the lapels, flapping the tails, turning around completely. "Of course maybe you'd like to pat me down anyway," I said, wiggling my ass. "You'd enjoy that, wouldn't you? I've heard all about you weight-lifter types. They say it's the steroids."

"You better watch it," he growled. "I don't have to take any more smart talk off you."

He looked at Martha Redfield, who was huddled in the chair, staring and open-mouthed. "You shouldn't of gone and brought this guy into things, got him meddling in the family's business," he said reproachfully. "Sister Amanda warned you. Now just look what you've made me do."

"You're crazy." Her voice was barely audible over the noise of the air conditioner and Harry's demented barking from the bedroom. "You can't do this."

"Sure he can," I said. "He's got Jesus in his heart and a forty-five in his hand, he can do anything."

"You thought Sister Amanda was asleep this afternoon," Mel told her, still keeping the gun on me. "You didn't know she heard you talking on the phone. You didn't even see me following you."

"For God's sake," I said, "can we skip the damn dialogue and cut to the chase? What are you here for, Mel? Just to wave a gun and run your mouth, or did you have something specific in mind?"

He smiled. It wasn't an encouraging sight. "Oh, yes. I'm here to bring you both with me. Sister Amanda wants this lady home where she belongs, and she wants to have a word with you." He glanced around the room. "She heard you say you had something to show Mizz Martha. Where is it?"

I pointed at the manila envelope, lying on the couch where I'd dropped it when he'd burst in. "Give it here," he said.

I picked it up and handed it over. He tucked it under his left arm without moving the .45 off me. "Okay, let's go," he said.

He herded us out the door. In the bedroom Harry was still barking. I hoped somebody would eventually come let him out. I hoped that would be me, but right now I had to admit the chances didn't look too great.

The white pickup truck was parked a considerable distance from the trailer, halfway up the gravel drive to the road. Martha Redfield had some trouble making it; she wore heels that kept sinking into the dirt. But then she wasn't too steady on her feet by now anyway. She was crying quietly and she seemed barely able to see where she was going.

"You drive," Mel told me when we got to the truck. "Keys're already in the lock. You sit between us," he said to Martha.

He gave me his big ugly grin again. "Case you think I won't shoot you while we're moving," he said, "you're right. You try anything, or don't go where I tell you, I'll hurt the lady. You know I can do it."

He looked at Martha. "Sorry," he said, "but like I say, you brought all this on yourself."

The traffic was heavy and slow all the way across the river and along the expressway. By the time we rolled through the streets of Broken Arrow's rich-asshole ghetto it was getting visibly late, and when I finally turned the pickup into the Redfield estate's drive, the setting sun was spilling pink tints over the white trim of the front porch.

Mad Mel followed us up the walk, gun in hand. The door opened and Amanda Redfield stood there with something on her face that was nearly a smile. "Answering the door myself this evening," she said almost apologetically. "All the help has been given the night off, you see. I thought we should have privacy for our . . . meeting."

Martha Redfield said, "What do you want? What do you think you're doing?" Her voice was very thin, on the edge of hysteria.

Sister Amanda ignored her. She was looking at the big manila envelope in Mad Mel's left hand. "What's that?" she asked sharply.

He held it out and she took it. "This is what he called her over there for," he said. "He was getting ready to show it to her when I busted in."

She peered into the envelope, riffling the edges of the papers, squinting in the bad light. "Well, well, Mr. Roper," she said, "you had to keep digging, didn't you? You would have done better to heed my warning, but you thought you were too good for that. *'The way of a fool is right in his own eyes, but he that hearkeneth unto counsel is wise.'* Proverbs 12:15," she added didactically.

I said, "Going to kill me yourself, the way you did Lorene Matson? Or have King Kong here do it for you?" I turned and looked at Mel. "Of course I'm just assuming you didn't have him do Lorene, too."

Everybody stood very still for about a second and a half.

"Come inside, Mr. Roper," Amanda Redfield said at last. "You'd better tell me what you think you know."

TWENTY

Sister Amanda led the way down the shiny-floored main hallway into a spacious living room. The walls were painted ivory white and the deep carpeting matched the walls. With all the light from the big chandelier overhead, you almost needed shades in there. Long drapes half-covered windows Mad Mel could have driven his pickup truck through.

She turned sharply, as we all came in, and looked me up and down. "Has he been searched?" she said, evidently to Mel.

"Well—" Mel looked embarrassed. "He's clean," he said.

"Meaning you didn't bother," she said. "Do it now."

He took a step toward me. I said, "Inside jacket pocket." I didn't particularly want him pawing at me with those great hands.

He pulled my jacket back with his left hand, keeping the .45 back out of grabbing range, and poked at the jacket's lining. His hand was too big to fit into the inside pocket; I heard fabric tear slightly. Finally he managed to drag the .38 free. "Smart guy," he growled, stepping back.

Sister Amanda snapped her fingers and held out her hand. After looking confused for a moment, Mel handed her the .38.

She took it with a confident motion that said she'd handled guns before. That didn't surprise me by now.

She looked at the snub with mild interest. "Were you prepared to use this, Mr. Roper?" she asked dryly.

"Ask Mel's friend Buddy," I said.

"Yes." She gave Mel a brief glare. "I gave instructions for you to be warned in a way you'd remember. I had no idea Mel would use such incompetent help."

"Well, he's doing better now," I said. "Whoever took a shot at me the other night was pretty good. Or was that Mel himself on the trigger?"

She looked at Mel again, frowning. He shrugged massively. "I don't know anything about anybody shooting at Roper," he said, sounding sincere. "Sure wasn't me."

"Hm. Well, no matter." She gestured with the gun in her right hand, still holding the big envelope in her left. "Let's sit down."

She eased herself down in an old-fashioned armchair, all carved dark wood and flowered upholstery and bowed legs. Following her gesture, I went over and sat down on a long low couch that matched the armchair. After a second Martha Redfield joined me. Her eyes were huge and her face was papery white.

Mad Mel took up station behind Sister Amanda's chair, over to one side to give himself a clear field of fire. He still had that .45 in his hand and it was still looking straight at me. I wondered if he was any good with it. A cannon like that, he wouldn't have to be a target-grade marksman. And he just barely needed a gun to begin with.

A big round knee-high table stood between the couch and the armchair. Sister Amanda tossed the manila envelope onto the table and then, more carefully, laid the .38 on the marble top close in front of herself. She looked at me with a chilly little smile. "If you try to grab it, Mr. Roper, Mel will kill you."

She sat back and folded her bony hands in her lap. "Now," she continued, "begin."

I turned my head for a moment to look at Martha. She didn't

look at me; her eyes were fixed on the old woman in the arm-chair, like the bird in the myth watching the snake. I faced front again and said, "Well, to start with, I never did entirely under-stand why this business with Lorene Matson was supposed to be such a catastrophically big deal. Oh, I know, adultery and all that, but after all, it was something that happened a long time ago. And it wasn't as if the Reverend tried to duck his responsi-bilities. A lot of people would say it was pretty admirable, the way he made sure the child was properly supported and sent to good schools and so on."

"I'm not really interested in your ideas on morality, Mr. Roper," Sister Amanda said coldly. "Get on with it."

"All I mean," I said, "I couldn't quite see that it was so terrible that a man like Jack Redfield would kill to cover it up. And then, too, as I've been saying from the beginning, why wait twenty years and then do it? It didn't add up."

Amanda Redfield's face was absolutely still. Her eyes watched me, black and unblinking as the muzzle of Mad Mel's pistol.

"There was something else," I went on. "Lorene Matson, back in March, told her daughter something about having a new angle, a way to get a lot more money out of what she called her 'insurance policy.' That was right after she got back from Phoenix, where she visited her mother in a nursing home and also her father in a VA hospital. But I didn't find out that part until the other day.'

I leaned forward and stretched out my hand. "I want to get something out of that envelope," I said.

Mad Mel said, "Be real careful."

I pulled the envelope toward me, fished about inside and took out the letter from Lorene Matson to her mother. "Lorene was worried for her life," I said, "apparently because she was afraid of getting AIDS. She made up a package, copies of all the important documents on Amy's paternity, and sent it to her mother for safekeeping, with instructions to take it to a lawyer if anything happened to Lorene. She didn't realize that her mother was no longer in contact with reality, or that the nursing home director would intercept the package."

I scaled Lorene's letter across the table toward Amanda Redfield. It landed next to the .38 snub. She said, "Go on."

"There was something else in that envelope." I took out the four clipped-together pages. "A couple of file sheets from local medical offices—one on you, as a matter of fact, Sister Amanda—and an Army service-record sheet, and one from a VA patient's file. I spent a lot of time staring at these papers, you know. Couldn't figure out what they meant, until yesterday afternoon a big stupid hairy dog made me see it. The one thing they all had in common, the one item of information found on all four forms." I waved the photostats at her. "Blood type."

I tossed the forms onto the table. "Just to make sure, I checked with a doctor today. There's absolutely no doubt about it," I said. "Eugene Redfield, your husband, was not Jack Redfield's father. The blood types make it impossible."

I felt Martha Redfield move slightly beside me, heard her inhale sharply. Even Mad Mel looked startled. Only Amanda Redfield failed to register any response. The long Puritan face might have been cut from moon rock.

"I talked with Homer Matson Tuesday afternoon," I said. "He remembered you fondly, Amanda. 'Hot stuff' was his term. What happened? Did it get lonely out there on the farm, with Eugene away?"

I turned and looked at Martha. "There's your motive for murder. That's what all this was about. Adultery? Adultery hell, *incest!* Lorene was Jack's half-sister!"

The horror on Martha Redfield's white face was so great that I put my hand on her shoulder and said quickly, "He didn't know, Martha. He had no idea."

I looked at Amanda again. "That's why you killed her, wasn't it? She found out—I suppose her father told her something, she suspected the truth and somehow got the documents to check it out—and she knew she had the brass ring now, a first-class ticket to ride, for herself and her daughter and even her mother. But then she made a mistake. She came to you first, instead of Jack."

I gestured at the papers on the table. "Didn't you realize she'd have other copies somewhere safe, for protection?"

"I had no choice." Amanda Redfield's voice was like something coming from an open grave. "She approached me wanting money, more money than I could possibly lay hands on. All the family money, you see, it's tied up in various complicated ways because of the Ministries and the tax laws and so on. I couldn't have raised the sort of cash she demanded without being found out. At the very least I would have had to get my son's approval, which I could hardly do."

"You didn't know Jack had been paying her off?"

"Mr. Roper, until she called me that day at home, demanding I meet with her, I hadn't even thought about the wretched girl in years. I didn't know she was living here in Tulsa—this is a good-sized city, and after all we did not move in the same social circles," she pointed out dryly. "I didn't know she was living at all, or care. In fact when she first contacted me I had to think for a moment before I realized who she was. And I certainly had no idea my son had fathered her child, let alone carried on such an arrangement—"

She paused. Something close to wonder seemed to appear in her eyes. "I still can't understand how he managed to keep something like that from me all those years. Even as a child he never had secrets from me. I must admit, Mr. Roper, that it came as a painful shock when he finally confessed the whole business to me."

"Lorene Matson didn't mention it to you?"

"The matter never came up. Possibly she thought it would hurt her chances of getting money from me, if I knew she was already getting it from him. Possibly she simply assumed I knew. Our conversations were very few and never very long, even the last one. I went to her shabby little house," Sister Amanda said, "and tried to reason with her. She didn't believe me when I explained why I couldn't raise the money. She laughed in my face, waved papers at me like those you have there—the originals, I think. She said if I wouldn't pay up she knew who would. She said Jack was on his way and she was going to tell him the truth about his . . . conception, and their relationship."

"So you stopped her."

Her hands moved a few millimeters. "I shot her, yes. I am a good shot, Mr. Roper. My late husband taught me. It was his pistol I used, one he brought home from the war. I used to shoot rats in the barn with it. I threw it in the river on my way home."

"You took the papers?"

"The ones she was holding, yes, of course, and burned them when I got home. I didn't know about the others, the records you found in her house and gave the police, or the copies she had sent to her mother. There was no time to search the place," she said. "I could only hope that any other copies would not be found, that the police would treat the matter as just another sordid crime in the world of prostitution. And," she added, "of course I knew that the Lord would protect me."

Martha Redfield said incredulously, "You killed that poor woman and you expected God to help you get away with it?"

"She was an evil person," Sister Amanda said. "A scarlet Jezebel who sold her body for money, and a blackmailer besides. She was about to destroy a man of God, and to deal a terrible blow to God's work. I feel no guilt whatever for what I did that night."

"And for what you did forty years ago? Or rather what you and Homer Matson did? No regrets there either?"

Something changed at last in her face. A kind of strange cold joy radiated from the stony features. "It was God's will," she said in a softer voice. "My husband could not give me a child. He would never admit the problem was his, but I saw a doctor secretly and made sure I was not barren. And we tried enough," she added, her face going momentarily ugly again. "My husband was a man addicted to the disgusting lusts of the flesh . . . but finally it was shown to me in a dream what I must do."

"So you did it with Homer Matson," I said. "Lucky Homer."

"He was merely the instrument of the Lord," she said serenely. "An unworthy instrument, I agree, but the Lord sometimes does things in ways we do not understand."

"Did Homer ever know the boy was his?"

"Of course not. At least I never told him, though he may have suspected something in time," she said. "One reason I persuaded my husband we should move to Tulsa was that Jack and Lorene were reaching a dangerous age, and were dangerously close."

"Obviously you should have killed her then," I said sarcastically.

"Possibly," she said, quite seriously. "I've thought about it."

Mad Mel suddenly made a choked noise. Everybody looked at him. His mouth was hanging open. The gun in his hand was still pointed at me, though.

He said hoarsely, "It's true? It's all true? You did it?"

"To save Reverend Jack," she said, not looking around. "You know what it would have done to him, Mel. Look what it *did* do to him, when only a small part of the truth came out because of this man's meddling. I was trying to prevent that."

"Yeah, but—" Mel's pale blue eyes were full of confusion. "You never told me," he said. "You never said you murdered that woman. I never knew that was what all this was about." He waved his hand toward Martha and me. "I don't know, maybe we ought to—"

"I told you we had to stop Roper," she said. The ice was back in her voice now. She turned around and gave Mel the full benefit of her basilisk stare. "I told you these two were going to bring even more shame upon Jack's memory, if we didn't stop them. You said you were ready to do whatever had to be done."

Mel nodded unhappily. "Sure, only—"

"Mel," Sister Amanda said urgently, "do you want the world to remember Reverend Jack Redfield as a man who fornicated with his own sister? Do you want to see me go to the electric chair?"

Mad Mel's face crumpled. For an instant he looked like an enormous child trying not to cry. "No," he said in a tiny voice, and then more strongly, "No, I couldn't stand that to happen. What do we do?"

Sister Amanda looked at Martha and me. "You know the answer to that, Mel," she said. "What else is there to do?"

There was a long frozen pause. The big room was as silent as death. Which had come into the room, just now, leaning a bony elbow against the door frame, grinning at everybody in ghastly anticipation: Who'll be first?

"That's pretty rough," Mel said finally. His voice was uneven. "I mean, cold blood and all, I never did anything like that before."

"He killed Reverend Jack, Mel," she said, "as surely as if he did it with that pistol he was carrying. He destroyed all the great works the Reverend was doing for the Lord. And if he leaves here alive, he will do even worse."

Mel nodded jerkily. "Damn," he muttered.

"Don't curse," she said.

"Sorry. What about her?"

"She made her choice," Amanda said flatly. "She's the reason he kept prying. She's as bad as he is. I wouldn't be surprised if they're having some sort of affair. Anyway, she knows too much now."

But Mel was shaking his head emphatically. "I don't think I could do that," he said. "Him, okay, you're right, but not a woman. Not Mizz Martha. Maybe we never got along, but I've known her for years. I just can't do it."

"Hm." Sister Amanda made an impatient sound in her throat. "I suppose there's an alternative. We could have her committed to a mental institution. Then no one would believe anything she said."

"Could you do that?"

"Why not? Surely you can keep her here, lock her in her room, for a day or so while I make inquiries. With the kind of money I can offer, I don't think it will be hard to find a private institution with an accommodating administration."

"Yeah," Mel said, "I know a guy can fix us up with some pills, keep her out of it till you can get it worked out—"

They made a grotesque pair, the hulking brute and the mad

old woman, calmly discussing the details of murder and kidnapping; they might have been kicking around ideas for the Sunday-school picnic. I felt as if I'd swallowed a big icicle and now it was trying to come back up.

"How do you figure I ought to do it?" Mel asked. "Take him down to the river, or what?"

"For heaven's sake," Sister Amanda snapped peevishly, "why do I have to tell you how to do everything? Use your own—"

Martha Redfield screamed.

I mean, she *screamed,* not just a normal scared-woman scream, but a long rising-scale banshee shriek that went on and on and up and up. It stood the hairs on end all over my body; when it hit the upper registers my teeth started to hurt. Mad Mel jumped and even Sister Amanda's eyes got wider.

"Nooooooooooooooooooo," Martha wailed, *"no no no no no no no no—"*

And went flying past me, still screaming, in a wild arm-waving charge, leaping across the table, straight at Sister Amanda, slapping and clawing and snatching, while the old woman began screaming too, trying to fight back, and then just trying to cover up against her daughter-in-law's flailing hands. Now Mad Mel was in there, grabbing Martha from behind, dragging her back, shouting at her, lifting her off the floor, while her heels kicked viciously against his knees. "You stop that," he roared, "you stop that—"

He turned then, letting her go, maybe catching the movement out of the corner of his eye as I dived across the table and grabbed up the .38, and he started to raise the .45, but it was too late.

I shot him in the middle of his huge barrel chest, three times, rapid fire, the snubby revolver bucking violently in my hands and making a deafening blast in that enclosed space. Mad Mel took a step forward and then another. He didn't seem to be trying to raise his gun now; he seemed to have forgotten it, to want only to get his hands on me. He took a third step and I emptied the .38 into his chest and then leaped back and vaulted over the couch as he lunged at me. Somewhere in mid-lunge his face suddenly went blank and he crashed to the floor, arms and legs spread wide, face down. The impact shook the whole room. Even the chandelier overhead made tinkling sounds. Mad Mel's head came up for an instant and then fell back with a soggy thump.

Martha was still screaming, hands to her face. I went over and put my arms around her. "Hush," I said, and to my surprise she did. "It's all right now," I said in the sudden silence.

A voice like a spider's said, "Not for you."

Sister Amanda stood there, no more than seven or eight feet away, holding Mad Mel's .45 in an efficient two-hand grip, covering both of us. She had the hammer all the way back.

"Let it go," I said. "Can't you see it's over?"

"It may be," she said. "The Lord's will be done. But first, I'm going to kill you. Both of you."

Her thumb moved. The .45's safety snicked off with a little smooth sound. The muzzle steadied on my chest. "Goodbye, Mr. Roper."

Somewhere behind me there was a loud crash of breaking glass and then a gun went off, something big and powerful, so close the muzzle blast nearly burst my right eardrum. Sister Amanda stood there for a moment, a look of deep puzzlement on her face. A dark spot had appeared in the middle of her forehead. The .45 suddenly fell from her hands and hit the floor, muzzle down. The soft carpet cushioned the fall and it didn't go off.

Sister Amanda went limp all over, all at once. She didn't so much fall to the floor as simply collapse upon herself. She made only the smallest sound going down, the rustle of stiff black fabric masking the soft impact of her thin body.

I turned around just as Wiley Harmon climbed through the shattered window, a big shiny pistol in his hand. "Ding dong, the witch is dead," he said cheerfully.

I said, "What the hell are you doing here?"

"Well, that's kind of a long story. I was over near your place, taking care of some business—never mind what—and I remembered there was something I wanted to tell you, some news I figured you'd wanta know. You weren't there and the fucking dog was barking his ass off in the bedroom, and I knew you wouldn't go off and leave him locked up in there. Also the front door had been busted in and there was this Lincoln parked in your yard. I don't hafta point out," he said, "you don't exactly know that many people, drive Lincolns. In fact I could only think of one. Put it all together, I figured I better get my ass over here fast and fuck calling the Broken Arrow cops. Got here just in time to see you waste ape-shape, there." He pointed at Mad Mel's body with his toe. "You gotta fill me in later. Looks real interesting."

"What happened—"

"No, no," he said, "don't *tell* me what happened. I'm the fucking detective here. I'm supposed to figure *out* what happened."

He walked around the room for a minute or two, studying the scene. At length he came back and stood over Mad Mel.

He held up the revolver in his hand, showing it to me. "Look at that," he said. "Smith and Wesson Combat Magnum. You know where I got it? I took it off a fucking sixteen-year-old kid. Along with enough crack to kill a herd of whales. Don't know what the world's coming to."

He raised the Magnum suddenly, aiming toward the broken window where he'd entered. There was a loud bang and the long barrel jumped upward. Wiley fired again and lowered the revolver, nodding in satisfaction. Two fresh holes had appeared in the wall next to the window.

"Punk had armor-piercing slugs in it, too," he observed. "Go right through a flak jacket. You see how that one punched through the old bat's head without expanding? Just left a neat little hole. Don't leave Ballistics much to work with, but fuck 'em."

Beside me Martha made a gagging sound. Harmon didn't appear to notice. He took a handkerchief from his pocket and wiped the Magnum carefully all over. Holding it by the barrel, still using the handkerchief, he bent down and put the handle in Mad Mel's hand, using his other hand to force the big fingers into position around the grips and trigger. When he let go Mad Mel's hand relaxed and the Smith fell to the carpet beside his outstretched fingers.

"Now," Wiley Harmon said, stepping back and looking around, "what I believe happened here, using my trained investigative eye, is this. I believe this oversized shitbag here killed the late Lorene Matson, possibly in a misguided attempt to protect the late Reverend Redfield. I think he got it into his little pea-sized brain that the famous author and journalist Taggart Roper, of scenic and historic Yuchi Park, either knew he did it or was about to find out. Possibly this was because the said Rev's widow had been conferring with Mr. Roper over the chances of doing an investigative-type book about the murder and trying to clear her late husband's name."

Martha started to say something. I squeezed her hand to indicate silence.

"I further believe," Harmon continued, his voice very stiff and pompous now, "this big asshole finally went completely crazy, not a long fucking trip for him, and kidnapped the said noted novelist and also the widow, and brought them here with the intention of committing homicide on their persons, contrary to the statutes of the fine state of Oklahoma. After bringing them here he admitted in their presence that he was the one who killed the departed hooker."

He paused and looked intently at me and then at Martha and then back at me. "That part's kind of important," he added in his normal voice. "Okay?"

He pointed at the crumpled body of Amanda Redfield. "But a study of the evidence shows me that who should walk in but the saintly mother of the late Reverend, who made a brave attempt to stop the gorilla from what he was about to do. This only got the dear sweet old bitch a slug right through her lovable gray head. A slug which, if they ever find where the fucker went, will no doubt prove to have been shot from this howitzer which we find prackly in the perp's hand."

He turned and gestured melodramatically at the wrecked window. "But meanwhile, speeding toward the scene, we see the brave and handsome Detective Sergeant Wiley P. Harmon of the Tulsa PD, who has gone by to see his good friend the noted novelist and discovered evidence of foul play and all that good shit I just told you. Gimme the fucking thirty-eight."

I handed it over. He swung the cylinder out and looked at the cartridge heads. "Boy, you didn't fuck around, did you? Gave him all six. Way to go, even though it's gonna make a little trouble for me."

He clicked the revolver shut without ejecting the empties. "And so," he said, shifting back into his courtroom style, "the heroic police officer arrives on the scene, unfortunately too late to save the life of poor old Saint Amanda, though he does witness the slaying just as he comes up to the window. Naturally he attempts to place the perpetrator under arrest and inform him of his rights against self-incrimination under the U.S. Constitution."

He pointed at the bullet holes by the window. "But he gets fired on and narrowly missed, which forces him to return fire with his trusty off-duty revolver"—he held up the .38 snub—"with fatal consequences for the said perp." He stuffed the snub into his waistband. "Have I reconstructed the crime or what?"

"With your usual deductive genius," I said.

"No shit," Wiley Harmon agreed. "L.E. fucking Mentary, Watson."

Martha Redfield said faintly, "I don't understand."

I said, "Look, Wiley's right, this is better for everybody. The way it actually went down, there are some questions that will have to be asked. Some of the answers leave me open to trouble, maybe even to prosecution. At the very least I'd be blown, I couldn't operate the way I do around this town any more."

I put my hand under her chin and raised it until I could look into her eyes. "And do you really want the truth to come out? Do you want an even worse scandal attached to your husband's memory?"

She hesitated. I said, "Also, do you want Amy to know that her parents were brother and sister?"

"No," she said then, "you're right. She's got enough to deal with as it is."

"I don't know what the fuck you two are talking about," Wiley Harmon said. "Me, I just don't need it on my record that I shot an old lady. No matter what the circumstances were, that's gotta look like hell."

He looked at Martha. "You sure you can carry this off?" he said. "Maybe, I dunno, he had you locked in another room while all this went down."

"I'll be all right." Her voice was stronger than I'd ever heard it. She was even standing up straight. "I'll tell it the way you said."

"Yeah?" he said doubtfully. "Okay, but I think you better be pretty bad hysterical when the Broken Arrow cops get here. Not making any sense, in shock, in no condition to be interrogated. You can do that, can't you?"

"Believe me," she said with feeling, "it will be easy."

"All right, then," he said, and to me, "Come on, let's clean up the scene. Some shit here doesn't need to be on the premises when my colleagues show up." He bent down and picked up Mad Mel's .45. "Hey, look at this. I was gonna say you owe me for what that Magnum was worth, but fuck it, I'll call it square. You got any idea what a clean forty-five goes for these days?"

I started picking up the papers from the table and the floor, stuffing them back in the manila envelope. Wiley picked up a couple of sheets and glanced at them before handing them to me. "You figure you'll ever tell me what this shit was really about?"

"No," I said.

"What I thought. Well, let's go stash this junk in my car. Then I gotta put in a phone call to the Broken Arrow guys. They ain't gonna be happy about this at all. They ain't gonna be happy about all this bloody shit going down in their territory, and they're gonna be even unhappier about it being a Tulsa cop that wrapped it up."

He laughed suddenly. "Boy, this is gonna put me in good with Lieutenant Birdshit for a change. The one human he hates worse than he does me is the Chief in Broken Arrow." He shook his head, laughing, as we headed for the door. "Plus I nail a perp prackly in the act of a really evil-ass murder, *and* we get to close the books on an unsolved homicide that got a lot of bad publicity. I'm gonna come out of this looking pretty fucking good."

He clapped me on the shoulder. "You know, Roper, sometimes it's a real pleasure doing business with you."

TWENTY-ONE

Things got a little tense for me for a while there, but not too bad, and not for long.

The Broken Arrow cops kicked my story around and poked at it some, made the usual why-don't-you-tell-us-the-truth noises, but their hearts weren't in it. They were just taking out their annoyance at having something like this blow up under their noses, in a part of their turf that was supposed to stay quiet and peaceful. They were pissed off at Wiley Harmon, too, because he'd come into their jurisdiction and done a one-man cowboy number without calling them in.

But there was no way they could really lean on me without leaning, indirectly at least, on Martha Redfield; and, considering who she was and what kind of money she represented, they weren't about to do that.

Nobody wanted to look too hard at the story, anyway. Everything was wrapped up in a nice package, victim and perpetrator and witnesses and even a heroic cop. There would be no trial to cost the state money and risk the reputations of public employees. As a bonus, the Lorene Matson case could at last be officially closed, giving the Tulsa PD another solved homicide for their annual batting-average report, and ending at last the accusations that the authorities had shown favoritism in not arresting Reverend Redfield.

The religious community was a bit happier, too; at least their man hadn't been a murderer after all. The Christian Martial Arts Association issued a statement that Mad Mel's mind had been disturbed by the use of steroids and other dangerous substances. A huge contingent of the faithful turned out for Sister Amanda's funeral. I heard the service was a piss-cutter, but I don't know; I didn't attend.

The TV and press people came to town again, but not in very heavy numbers, and they didn't stay long. The spectacular murder made a good story, and they played it for all it was worth—a couple of network shows somehow got hold of copies of Mad Mel's sermonette tape and showed the part where he smashed the bricks—but nobody tried to go any deeper, or questioned the official story. That might have drawn attention to their having tried and convicted Jack Redfield, by innuendo and implication, only a few weeks ago.

"They don't want to admit they fucked up," Rita Ninekiller said.

"Hell," I said, "when did they start worrying about that? Remember Tienanmen Square? Did you see even one of the journalists and correspondents and writers who'd been telling us how wonderful things were in the People's glorious Republic—did you see one of those assholes stand up and say, 'Okay, we were full of shit, sorry'? Or that last war, remember? They all made a nightly ceremony of predicting a horrible bloodbath, turned thousands of relatives of GIs into nervous wrecks, but when Schwarzkopf's guys went in there and did it and the enemy cracked wide open and ran like hell, did any of the bastards say, 'Hey, we told you people a lot of bullshit'?"

"You're a fine one to be talking about bullshit," she said. "I don't know why you're not a better-known novelist. After that piece of fiction you and Martha Redfield and Wiley Harmon cooked up."

"Naturally," I sighed, "I don't know what you're talking about."

"Naturally," she said.

We stopped talking then to do some other things. Later, though, she said, "You're not ever going to tell me the real story, are you?"

"Probably not," I said. "Maybe if other people weren't involved—"

"No, that's okay," she said. "I figure you've got your reasons. When you shut the door on me like that, I've got to be able to walk away and not stand there rattling the knob. Considering what I do and what you do, that's the only way we can keep going."

She pushed her hair back from her face and looked at me. "We are going to keep going, aren't we?" she said.

"I guess so," I said. "Looks that way, doesn't it?"

"That's what I like about you, Tag Roper," she said, laying her face against my chest. "You say the most romantic things."

Martha Redfield and Amy Matson left town together. I got a letter from Martha, around the end of August, postmarked Phoenix. She said Amy was trying to get Rose into a better home and Homer into the AA program. They were buying a condo together out in Tempe. Amy had decided to wait a year or two before going back to finish college. The house in Broken Arrow was being sold and the Jack Redfield Ministries would soon be closed down for good.

It was a chatty, casual sort of letter; reading it, you'd never have guessed that the writer and the reader had once shared a terrible and memorable few hours. Enclosed with the letter, however, was a check, and when I got through re-counting the zeros, I decided Martha Redfield had expressed herself in an admirably sensitive and sincere way.

I never heard from her, or Amy, again.

Ceremonies of the Horsemen came back early in September. The editor who had read it—or claimed to have done so—was very impressed with my writing and my knowledge of the subject, but didn't feel it was quite suitable for the present market. He suggested I might have better luck if I'd rewrite it as a historical romance and make the lead character a woman. He suggested that I use a feminine pen name while I was at it.

I bundled the God-damned thing up and sent it out again. By then I was halfway through the new one, anyway.

It was almost the end of summer when I finally remembered to ask Wiley Harmon something that had gotten past me that night in Broken Arrow.

"You said you were coming by to tell me something," I said. "When you came to my place and found the door broken in and the rest of it. What was it you were going to tell me?"

"Oh, yeah. That's right, I never did tell you, did I?" He laughed and drank off an inch of his beer. We were sitting in the Copper Bottom and it was late. We'd been conducting some business concerning a new job I was working on, never mind what.

"What it was," he said, "you remember that punk Larry, the one used to be shacked up with Lorene's daughter, back when all this shit started? You knew he was working for Shelby?"

I nodded. Harmon said, "Well, that Monday night while you were out in Phoenix, Larry wigged out completely. Got in a beef with a customer, then yelled out a bunch of shit at the band, I mean he was really apeshit. Barmaid told me you could see the white powder on his nose from across the room." Harmon grinned. "Shelby came out, told him he was fired. Damn if Larry didn't pull a gun, little twenty-two automatic. Threatened Shelby, fired a shot into the ceiling, finally made the bartender give him the cash from the register and ran out the door. Drove away like he thought it was Daytona."

He drank some more beer. "Guys in a patrol car saw him, got on his tail, called in reinforcements, wound up with this wild-ass high-speed chase all the fuck over town in the middle of the night before he finally lost it and crashed his car into the side of somebody's parked van out near Skelly Stadium. Surprisingly, the punk wasn't hurt all that bad."

I started to say something but he waved a hand at me. "No,

wait, that's just the setup, you ain't heard the good shit yet. See, when they got him downtown, he was still flying eight feet off the ground and talking a mile a second. Told some real interesting stories, too. When he was through talking the guys in Burglary were able to close the books on a whole string of break-ins and ripoffs in the area, and the narcs had the name of Larry's coke supplier, and other good shit like that."

He leaned his elbows on the table. "Reason I thought you'd be interested," he said, "couple of things he said, nobody else paid much attention to, but I recognized the basic details. You know when you got into Lorene's place the first time? The guy that sucker-punched you in the dark?"

"Larry?" The idea had never occurred to me.

Harmon nodded. "He'd gotten enough from Amy to figure out that there was maybe something in that house that was worth money. Found out she'd hired you to look for it, he figured he'd get there first, grab it himself, go into business on his own."

"Son of a bitch."

"Yeah, a lot of people around this town would agree with you. Anyway," Harmon said, "the other thing, that was him took a shot at you that night at your place."

"Hm." I turned the information around in my mind and then fitted it into place. The last missing piece, and I'd forgotten it was even missing.

"Don't sweat it," Harmon added. "Nobody but me ever made the connection with you and the Redfield case. The way he was babbling, didn't make much sense unless you already had an idea what he was talking about."

He raised his glass. "Here's to Larry. The boys down at McAlester ought to have him just about broke in by now."

Summer came to an end and the nights turned cooler. One day I failed to close the door completely and Harry got loose long enough to impregnate Mr. Berryhill's beagle.

I took to sitting out in the yard in the lengthening evenings, playing my harmonica and watching the sun go down over the flats. The leaves were already starting to flutter down on the wind and soon they would be building up in earnest around the trailer. I didn't plan to do anything about them. I like leaves on the ground in the fall. Like the snow that comes after them, they cover for a time a world where a lot of things need covering.